PLAYING FOR PAYBACK

PLAYING
BOOK 2

LAINEY DAVIS

CONTENT NOTE

This is a light-hearted hockey romance meant to entertain readers. However, the story includes:

- Discussion of body image, including instances where the heroine experiences negative self-talk and encounters body-shaming comments from other characters.
- A beloved pet experiences a health emergency that may be distressing to some readers, though the animal ultimately recovers fully.
- Instances of biphobia and bi-erasure, including harmful stereotypes and questions about the validity of bisexual identity. These attitudes are challenged within the story.
- Brief references to financial stress and student loan debt.

All these themes are handled with as much care as possible and addressed as part of the characters' journeys toward acceptance and joy. Please take care of yourself, but remember that all Lainey Davis novels end with a happily ever after!

PROLOGUE
ALDER

There's blood on the ice. Is it mine? I drop my stick and pat myself uselessly—no pain. I'm aware that the ref has stopped the game, probably due to the blood. I glance at my brother Gunnar in the goal. He's swigging water from his bottle, helmet off, and his face is tight.

Where's my twin?

Last thing I knew, I was shouldering some Montreal asshole into the boards, snatching the puck from him, and sending it to Tucker. Without looking, obviously, because I never need to look with Tuck.

That twin connection? I swear it's real.

I shove my way toward the refs, aware that one is whistling for the medical team. I see a pair of legs wiggling on the ice. Whoever it is, they're sitting up. A few fingers of the fist around my heart loosen up.

I shove closer and freeze. I clutch my face, seeing my twin bleeding from the mouth. Tuck's blond hair is dark with sweat, and the electric blue eyes that mirror mine are filled with fear. As I meet his electric blue eyes, he stops groaning. I try to get closer to him as our new dentist approaches him in purple gloves. She's got a light strapped to her forehead, and people are all around her holding supplies.

I skate closer to my brother and watch him spit a tooth into her hand. He looks up at me and grins, missing one of his choppers. I bring a hand to my scruff-covered jaw and have to look away.

Someone gives me a water bottle, and I squirt it into my mouth while glancing at the big screen above center ice. The arena blasts music, and fans dance and apparently kiss. Yep. There goes the kiss cam.

Predictably, it scans over to the Partners and Wives section, where my older brother's girl blows a big kiss to Gunnar. They're so in love it's almost gross. Like one of those exaggerated relationships in the Fae smut books the women in my family keep talking about. The crowd freaking loves it when Em and Gunnar act all swoony.

I glance back at Tuck, but he still has a mouth full of dentist hands—Lena's hands. She's more than capable of managing him right now.

I chug some more water, and my eye is drawn to the jumbo screen again. My boyfriend is here today. Adam wouldn't sit with the PAWs, but I got him tickets right off the ice, near the team tunnel.

Am I jealous that the camera isn't panning to him, and he's not blowing me a kiss? Yeah. I'm fucking jealous. But after the barbecue incident, I'm also grateful he showed up. My family hates that Adam won't commit to me in any mean-ingful way. They all want me to end things with him, but none of them has ever navigated dating outside the hetero norm. Adam says he's not ready to be out with a celebrity. I have to respect that, especially now when I might have seri-ously damaged his career with my big mouth.

I sigh as the kiss camera hovers on a pair of dudes making out. They're receiving just as much applause as all the straight folks. I raise my fist to join in the whooping when I notice something familiar about one guy's dark hair.

I stare at the screen, realization growing that I recognize

the scruffy stubble, the collared shirt, and the hairy hand clutching the second dude's face like he can't bear not to be touching his lover.

Because that's Adam making out with Brad Reid, the guy I met last month at a barbecue at Coach's house. The same guy who was so bored and judgmental he couldn't even pretend to be proud of his girlfriend–the pretty dentist with her hands in my brother's mouth.

This isn't random.

The calculated look Adam flashes toward the camera tells me everything I need to know. After the PR disaster I caused him at the barbecue, he's making sure I feel the same public humiliation. He wanted me to see this; he wanted everyone to see this.

I look over to Lena, who glances up from Tucker right at that moment. Our eyes meet, and I tilt my head toward the screen. Then I watch her notice.

This is really too much. Our boyfriends are sucking face at my playoff game while my twin gets treated for dental trauma.

The longer I stare at the screen, the more I realize people are staring at me. I glance at the goal and see Gunnar wearing a pained expression. He mouths something to me. What?

I dropped my gloves and helmet at some point while a bunch of cameras are flashing at me. The video feed on the Jumbotron is frozen, Adam's illicit kiss highlighted in 800 square feet of bright pixels.

I grab my hair, tugging and trying to understand what's happening here.

At some point, an arm drapes over my shoulders. I try to punch it away, but I see it's Tucker. He's got bloody gauze in his mouth as he rests his forehead against mine.

"Bro." His word is garbled. "Thith thuckth."

Cappy skates over and hands Tuck his helmet, which he secures back onto his head. Banksy has my helmet and shakes my shoulders. "Come on, A-Stag. We've got a game to win."

Are they serious? Are they really going to carry on right now?

Of course, they are. Tucker can deal with his tooth later. Nobody cancels a pro hockey game over something as insignificant as a lost tooth, and they certainly don't stop when their bisexual defender sees his boyfriend cheating on him in front of 18,000 people.

I'm barely aware of the whistle-blowing to restart the game. I hear the puck hit the ice and the slap of Cappy's stick as he sends it up to Banksy.

I'm vaguely aware that Montreal gets control, and their winger is blasting toward me. I try to focus, but my legs feel like goo.

By the time I spring into action, chasing him down, it's too late. He's past me. He's past Tucker. And the puck is in the back of the net, past Gunnar's outstretched glove.

We lost.

Our season is over, and it's my fault.

"I just don't see why you can't work this summer, Brad." I groan as the waist of my new scrub pants digs uncomfortably into my skin. I'll have to ask for a size up, which means trading in all the pairs the hospital issued me yesterday. At least the tops fit.

My boyfriend pinches the bridge of his nose. "And I don't see why you can't understand how much work it is to finish a dissertation, Lena. The sooner I do that, the sooner I can get on the job market, and we can start our next chapter."

He acts as if academic professionals wait until graduation to start searching for tenure-track jobs. But I don't say that to him. What's the point? I need to leave, especially considering I need to grab new pants before I embark on a twelve-hour shift at the trauma center.

As the newest member of the emergency dental squad, I've encountered some pretty gnarly mouths already. Even though it's only been a month, I'm proud of how infrequently I've had to step away to compose myself.

Brad has been less proud of this achievement. I frown, remembering how he insisted that I stop discussing my work when he's trying to concentrate.

He's already returned to his book, and I take a deep

breath, remembering that all couples go through difficult stretches. The stress of both of us being in graduate school has been intense. Interestingly, a PhD in philosophy takes longer than a doctorate in dental medicine. I'm just glad I was able to find a good-paying job in Pittsburgh while he finishes his degree. There's no way we could cover rent in two cities with my loan payments coming due. Brad's stipend is barely enough to cover his Paleo diet requirements, so I've been floating the bills.

I sigh. "Right. Well, I'll be pretty late."

He nods. "I'll probably sleep in the office so you don't wake me with all the lights and running water."

I wince at this. I take extraordinary care when I return home. Obviously, I shower off the gore of the emergency department, but I don't even turn the fan on, so it's as quiet as possible. Brad and I need to have a conversation soon. An honest, sit-down heart-to-heart so we can hash out this tension between us and figure out some solutions to these perceived slights on both our parts.

"I love you," I say, but he's bent over his book and doesn't hear me. The words feel more hollow than usual.

I step out of our apartment into the spring sunshine and walk a few blocks north to General Hospital. It's an absolutely gorgeous day, and I let the weather lift my unease. This is just normal couple stuff, part of the growing pains in any relationship where both parties are career-focused and trying to find their footing.

By the time I reach the sliding glass doors of my workplace, I feel much better about everything. "Morning, Luis!" I smile at the security guard, who suspiciously eyes my bundle of scrub pants.

"You bringing your laundry into work, chica?"

I shake my head. "Nah. Gotta switch out for another size."

Why I'm telling the security guard my ass is too big for my pants? I have no idea. But he winks at me. "No shame in that, mami. Better to be comfortable while you're walking around fine like that."

I blush, surprised by how his compliment affects me. Most people in my life have a different perspective on my size. "Thank you, Luis."

"Any time, Doc!"

I swing through the linen room to swap my extra-large pants for a set of two-X. Thankfully, the curvy woman at the counter gives me a supportive hand pat, lets me change into one of the new pairs, and quickly turns in the pair of pants I arrived wearing.

Outfitted, I stop by my locker, drop off all my crap, pull my hair back into a long ponytail, and prepare for whatever mayhem the day may bring. Will I start with a skateboarding accident? Siblings fistfighting? An alcoholic who tripped and fell off a curb? I sort of like that it could be any or all of these things in addition to horrors unimagined.

I have no idea why trauma dentistry appealed to me when searching for a job after graduation. It's probably weird that I find the work to be soothing. I'm definitely seeing people at their worst, but I pride myself on my ability to keep them calm, to reassure them that I'm going to get them feeling better, and, if they let me help, chewing food normally in no time.

I consult on a rollerblading mishap and a college rugby fiasco before lunch, and I am just about done wolfing down some soup when I see a nurse sprint-walking toward me with a phone. She's got the determined pace of a woman on a mission, so I shovel another bite of chicken noodle into my mouth and stand to meet her.

"Lena." She heaves out a breath. "Urgent call for you."

My brows shoot up, and I reach for the phone. "This is Dr. Sinclair." The nurse mouths that she has to get back to the floor, and I wave, hoping she understands that I will return the phone as soon as possible. I start to follow her, but I pause at the elevator bay as the voice begins shouting in my ear.

"Lena Sinclair, this is Sarah Collins, assistant coach of the Pittsburgh Fury. We have an emergency."

I absolutely did not have to "get picked up by a fancy black car and driven to the hockey arena for a job offer" on today's bingo card. Another reminder that no two days in dentistry are alike! I run my hands over the smooth leather interior as I'm chauffeured to the Hill District. I stare at the sun glinting off the windows of the giant arena, briefly remembering my mother once saying that girls "my size" never get very far in the world. Her words seem hollow as I'm ushered through a fancy door, an even fancier elevator, and into an office suite full of very-fancily-dressed people.

It hadn't occurred to me to feel self-conscious in my scrubs and Hokas, and I was just about to squirm when a white woman in track pants and a T-shirt burst into the door.

"Dr. Sinclair. Thank goodness. I'm Sarah." She holds out a hand, which I shake, impressed by her rough palm and firm grip. "We've had a tragedy."

A throat clears from behind the mahogany desk. "Tragedy is a strong word. No one has perished." A balding white man stands and adjusts his suit jacket. "Dr. Sinclair, I'm Charles Sutton, owner of the Pittsburgh Fury. Please, take a seat."

I see someone has brought a leather chair right up behind me, and I lower myself into it as Sarah sits in the chair to my right. Mr. Sutton taps his desk and sits back down. "Are you aware, Dr. Sinclair, that the professional hockey league is required to employ a dentist and have one present for all practices and home competitions?"

I shake my head. "I never thought about it before. But it makes sense! I bet you see a lot of mouth trauma."

Sutton coughs. "Indeed."

Sarah groans beside me and slaps the desk. "I don't have time for all this. My guys are suited up and waiting for the morning skate." She turns to face me. "Doc Bowman had a heart attack this morning. He's over at General. They placed a stent, and he's fine. He apparently badgered the staff to ask who was the best with the brutal mouth cases, and they named you. We're offering you a job. Starting immediately."

I blink, processing her words. "I'm sorry? A job?"

Sutton waves a hand. "We have arranged for someone else to fill in your current position at the hospital. We require a specific temperament, and we believe you are uniquely suited to meet our needs."

I glance at one wall of his office, covered floor to ceiling with television monitors, each showing footage of a different hockey game somewhere in the world. I gesture at the screens. "I'm not really … cut out for a public role with a lot of attention…" I drift off, not wanting to spell out that a chubby dentist will not be great for optics on air.

Sarah frowns and recoils. "Dr. Sinclair, yours is a role where–if you're doing it well–nobody will even know you exist. Ideally, we never need you at all!"

Sutton nods.

I frown. "I can't imagine that's true."

Sutton taps the desk. "Dr. Sinclair, truly, the most likely scenario each game is that you stop the bleeding as quickly as possible so play can resume." He snaps his fingers, and a young Black man in a suit approaches with a folder, leather, of course. "This is our compensation offer."

I crack open the folder and gasp when I see the bolded number at the bottom of the page.

CHAPTER 2
ALDER

I pull up to Coach Thompson's suburban McMansion with the Fury banner hanging above the driveway, scratching at the scruff I've been cultivating for the past two weeks. The beard isn't looking great yet—patchy in places, too thick in others—but Adam says it makes me look like a Viking warrior, and I'm desperate for him to see me as sexy like that.

I recheck my phone. No text from Adam saying he's on his way.

Instead, there's a message from my dad:

> I'm thinking of you bringing Adam to the BBQ! Just be yourself. I love you, kiddo.

I swallow the lump in my throat. Ty Stag, hockey legend and tough guy extraordinaire has no problem with his son dating a guy. He just has a problem with his son dating *this* guy—the one who still hasn't arrived twenty minutes after I texted him I was here.

My phone rings, and Adam's name flashes on the screen.

"Hey, you close?" I ask instead of hello.

"I'm at the end of the street. I just wanted to check..."

After six months of dating, Adam hasn't met a single

teammate of mine outside of accidental run-ins. He hasn't been to a family dinner, hasn't attended a home game, and won't even let me tag him in private social media posts.

"I've been waiting for you in the driveway," I say, trying to keep the frustration from my voice. "The guys want to meet you. And the new dentist is coming—Coach is making a big deal about Doc Bowman's replacement."

A sigh crackles through the speaker. "I'm not comfortable with this kind of group party, Alder. I've told you that repeatedly."

"It's important to me." My voice comes out smaller than I intended.

Another sigh, then: "Fine. I see your car. I'll park behind you."

I watch in the rearview mirror as Adam's sleek Audi slides in behind my Escalade. He emerges looking like he stepped out of a magazine—crisp chinos, blue button-down rolled precisely at the elbows, artfully tousled hair. I suddenly feel underdressed in my Fury t-shirt and cargo shorts.

I hop out of my SUV and approach him with a smile. "You made it."

"For you." His lips tight, he taps away at his phone. "But I can't stay long. I have a client crisis brewing."

"You always have a client crisis brewing." The words slip out before I can stop them.

Adam finally looks up, his expression softening slightly. "It's how I can afford this car, babe." He pockets his phone and gestures toward the house. "Let's get this over with."

I reach for his hand as we walk up the driveway, but Adam deftly sidesteps, pretending to check something in his pocket. My hand hangs awkwardly between us for a moment before I shove it into my pocket.

"It's fine," I mutter. *He's just nervous. This is a big step.*

Coach's backyard is packed with my teammates and their partners. The grill is working overtime, smoke billowing as

Coach flips burgers with a spatula in one hand and a tongs-speared hot dog in the other.

My brothers spot me first.

"Aldy!" Tucker calls out, his grin wide and genuine. Gunnar waves from where he's helping set up lawn games. Their initial smiles fade slightly as they notice Adam trailing three steps behind me, already back on his phone.

Cappy, our team captain, approaches with his usual easy warmth. "A-Stag! About time you made it." He turns to Adam, extending a hand. "You must be Adam. Heard a lot about you."

Adam extends his hand with a perfunctory smile that doesn't reach his eyes. "Nice to meet you."

An awkward silence follows until Coach Thompson saves us, appearing with a plate of charred meat in one hand and a clean spatula in the other.

"Adam, right? Good to finally meet you," Coach says, balancing the plate to offer his hand. "Alder's one of our best —great to see him bringing someone important to him."

"Thank you for the invitation," Adam says with practiced politeness.

I grin and rest a hand on Adam's shoulder. "Adam's handling the media strategy for the Pittsburgh Athletic Media merger with East Coast Sports Network," I explain, proud to talk about his work. "It's a huge deal for him—" Adam freezes beside me, his smile vanishing.

Coach Thompson's eyebrows shoot up. "East Coast? My brother-in-law sits on their board," Coach says, interest piqued. "He didn't mention any merger."

"He wouldn't," I continue, despite Adam's increasingly rigid posture. "It's all under wraps until the press conference on Tuesday."

"Alder." Adam's voice is as tight as steel. "A word." Before I can respond, he grips my elbow, steering me toward the side of the house. I catch Gunnar and Tucker exchanging a look, and something twists in my stomach. Once we're out of earshot, Adam turns on me, eyes blazing. "What the hell are you doing? That information is completely confidential!"

I feel my cheeks heat. Pretty sure I just fucked up when I was trying to show off. "I was just making conversation—"

"You just told the coach of a major sports franchise about a confidential corporate merger! His brother-in-law is on the board! Do you have any idea what you've done?"

The cold realization of my mistake washes over me. "I didn't think—"

"That's the problem, isn't it? You never think." He yanks his phone from his pocket and glares. "I have to deal with this now. This could tank the entire announcement strategy." I watch as he walks away, phone pressed to his ear, his voice shifting to damage-control mode. I stand there, the weight of my carelessness settling like a stone in my gut.

I wander back to my brothers, who are still talking to Coach. All of them look at me, their expressions uncomfortable. Coach's eyebrows shoot up. "Where's your guy?"

I force a smile that feels more like a grimace. "Work call. He's around somewhere…"

I wince, but Coach sighs. "Well, boys, the water's cold, and the meat's hot." He turns to me. "Gatorade and seltzers in the coolers. No booze until after we win the Cup."

I catch Gunnar and Tucker exchanging a look, and something twists in my stomach. I hate that my brothers see precisely what they expected. Coach claps my shoulder. "Go grab a drink, son. More food's coming up soon."

I head toward the drink station, trying to shake off the embarrassment. There's a woman standing by the coolers, struggling with the cap of a probiotic seltzer. She's wearing a jean skirt that hugs the ample curve of her gorgeous backside and a flowing top that catches the breeze. Her brown hair is pulled back in a loose ponytail, and she's biting her thick lip in concentration.

"Need some muscle?" I offer, approaching with what I hope is a friendly smile.

She looks up, surprise crossing her face. "Oh! Thanks, this thing is determined to resist me." She hands me the bottle.

I twist it open easily and hand it back. "Sadists design those caps."

"Or dentists looking for business when people chip their teeth trying to open them with their mouth," she laughs.

"You must be Dr. Sinclair." I extend my hand. "Alder Stag. I play defense."

"Lena," she says, shaking my hand with a firm grip. "And yes, I've been studying the roster. You're the one with the twin, right?"

"That's me. We come as a package deal." I gesture toward Tucker, who's now operating the grill while Coach takes a break. "He's the better-looking one, but I've got the better slapshot."

She laughs a genuine sound that puts me at ease somehow. Up close, I can see she's wearing minimal makeup, just enough to make her eyelashes seem longer and her cheeks slightly flushed. I shouldn't be looking at her like that, though.

I reach into the cooler and grab a lemonade. "What's your professional position on this sugar-laden lemonade versus the probiotic stuff?"

She considers the question with mock seriousness. "It depends how many of those teeth are your own and how many are crowns."

"Knock on wood. All the Stag brothers still have all our originals," I say, rapping my knuckles against the wooden table. "Hockey miracle, I guess."

"Well then, I'd say life's too short to drink probiotic seltzer. Though I would recommend a good rinse afterward." Her smile is easy and confident. "Congratulations on making the playoffs."

We chat for a few minutes about the upcoming series against Montreal. She knows hockey surprisingly well, asking smart questions about defensive strategies and our opponents' scoring patterns. It's refreshing to talk to someone who gets it without being in the business — although I guess she's in the business now.

I find myself relaxing for the first time since arriving. "So...what's your deal? Are you a local? Family close by?"

A shadow passes across her face. "My boyfriend Brad is here somewhere." She glances around, then adds with obvious discomfort, "He needed to step away to 'center himself.' The sports talk was somewhat overwhelming for him."

I watch her shrink slightly as she says this, her shoulders curving inward, her voice growing softer. It's like watching someone dim their light.

"I get that," I say, nodding toward where Adam disappeared. "My boyfriend had to take a 'work call' two minutes after we arrived."

Her expression shifts to one of surprise, then recognition, then something like relief. "Boyfriend, huh? I do remember reading that there were a few guys on the Fury who are LGBTQ."

I nod. "I'm the B in that alphabet soup."

She grins. "So is Brad. Bisexual, I mean. He's finishing his dissertation in philosophy, so he's... particular about social settings."

"Adam works in sports PR, ironically enough. Just not comfortable with the spotlight himself." I try to sound understanding rather than disappointed.

She nods, offering a rueful smile. "Sometimes I think Brad agreed to come just so he could tell people he was at a 'professional athlete gathering' later."

We share a laugh that feels almost conspiratorial. There's a comfort in this shared experience, even if it's not a positive one.

"I should probably find him," Lena says, looking toward the house. "Make sure he hasn't started debating existentialism with your teammates."

"I'll help you look," I offer. "I should check on Adam anyway."

We wander toward the sliding glass doors leading to the kitchen. Through the window, I spot two figures by Coach's fancy bar cart in the corner of the dining room. Adam and another man—could it be Brad?—are examining a bottle of brandy, their heads bent close in conversation.

Adam gestures animatedly, a genuine smile on his face that I haven't seen in weeks. The other man—wearing a blazer despite the heat—is nodding enthusiastically, seemingly hanging on every word.

"Found them," I say unnecessarily.

Lena follows my gaze, her expression unreadable. "Of course. The one place with alcohol."

We watch for a moment as our boyfriends continue their intense conversation, utterly oblivious to our presence or the party around them. Adam says something that makes Brad throw his head back in laughter, his hand landing casually on Adam's shoulder.

"He seems to be enjoying himself now," I comment, trying to sound positive. Yet something cold and uncomfortable settles in my stomach.

Lena looks at me, and our eyes meet in silent understanding. I feel as though we are both thinking the same thing— that our partners seem more animated with each other than they've been with us all day.

CHAPTER 3
ALDER

You're still going to come, right?

I stare at my unanswered text much longer than is healthy, well past the time I should power it off and get dressed for the morning skate. I mean, shit. I'm a pro hockey player preparing for game seven in a playoff series. I have zero time for my love life to be fucking with my head.

It's been three weeks since the barbecue disaster, and Adam's responses have been increasingly cold and distant. The few texts I've gotten make it clear he's still dealing with the fallout from my loose lips. According to social media, the merger announcement had been rushed out a full day ahead of schedule, with stock prices taking a hit due to the "unplanned disclosure."

I fucked up. Royally. But I've apologized a dozen times, and I'm unsure what else I can do to make it right.

Finally, mercifully, Adam texts me back.

I said I'd be there.

The curt response makes me wince. No emoji, no elaboration—just the bare minimum acknowledgment. I purse my lips. I know this isn't working. I know. But I can't seem to quit this guy. Another text comes through before I can respond:

> Unlike some people, I understand the importance of professional commitments.

The dig is unmistakable. I type and delete three different responses before settling on:

> I really am sorry. What can I do to make it up to you?

The response is immediate:

> You've done enough.

I stare at those three words, feeling the chill through the screen. Part of me wonders if I should just end things now, cutting my losses before game seven. However, the thought of facing both a playoff elimination game and a breakup on the same day is too much.

Besides, maybe watching me play will remind Adam why he was with me in the first place. Perhaps I can still salvage this.

This is what I get for chasing a PR professional, right? From the moment I saw Adam at a post-game team event in a crowded bar, I've been following after him like my dog, Gordie, going for a butterfly.

Gordie is a lot to love, as my mother puts it, but I am, too.

I decide I need to see that ball of smelly fluff before I suit up, so I call my dog sitter, LeMarcus. Dude lives with his mom in my townhouse community and loves crashing in my guest room when I'm on the road. He's well worth every penny I give him.

"Yo, Aldy!" LeMarcus answers with the screen facing Gordie, and I break into a massive smile at my little scrappy Pughasa. The shelter believed he was probably a pug mixed with Pekingese and Lhasa Apso. But now he's all mine. Man, I love this dog.

"Hey, big guy! You being good?" Gordie wags his tail and woofs at the sound of my voice. "LeMarcus, do you have my face aimed at Gordie? Can he see me back?" My dog starts pawing at the screen.

I hear my teenage neighbor mumbling something about me being a boomer. "Yeah, man. Chill. He sees your ugly mug."

I wave, and Gordie woofs again. "I miss you, bud."

LeMarcus adopts a lower, goofy voice. "Dad, it's been like three hours since you left. I've barely been awake. I don't miss you at all."

"Tough crowd," I mutter. "Hey, thanks for showing me my good boy. Did he go out this morning?"

"Alder, I'm not discussing your dog's toilet time with you while you're in the locker room. Go bring us a win, man. Me and Gordie will be watching on your big-ass TV."

He flips the camera back, so I'm looking into his deep brown eyes. He sticks out his tongue, and I laugh. "Thanks for watching him. You find out about that culinary program yet?"

LeMarcus rolls his eyes. "Do you have any focus at all? Don't you have hockey shit to worry about right now? You can hear all about my life when you and my ma are out sittin' on your lawn chairs."

I love that this kid shows me absolutely no deference. It's refreshing, especially in a hockey-crazed town like Pittsburgh. Most people are all up in my business, trying to get me to sign their boobs and pecs and leave their phone numbers on Gordie's dog poo bags.

I hang up with my dog sitter, take a leak, and lace up my

skates, wondering where my brothers are. My twin, Tucker, and I are the youngest of four kids. Three of us play hockey for the Pittsburgh Fury, the team our dad played for and won a handful of Cups. He's a legend in this town, and I know my brother Gunnar lets that mess with his head, but he's a goalie, and they're weird.

Tuck and I have twin mojo. A coach would be nuts to break us up. Hell, I thought Tuck was nuts for wanting his own bachelor pad, and it's been a big adjustment living separately from him this year. I would probably have been content to room with him forever, but I get that we're adults now, and we're supposed to differentiate.

Tuck bursts into the locker room and slides onto the wooden bench beside me, planting a kiss on my cheek. Which I allow because I love him. "Hey, Fucker."

He flinches. "Why does everyone call me that?"

"Because it rhymes with your name, and you're a fucker." He's been trying to think of a suitable annoying nickname for me for the several decades we've been alive. What do I care if he calls me Derpy? Doesn't have the same impact.

Tuck glances toward the door, shakes his head, and starts suiting up. "I just had the best fucking massage. I think I slept through half of it. Not even sure how I rolled over." He stretches his arms above his head. "I have a good feeling about today's game."

I run a hand along my scruffy jaw. I sort of hate the requirement to stop shaving when we make the playoffs. I know beards are hot right now, but I find them itchy. At least Adam seems to think it's hot.

Tuck and I match each other's pace, getting dressed as the other guys file in, suit up, and head out to the ice. The goalies must have gone out early or something because I don't see any sign of Gunnar.

Tucker tosses his bag into the locker above his cubby and

slams the door. "Who all is here today? From the family, I mean."

I glance up, considering. "Mom and Dad. All the uncles... honestly, I think everyone."

Our oldest brother, Odin, just moved back from England with his girlfriend. Our cousin Stellen just finished law school. When I say everyone is here, I mean there are 25 members of the Stag family in the stands, ready to make some noise.

Tucker gives me a pointed look. "He going to show this time?"

I swallow the hairball that his question creates in my throat. "He'll come. He's sitting somewhere different, though."

"It's insane that you've been with this guy for six months, and I, your more-handsome twin, have only met him in passing. You know that, right?"

"Jesus, Tucker, I know. You know it's still scary to be queer in this society, right? Cut him some slack."

My brother shakes his head. "Of course I know that. And any person you date should know our family is a safe place, Bruh."

I close my eyes, think of my dog, and take a few deep breaths. "Look, I can't talk about this now. Let's just focus on beating Montreal, okay?"

He pushes to his feet. "You're right. But we *are* talking about this after we win tonight, okay?"

I follow him out to the ice, wondering how annoyed I should be that he's giving voice to all the quiet concerns I've been afraid to name for months. I truly believe if I give Adam enough time and space, he'll come around. Like, he will literally come around to family dinner. I don't need to trot him around town on my arm. I don't need him to be my date at the hospital gala. But my brother is right. Our family is the best, and pretty much all I want in the world after a Cup victory of my own is to bring the person I'm dating to a lazy summer day at our vacation house, where we all fight over card games and shove each other into the pool.

I glance up at the empty arena and emerge from the tunnel toward the ice. I look to the seat I reserved for Adam. He'll be there. I know he will. And maybe, when we win, I can skate up to the glass, press my glove against the barrier, and he'll lean in and smile.

CHAPTER 4
LENA

THE CASE SNAPS SHUT WITH A SATISFYING CLICK. EVERY instrument was in its place, every tool properly sterilized, and every emergency medication was measured and ready. If nothing else in my life is predictable, at least I have this—the beautiful order of my profession.

I run my fingers over the embroidered logo above my pocket: DR. SINCLAIR, PITTSBURGH FURY. The branded scrubs actually fit my plus-sized frame, a luxury I hadn't expected when I took this job. It's a real treat to just grab work clothes that fit comfortably.

"Everybody in this organization is king-sized," Coach Thompson commented during my orientation, gesturing to the equipment room stocked with gear for every possible body type.

I hadn't been sure if that was a compliment, an observation, or something else entirely, but the following wardrobe allowance made me too grateful to question it. Plus, now my salary is nearly double what I made at the hospital, enough to actually make progress on my mountain of student loans instead of just treading water with minimum payments. Thompson can say whatever he wants.

Through the open door of my office, which is attached to

the locker room, I can see the players gearing up, stern and quiet beneath heavy padding. It's playoff game seven. The culmination of a season's worth of work, hope, and sacrifice.

My mind drifts back to the last game when Anton declined pain medication during an emergency extraction after taking a puck to the mouth.

"No drugs," he'd insisted through a mouthful of blood. "Need head clear for third period."

I'd done it—removed the shattered pieces of his lateral incisor while he gripped the arms of the chair, his knuckles white, eyes watering but determined. Afterward, he'd thanked me with a nod and returned to the ice to score the game-winning goal.

These men are formidable.

And Sutton was right so far. To my knowledge, I haven't appeared on television, and my name hasn't surfaced in any kind of internet search. I get to be incognito while working dental magic on the gnarliest mouths in the business.

As the team warms up, my gaze lands on number 14, Alder Stag, as he sends a puck flying toward his twin at the blue line. My stomach does an unwelcome flip that has nothing to do with pre-game nerves. I mentally scold myself for my attraction to his athletic competence. Unprofessional, Lena. Completely unprofessional.

Additionally, he has Adam, and I have Brad—theoretically, at least.

I recheck my phone. Again, there is no message from my long-term boyfriend confirming he's using the ticket I arranged. When I asked him to come to tonight's game, he sighed heavily as if I'd suggested he endure root canal surgery without anesthetic.

"Another sports game?" he'd said, not looking up from his dissertation notes. "I have actual work to do, Lena."

I pressed the issue, explaining that this was different—a playoff elimination game, a chance to see what I actually do in my new role. Finally, he agreed, but only after I promised to get him a seat away from the "sports fanatics" in the Partners and Wives section.

Just like Alder had done for Adam...I overheard him saying so in the locker room. I shouldn't eavesdrop, but our conversation at the barbecue stuck with me—the recognition of our parallel situations. Alder Stag and I have an understanding...or some sort of shared relationship strife. It's not that I'm thinking about Alder often, exactly. It's just that certain moments replay in my mind when I least expect them.

The buzzer sounds, signaling the end of warm-ups—time to focus.

I join the medical team at our station near the bench as the players take the ice for introductions. Dr. Martinez, the team physician, nods in greeting.

"Ready for whatever dental disasters await, Sinclair?"

"Always," I reply, adjusting my stash of purple nitrile gloves. "Though I'm hoping for a quiet night."

"Playoff hockey?" He laughs. "Good luck with that."

The arena erupts as the starting lineup is announced, the noise rising to a physical force when the Stag brothers' names boom through the speakers. I scan the crowd absently, wondering if Brad actually showed up when I spot him—miraculously—in the section I'd arranged. He's looking at his phone, completely detached from the excitement around him, but he's here.

I wish things had improved between us since I got this new job, but if anything, we're growing even further apart. I no longer feel like we're connecting, and I also have no idea how to start a conversation about it.

The game begins with the controlled violence unique to

hockey—bodies colliding, sticks clashing, and skates carving sharp patterns in the ice. I watch with the clinical detachment I've been practicing, assessing each hit for potential injury and mentally cataloging the force and angle of every check into the boards.

Montreal plays aggressively from the first drop of the puck, targeting the Fury's top scorers. I find myself holding my breath when Alder shoulders a particularly nasty opponent into the boards, stealing the puck, and sending it to his brother without even looking. This happens 100 times a game; I should be used to it. But I've seen enough hockey this month to know that the telepathic connection between the twins is something to behold.

The first and second periods pass without incident—a minor miracle in playoff hockey, according to Doc, since the stakes are so high. I fiddle with my kit out of habit during the intermission, though nothing has been disturbed. I briefly glance at Brad, wondering if he's texting his advisor, perhaps one of his study group members, or just playing Candy Crush instead of watching the game.

The third period begins with heightened intensity, the desperation of both teams evident in their play. Five minutes in, I see it happen—Tucker Stag takes the top of a stick to the face as he battles for the puck. He drops immediately, a spray of red on the white ice. The whistle blows, and the ref starts waving his arms frantically.

"A-Stag is down," one of the assistants says, already gathering supplies.

My heart lurches before I can stop it. "T-Stag," I correct automatically.

The assistant gives me a curious look, but there's no time to explain how I can distinguish the brothers apart from a distance. We move quickly onto the ice, adrenaline sharpening my thoughts to a fine point.

Tucker is sitting up by the time we reach him, blood dripping freely from his mouth onto the ice. I kneel beside him, snapping into complete professional mode.

"Let me see, Tucker," I say, keeping my voice calm and authoritative tone.

He opens his mouth, revealing a partially fractured incisor, the jagged edge already cut into his lower lip, causing the bleeding. His eyes seem to calm when he recognizes me.

"Doc Thinclair?" he manages through the blood.

"Exactly so. Hold still."

I work efficiently, applying gauze to control the bleeding while examining the broken tooth. Thankfully, it's a clean break,—no root exposure, although the edges are sharp enough to cause further tissue damage if left untreated.

"I'm going to file down the sharp edges," I explain, reaching for my hand tool. "It'll be temporary until we get you properly treated off-ice."

Tucker nods, his eyes darting to something—someone— behind me. I sense Alder's presence before I see him, and the shift in Tucker's expression tells me his twin has arrived.

"He okay?" Alder asks, his voice tight and edged with concern.

"Broken tooth, but nothing that can't be fixed," I reply without looking up, focusing on my work. "He'll be ready to go in a minute."

I feel Alder hovering, watching as I smooth the jagged edge of his brother's tooth just enough to prevent further injury. Our shoulders nearly touch as he leans in to check on Tucker, and I force myself to maintain absolute professional focus despite the proximity. Then, I sense when Alder skates away from the scene.

"All set," I say, backing away as Tucker spits one last time and accepts his mouthguard from an assistant. "We'll do a proper fix tomorrow."

Tucker nods, and I'm aware of the crowd yelling and the cameras flashing, a low hum traveling through the arena, but I'm assuming it's due to the injury.

I glance up into the ice-blue eyes of Alder Stag, who tips his chin toward the giant screens above the ice. I expect to see a replay of Tucker's injury. Instead, I see … Brad. Brad is on the kiss cam, but he's not alone and certainly not uncomfortable. He's enthusiastically kissing another man, their hands clutching at each other's faces with unmistakable familiarity. It takes my brain a moment to process what I see, to reconcile the image on the screen with what I know to be reality.

The man Brad is kissing is Adam… Alder's boyfriend.

My lungs stop working. The sounds of the arena fade to a distant whine as I stare at the frozen image on the screen: eighteen thousand people watching my boyfriend kiss someone else—someone I know.

I feel myself sway slightly, grabbing the arm of the ref for support. There's commotion throughout the arena. I look away from the screen to see Alder standing motionless, staring up at the same image, his gloves and helmet discarded on the ice. His face contorts in what might be rage, anguish, or both.

Our eyes meet across the distance, a silent exchange of shock and betrayal that needs no words. In that horrible moment, we're connected by the same wound inflicted by the same hands.

The crowd's reaction shifts from excitement to confusion, and murmurs grow as people realize something is wrong. Cameras flash, capturing Alder's reaction while I stand frozen in relative anonymity.

I watch as Tucker approaches his twin, blood-stained

gauze still visible in his mouth, as he drapes an arm around Alder's shoulders. The medical staff around me are talking, asking questions I can't process.

"Dr. Sinclair? You okay?"

I nod mechanically, forcing myself back into professional mode through sheer will. "Fine. Just—worried about Tucker's follow-up care."

They accept this explanation, turning their attention back to the ice where the referees are preparing to restart play. I stand there, somehow both present and absent, my body going through the motions while my mind replays the kiss in an endless, excruciating loop.

The whistle blows. The puck drops. The game continues as if the world hasn't just shattered.

I watch Alder attempt to resume play; his movements suddenly seem wooden and unfocused. A Montreal player blows past him, then Tucker, then scores on Gunnar. The buzzer sounds, and just like that, the game is over. The season is over. And somewhere in the arena, Brad is with Adam, unaware or uncaring of the devastation they have just caused.

CHAPTER 5

ALDER

I wake to the sensation of what I hope is my dog's tongue on my face. "Gordie, chill." I groan, the effort of speaking too much for my pounding head. My entire body is one giant cramp, and I realize I'm folded in half on a sofa.

I peel open one eye. I'm in my living room, on the couch. The room is cluttered with empty alcohol containers, and … I groan. Two of my brothers are sprawled on the floor, and another is in my recliner.

Gordie whines and keeps licking. Shit. He probably needs to go out.

I rescued Gordon mid-season, and I never get hammered while I'm in season. Nobody could have prepared me for the horrors of having a small creature depend on me while I'm hungover as fuck.

I sit up, and Gordie starts yipping, which feels like tiny needles hammering into my eyes. I have no idea how Tucker and Gunnar are sleeping through this, but they're probably still plastered. I glance at my body, see that I'm wearing sweatpants and a T-shirt, and decide that's plenty to take a dog outside.

I rise to my feet, feeling the ache in my ribs where I was checked extra hard last night. Last night. Fuck.

"Come on, Gordo." I hobble toward the sliding door and onto the small patio, wishing I were farther along in Gordie's training so that I could just let him loose and know he'd come back. I clip his leash onto his collar and try sitting on the step, but Gordon Howe Stag can't just piss in the grass by the porch. My picky-ass dog wants to do his business where other dogs in our neighborhood can see and smell him. I assume.

He drags me toward the drainage ravine, and I mutter brief thanks that he's not pulling me toward the jogging path by the river where other humans are inevitably out and about. I don't even know what time it is.

Twelve hours past my public humiliation? Fourteen?

The dry, caked feeling in my mouth mimics the sensations in my brain as I think about watching Adam suck face with another guy. In a hockey arena. In the hockey arena where I was playing game seven. If I had just played things cool, people wouldn't have figured out that he meant something to me. If I had gritted my teeth and stared at my brother or something, this would still be a private pain.

But, remembering the post-match locker room screaming now, my brothers tell me my face twisted in rage, and I was howling louder than Tucker when he lost his tooth.

Shit. Tucker.

"Gordon, come on, boy." I tug him back toward the house. My twin needs to get back to the training facility today to get his mouth fixed, and Tucker is terrified of the dentist. I'll never understand it. I absolutely love having my teeth cleaned. The dentist gets all up in there with that scraper, and my mouth feels like a million bucks by the time I'm done.

Regular people only go to the dentist twice a year. But since we have one right there on site and nobody else takes advantage, I get my plaque scraped every few weeks. Tucker? Hell, he asks me to pretend to be him when it's his turn for mandatory oral health checks. It used to work with

Doc Boman. Something tells me the new dentist won't be fooled.

It's hard to imagine keeping my cool with a woman like that leaning over me, complimenting my gums. But I don't want to think about her right now. I should be focused on my enormous humiliation.

I walk back inside, and the stench of my living room almost knocks me on my ass. We seem to have blended whiskey with strong beer. No wonder my guts feel like there's a rip tide in there. I concentrate on focusing my eyes on the microwave clock and see that it's just past nine.

This is fine. We have time.

I offer Gordie a biscuit and tread carefully back into the living room, where Tucker is starfished on his stomach on my rug. I nudge him with my toe, which is wet from the grass. I'd laugh at how gross this is, but I'm too fucked up. "Fucker, bro. We gotta get your mouth fixed."

He grunts.

I crouch next to him and manually peel open one eyelid. "Don't make me spit on your eyeball."

His pupil contracts, and Tucker springs into a sitting position. "How are we related? You're vile."

"Apparently." I think again of chasing after Adam for six fucking months. Six months of me calling him and initiating our hangouts. And then I was so overjoyed by any scrap of attention I wrecked everything by blab-bragging.

Sure, Adam was always down for the physical stuff. I guess that's all I'm good for. Although, evidently, not even that good if he's so eager to do that shit with someone else.

A thought invades my brain fog. "Tuck, what if he gave me a disease?"

My brother sighs, fully awake now. He claps a hand on my shoulder. "You're safe, right? You use the basket?"

I sigh. Our parents always insisted each Stag kid had a "safe and satisfied" selection, no questions asked. Even now that I'm a grown-ass adult, Mom still restocks the wicker basket on my fridge whenever she drops by. Condoms, lube, pamphlets for HIV prevention...

I nod. "Yeah. I use the basket. But, you know, none of that stuff is foolproof."

Tucker flops over with his head in my lap. He drags his palms down his face. Then he winces and opens his mouth, revealing the jagged edge of a tooth broken off near the gum. "When's the last time we got tested for shit? Not since preseason?"

I shake my head. "I don't even know. I didn't get called for randoms this year."

Tucker sits up, then stands, clutching his ribs in the same spot where mine ache. "Well, you're taking me to get my face fixed. You can just ask Doc to check your junk while we're there."

With this extreme vote of confidence, Tucker and I shove our feet into shoes. I grab a baseball cap from the peg near the door, and my brother helps himself to get another one, which was probably his first time. I pull my phone and keys off the table by the door and see that I've missed approximately 7,000 calls and messages.

"Fuck me. I need to change my number."

Tucker peeks over my shoulder and looks at his phone. "I only missed 45 messages from Mom. And twelve calls from Brian."

At the sound of our agent's name, it appears on my phone screen as the device vibrates in my hand. I lean against the wall by the door and answer.

Brian, as usual, does not waste time with greetings or small talk. "A-Stag, this is a shit show. Oy vey, this guy you were schtupping is making problems. Did you know about any of this? Don't answer that. I'm meeting you at the facility."

He hangs up, and Tucker and I leave the apartment. Gunnar and Odin will let themselves out later.

Tucker squints into the sun as we walk toward my Escalade. "Did Bri say shtoop? What's that?"

I unlock the doors and slump into the driver's seat. "Using context clues, I'm guessing it means fuck, Fucker."

"Yeah. Probably."

I shake my head and start to drive. Coming out as bi when I was in college was, thankfully, a non-issue for my team-mates and has remained that way. There's another out-player on the Fury, too, although people usually refer to us both as gay, even though I'm super bi.

Brian has been great about setting up opportunities for Banksy and me to talk with youth hockey players about the importance of inclusivity in hockey. It's all been rainbows and Pride flags until I got cheated on.

Tucker must be scrolling through social media because he starts making all sorts of noises while I'm driving north.

CHAPTER 6
LENA

I'VE LOST TRACK OF HOW MANY TIMES I'VE THROWN UP SINCE I saw Brad making out with someone else on the jumbo screen at my new job. The fact that Brad was even at a hockey game is surreal. I wish I felt more surprised that he was cheating.

Most of the nausea came alongside a deep certainty that he's never cared for me. Not like I cared for him. I clutch my stomach, glancing around the empty apartment where I slept a total of zero minutes last night. He hasn't answered his phone. He certainly didn't come home.

Home.

This place will never feel like home to me. It is a den of betrayal.

I don't know much right now, but I do know that.

I stare at my face in the bathroom mirror, at the dark smudges under my eyes, at my unkempt hair. I need to get my shit together and drive to the hockey facility—a special building north of the city where the players practice, work out, and sometimes seek dental care.

Since I don't know if I can bear to come back here ever again, I grab the first suitcase I can find and stuff a bunch of things into it: my laptop and some underwear, not my clothes because I'm between sizes right now and was counting on wearing scrubs most of the time.

I spit out a laugh, remembering all the zeroes on my new salary. Now that I'm not going to be funding anyone else's lifestyle, I'll be able to divert some of that money toward a plus-sized wardrobe that feels comfortable. After I take a whack at my student loan balance, I guess.

I rush through a shower, glance around the apartment again, and realize how much of it centers on Brad and his wants and tastes. The spare bedroom? His office where he can ponder his dissertation.

The living room? His furniture choices, his artwork. His dishes. His blender and specialty cookware. Like the clay tagine, he insisted on getting, donating our other pans, and then using them exactly once. I've been microwaving my pasta in a glass measuring cup for a year. A fucking year.

I swipe at the tagine on the counter and watch in satisfaction as it strikes the tiled kitchen floor, shattering into three pieces. "Good," I say to the empty apartment.

I climb into my beat-up Honda Civic, drive north, and head to my dental suite to wait for Tucker Stag.

This is what a dental suite might look like in a fantasy land, surely. Everything is painted in soothing beach tones. The artwork appears as if it came straight from a meditation retreat. And the equipment! It resembles a catalog we see at a dental conference, fully aware that any practice hiring us will likely only afford shabby, outdated versions.

I run my hand along a water pick, state-of-the-art 3D imaging devices, and modern X-ray machines. There hasn't been much time to explore since the team has been in the playoffs. My predecessor has a closet full of small drawers, each labeled with a name: G STAG, ROGERS. I pull open some of the drawers to reveal plaster mouth molds and, in some cases, loose teeth. Fascinating.

Well, if this is where I get to work, there's at least a small silver lining to my humiliation. I could sleep in this office quite comfortably, I'm sure. The desk chair alone is one of the five-figure options I used to laugh at with my cohort in dental school. I sink into it, noticing that I can widen the base to comfortably accommodate my hips.

Yeah, this is okay.

I hear male voices arguing and kick my bag under my desk. I tuck my hair behind my ears and straighten my scrub top as a third, angrier male voice joins the fray. Should I wait here for them to approach?

I don't have to wait long until a middle-aged white guy with dark hair sticks his head into the office. "You the new doc?" I nod. He presses his lips together. "Well, I'll let you go to town on Tweedle Dee here, but I'd appreciate it if we could talk after."

"Certainly, Mr…"

He smacks his forehead. "Sorry about that. Brian Klein. I'm the agent for these two." He hooks a thumb over his shoulder, and I glance around him to see two identical hockey players. Well, nearly identical. One has a bruised face, and I last saw him bleeding on the ice as I filed down the sharp edges of his broken incisor.

I slip into my work focus, forgetting everything else for the moment as I rise to greet my clearly terrified patient. "Tucker, I'm going to take good care of you today."

The non-injured twin slaps his brother on the back. "You should call him Fucker. He's going to be good."

Judging by his face, there's nothing good going on for Alder today. He looks about as healthy as I do after the kiss cam. Maybe he's just concerned for his brother.

"Tucker," I repeat. "How is your pain this morning?" His eyes dart rapidly around the room like he's searching for a drill. "Tell you what." I approach him and realize my head only comes to the shoulders of these massive athletes. I look up into his bearded face, wondering how someone could play such a violent, brutal sport, and feel so intimidated by the tiny tools I use to tend teeth. "Let's get you in the chair, and we can take a look at things. I promise I will only use my hands until we discuss a plan. Okay?"

Tucker looks at his brother, who rolls his eyes and shoves Tucker toward the exam chair. Tucker clutches his twin's hand in a move I find deeply endearing, and I'm glad when they both make their way toward the chair. Now, I need to set Tucker at ease… or at least distract him while I work.

"How are you today?" I reach for the box of gloves on the wall of the exam room. They're all XL, of course, but these will have to do until I can order smaller gloves to fit. At least my hands aren't plus-sized.

"Fine," he grunts and looks away.

"Okay, Tucker, Alder is going to stay right with you. I'm going to tip you back, turn on my light, and reach inside to check things out, okay?" Tucker shakes his head, but Alder places a hand on his shoulder. This is going to be a rough one. The twins are probably six-three, their frames occupying the entirety of the available space. Relatable.

Tucker opens his mouth a wee bit, and I nod, reaching a finger inside. "I'm just going to feel your gums for signs of swelling. Good." I touch the jagged edge of the broken tooth. "Breathe, Tucker." I didn't have time to grab a surgical mask, and I inhale a nose full of Tucker's leftover alcohol. I don't blame him. I wish I'd gone with him to the bottom of that bottle last night.

He clenches his jaw as I note the fracture lines in what's left of the tooth. "That's going to be sharp and sore," I say, checking for nerve exposure and finding none. "We have a few options. I could put a plastic cap over the remainder of the tooth. It would be pretty fragile…you'd have to be careful chewing, and you would lose it if you got hit in the face again."

Alder snorts. "You lost him at 'careful,' Doc. What's the other choice?"

I wince and nod. "Well, I'm afraid I'd have to extract the tooth and build you a removable one. I would advise against a permanent implant--"

"Implant?" Tucker's eyes fly wide, and he jerks his head away. Alder sighs and pats him on the shoulder.

Brian, the agent, tired of waiting, I guess, starts to yell. "Tucker, quit being a baby. She's going to numb you first and it's fine."

"Yes," I concur. "I'm assuming we don't want a permanent tooth until you retire." Tucker shrugs. I spin around in my chair, opening drawers until I find the supplies I need to numb Tucker's mouth so I can prepare his tooth for extraction. I grab the numbing ointment and a cotton swab, holding it up so he can see. "Numbing gel first, then a shot."

Tucker emits a wail. Alder leans toward me. "Just do it. He does better if you go fast and just do it."

I gaze into Alder's eyes, seeing pain there alongside compassion. I nod and swab Tucker's cheek, then quickly prepare the shot. "Little pinch," I say, shaking his lip to distract him. It doesn't work, and he clenches.

"Do it, Doc," Brian yells, and I sigh.

I lean closer. "Tuck, I promise this will only hurt for three Mississippis. Okay?" His eyes water, but he nods. I inject the gum as Tucker squeals, then stops.

"There." I sit back and peel off a glove. "Should be a few minutes, and we can get started."

Brian takes this opportunity to clear his throat and start talking. "Dr. Sinclair. Lena. I'm sure you've seen the headlines by now."

I furrow my brow. "Headlines?"

He mutters in Yiddish and holds up his phone.

There's a giant headline, *Fury Defenseman's Boyfriend Caught in Kiss Cam Scandal*, followed by a picture of Brad and

Adam making out at the hockey game, and another photo of Alder screaming in…is it rage or anguish? Humiliation?

Brian licks his lips. "According to my client, your boyfriend." He points at me. "Is fucking his boyfriend." He points his other hand at Alder, then smashes his fists together, mimicking an explosion. "The media is going nuts."

Brian launches into a rapid-fire discussion about how Alder is being dragged through a gauntlet of speculation, analysis, and criticism, with the worst of it coming from fans who claim he cost the Fury the season on purpose after realizing what his partner was up to.

"This is cruel," I shout, clapping a hand over my mouth.

Tucker sits up, drooling. "Thath what I shaid."

Brian shakes his head. "This is pro sports, ladies and gents. We need to control the narrative. It doesn't help that Alder refused to talk to the media after the game." He taps Alder on the back. "You're getting fined, by the way."

"Fuck if I care," Alder mutters. He meets my gaze and slumps against the wall, nearly falling off the rolling stool.

It seems so cruel to discuss his humiliation like this: the betrayal. I almost forget about my nightmare. I open my mouth to suggest… what? That there's an explanation? A reasonable excuse?

Brian mutters something about taking calls and waltzes out of the room. I wish I could slip away from the visible pain both these men are experiencing for different reasons. I thought I could quietly slip into this job. I believed this was a financial windfall that would help me regain my footing in my relationship. Instead, it's set me up for an extremely public analysis of all my deepest shame. My mother's refrain echoes in my head. Nobody will ever love me, not when I look like this. Nobody will ever take care of me. I will need to be more nurturing, more available, more, more, more, while striving to be smaller and take up less space.

I hear another whining sound and realize it's coming from

me. I shove a knuckle into my mouth. "I apologize," I say to Tucker, who reaches for my hand and squeezes it. I choke out a laugh, realizing what it means for him to work through his terror to comfort me.

Alder's blue gaze bores into me as I try to think. "I don't know what to do," I say to him. Not sure why I'm addressing him, but his face is in my line of vision. "I don't know what to do."

He swallows, the muscles of his throat working behind a scruffy blond beard. "You're going to fix my brother's mouth, and then we're going to get revenge on those assholes."

CHAPTER 7
ALDER

I'M PRETTY SURE MY BROTHER BROKE ALL THE BONES IN MY HAND while squeezing it during his tooth extraction with Dr. Sinclair. I have no idea what she's doing in his mouth, but she assures me he's numb, and she keeps singing softly to him with a lovely voice that I can hear above the humming of her tools.

After what feels like twenty hours, she leans back, flicks her ponytail over her shoulder, and confidently declares him to be all set.

Tucker flops around in the seat, meeting my eye and pulling his lips back. I squint, looking at his mouth, and see… a hole where his upper front tooth used to be. "Looks smooth," I tell him. He closes his eyes.

Dr. Sinclair—Lena—pats his hand. "You should be able to eat and speak normally once the anesthesia wears off. I'll get to work building a temporary tooth and bring you back to get fitted for that as soon as possible. Hopefully, we have a model of your 'before' mouth in here somewhere." Lena waves a hand toward a set of drawers. I cringe internally because I happen to know that mouth mold day was one of the times Tucker bribed me to come in place of him. So, I guess he's getting a tooth-shaped like mine…

Lena stands and walks to the sink, washing her hands while still humming to herself. She and I have a few things to discuss.

Brian reappears in the room and tips his chin at me, signaling with his hand to his ear in the universal sign for 'call me later.' He swats Tucker on the shoulder. "Come on, big guy. I'll take you home."

Tucker moans and shakes his head but rolls himself out of the chair and gets to his feet, following Brian, who is already talking to him about endorsement deals for orthodontia. I glance around the room at the heaps of dental tools and gauze that Dr.—Lena has started cleaning up. "Don't you have staff for that?"

She shrugs. "Probably? I think they're maybe all hungover after …everything…"

She drifts off, and I chuckle. Then, I hear her stomach gurgle loudly in the quiet room. "Right." I nod. "Well, we've got shit to discuss, and you're starving, so why don't we head to the cafeteria and kill two birds?"

"Mmm." She nods again, dumping a bunch of metal tools into the sink and wiping her hands on her scrub pants. "Lead the way."

We walk silently through the halls of the training facility, which resembles a ghost town. Makes sense since I ended our season last night, but I guess I assumed the staff would at least be here yelling at each other and threatening to bench me or send my ass down to the minors.

The cafeteria is pretty quiet, but I hear the sounds of someone washing dishes in the back, and there are a few meals in the grab-n-'-go cooler. So Lena and I help ourselves and sit at one of the booths along the window overlooking the training ice. It's dark down there, which seems fitting. I realize neither of us has anything to drink, so I grab a few mugs and find coffee in a carafe. I see that Lena has grabbed a small tray of cream and sugar, and I smile at her as I sink back into the booth.

I hand her one of the mugs, and then we reach for the creamer simultaneously. Her hand is warm and soft, and I retract mine as if I got burned. I clear my throat. "After you." I wrap my hands around my mug, grateful for the warmth.

Dr. Sinclair—Lena—stares into her mug as if it contains answers instead of caffeine. The silence between us isn't exactly uncomfortable, but it's heavy with the weight of shared humiliation.

She glances up, tucking a strand of dark hair behind her ear. "Is it always like this? Your life being... public property?"

"Only when I screw up spectacularly." I attempt a smile that feels more like a grimace. "Or when I'm doing something marketable. It's Pride Month, so I'd be getting attention anyway."

"That's right." She nods slowly. "You're out. I mean, clearly, since everyone knew about Adam."

I take a sip of coffee, wincing at both the heat and the memory. "Yeah. Since college. It's never been a big deal with the team. Adam, though..." I trail off, surprised by my sudden urge to explain everything to this woman I barely know. She sets me at ease, and I don't even think she's aware of doing it.

"Adam wasn't out?" she prompts, a dark brow raised in confusion.

"Not like I am. After six months of dating, I've never met his friends. He's never spent holidays with my family—which, trust me, is a whole circus you can't avoid in the Stag household." I stare at my hands. "I made excuses for him. Said he needed time."

Lena's quiet laugh holds no humor. "I know about making excuses. Brad was 'focusing on his dissertation.' That's why he couldn't work, couldn't contribute financially, couldn't help around the apartment..." She rubs her temple. "God, I'm an idiot."

"Hey." The word comes out sharper than I intended. "We're not idiots. We're just people who trusted the wrong people."

There's a moment of silence as she absorbs my statement, and both of us attack our food. I'm not even sure what she grabbed, but I've got some kind of oatmeal bowl layered with nuts and seeds. I make a mental note to stop for fast food later since it's the off season, and I can murder my guts with grease if I want.

"You know what kills me?" Lena says after several bites. "I paid for everything. His books, his conferences, our rent." She stabs what looks like a potato. "I even paid for his therapy because—get this—he said he needed to work through his commitment issues."

"While he was *committing* to someone else." I shake my head. "Adam always had reasons why we could only meet at my place. Never in public." I pour syrup over my oatmeal, watching it pool at the edges of the bowl. "I thought he was protecting me from fans and media. Turns out he was keeping his options open."

"Brad claimed I'm too boring for anyone else to be interested in," Lena says so matter-of-factly that it takes me a moment to register the cruelty of those words. "Said I should be grateful he saw past my size to the real me."

My spoon freezes halfway to my mouth. "That's fucked up."

"Yeah." She holds my gaze, and something shifts between us—a recognition that we're not just complaining about bad breakups. We're acknowledging genuine harm. "And you know what? That grad program he claimed took all his time? He was barely passing his program requirements. His advisor called once looking for a draft that was months overdue."

"Adam would always text during our dates. Said it was work." I shake my head. "Probably texting your boyfriend."

"Ex-boyfriend," she corrects firmly, and we share our first genuine smile.

I hop up to refill our coffees, and I find myself telling Lena about Adam's excuses for missing my family's Christmas, about the way he'd criticize my townhouse, and about the subtle digs at my intelligence.

She nods along, offering her own stories—Brad "borrowing" her credit card, Brad telling her friends she was too busy to hang out while she was working extra shifts to cover their expenses, and Brad criticizing her clothes while refusing to carry laundry down to the building's basement.

With each revelation, my embarrassment fades, and my anger grows—not the hot, blinding rage I felt when I saw them on the kiss cam, but something cooler and more focused.

"You know what's almost funny?" Lena sets down her fork, plate nearly empty. "I kept thinking if I just tried harder. If I had been more supportive, he'd have finally committed. Complete his dissertation, get a job, be a partner instead of a project."

"I get that." I lean back, suddenly aware I've eaten every grain in my bowl. "I thought if I gave Adam enough space, enough time, he'd eventually feel secure enough to let me in. To be part of my world."

"And then..." she begins.

"They became part of each other's worlds," I finish.

Our eyes meet, and there's a moment of perfect understanding between us—two people who've been played for fools finding unexpected solidarity across a sticky cafeteria table.

Lena wraps her hands around her coffee mug again, but it doesn't appear she's seeking warmth this time. She looks composed. "I spent this morning throwing up from the shock. Now I'm just... angry."

"Good." I nod decisively. "Angry is better than humiliated."

"Is it, though?" Her eyebrow lifts. "I mean...the whole city's watching?"

I consider this as I study the woman across from me—her direct gaze and the stubborn set of her jaw. Something about her reminds me of my mother, not in looks but in backbone. "Maybe we can turn this around somehow."

"How?" she asks, curiosity replacing some of the hurt in her expression

I lean forward, thoughts brewing. "Like I said, what if we get some revenge? Nothing illegal, but something... satisfying."

Her eyes narrow, but there's a spark there. "What kind of revenge?"

"I don't know yet, but we deserve to feel better than this." I tap my fingers on the table. "Got any ideas?"

"Actually..." A small, dangerous smile plays on her lips. "I've had a few thoughts."

"Let's hear them."

"Well, Brad's teaching a summer seminar on moral philosophy." She twists her napkin between her fingers. "Wouldn't it be poetic for someone to interrupt his lecture on ethics with a reminder of his moral failures?"

I let out a surprised laugh. "What did you have in mind? Skywriting? Billboard outside his classroom?"

"I was thinking more... musical." Her smile widens. "My college roommate's brother has a barbershop quartet. They do singing telegrams."

The image clicks instantly, and I'm grinning despite myself. "A quartet bursting into his classroom to sing about what a cheating mooch he is?"

"They could sing 'No Scrubs' by TLC."

I nearly choke on my coffee. "That's perfect. Imagine it in four-part harmony or whatever?"

"I bet his class would join in, sing with them," she finishes, and we're laughing now.

"What about Adam?" she asks when we've calmed down. "What's your revenge fantasy?"

I consider this, rolling a few possibilities around in my mind. "I'd love to let Gordie–that's my dog–piss in all Adam's designer shoes. Oh, or switch all his pants out for pants one size smaller."

Lena grins. "I could give you toothpaste that dyes his teeth blue."

"Yes!" I pump my fist. "I love that one."

Lena raises an eyebrow. "Would you do anything to him at a work event?"

"No." I shake my head. "I'm not that guy. But making him sweat a little? That's fair game."

"What about social media?" she suggests. "You could post about 'moving on' and 'finding someone who appreciates you.' Make him think you've already replaced him."

"I could," I muse. "Though knowing Adam, he'd just call me to figure out who I'm seeing."

"Block his number?"

"Tempting." I drum my fingers on the table. "What about you? What else can we do to Brad?"

She sighs. "I don't think I'm creative enough for this."

I wave a hand. "You're super creative. This is all gold. We could always do something classic. Change his Netflix password. Sign him up for embarrassing email lists."

"I like the email idea," she nods. "Especially since he uses his university email for everything personal."

We spend the next twenty minutes throwing increasingly ridiculous revenge ideas back and forth—most of which we'd never actually do, but it feels good to voice them out loud.

Eventually, our laughter dies down, and reality settles back in. Lena's expression clouds over.

"What's wrong?" I ask.

She hesitates, then says, "I just remembered I don't want to go home tonight. Or ever... really."

"Because of Brad?"

"Yeah." She stares into her empty coffee mug. "The thought of facing him, of sleeping under the same roof..." She shakes her head. "Maybe, I can find a hotel for a few days."

"Hotels are expensive," I point out. "Especially considering you were already floating his lazy ass."

"I know, but—"

"I have a guest room." The words are out before I can think better of them.

She looks up, surprise evident in her expression. "What?"

"I have a guest room," I repeat. "It's nothing fancy, but it's private. And, you know, Brad-free."

"That's..." She blinks. "That's very generous, but I couldn't impose like that."

"It's not an imposition," I assure her. "It's the first time I've ever lived without my twin and at least one other brother. It's too much space for just me and my dog."

"We barely know each other," she points out.

"True," I acknowledge. "But you're the team dentist. If you were an axe murderer, I'm pretty sure they would've caught that in the background check."

That elicits a small laugh from her. "Still..."

"Look, it would be temporary," I say. "Just until you find your place. And honestly?" I lower my voice conspiratorially. "It would give us more time to plot our revenge. Two minds are better than one."

She studies me for a long moment, clearly weighing her options. "I wouldn't be in your way?"

"There's plenty of space." I shrug. "And this way, when

Brad and Adam inevitably try to reach out, neither of us has to face them alone."

"What about rent? Utilities?"

"We can figure all that out later."

She draws a deep breath, then nods. "Okay. Temporarily. Until I find a place."

"Great," I say, surprised by how pleased I feel. "Do you need to get your stuff tonight?"

"I have a few things in my car." She pauses. "The rest... I don't know. Maybe I can go when I know Brad won't be there."

"Or I could go with you," I offer. "Moral support. Heavy lifting."

"Thank you," she says, and the genuine gratitude in her voice makes something warm unfurl in my chest. "For all of this."

"Hey, revenge plotters have to stick together," I reply lightly, but I mean it. There's something comforting about having someone else who understands exactly what I'm going through.

As we gather our things and head for the exit, I wonder what I've just gotten myself into: a roommate situation with a woman I barely know, a revenge scheme against our cheating exes without input from Brian, and a complicated web of personal and professional connections.

But as I glance at Lena walking beside me, her head held high despite everything that's happened, I can't bring myself to regret it. For the first time since seeing that kiss cam footage, I feel something other than humiliation or rage.

I feel like I might have found an ally.

CHAPTER 8

LENA

I GLANCE AROUND THE SUNNY TOWNHOUSE COMPLEX, GRIPPING my hastily packed suitcase with white knuckles. This is madness. Complete madness. Twenty-four hours ago, I was treating a hockey player's broken tooth on live television. Now, I'm moving in with his twin brother as part of an elaborate revenge scheme against our cheating exes.

My mother would be thrilled— or horrified; probably both.

A neighbor waves at me as I park in the space Alder texted me to use–a Black woman in a sundress watering the plants in her small plot of lawn. "You must be Lena. Alder said he was getting a roommate." She smiles and waggles her eyebrows.

Of course, he did—so, much for slipping into his home unnoticed. I force a smile and wave back, glancing around again. The townhouse community is situated right along the Allegheny River, with a paved bike and jog path along the water. Each unit has a small lawn and patio, and the whole complex is fenced in, featuring a gate that leads out to the river. This is a huge step up from the kind of place where a dental school graduate with crushing student loan debt gets to live.

"I'm Kim," she says, waving with her non-hose hand. "You're aiming for that one with the big wreath on the door." She gestures toward a unit adorned with a gaudy gold wreath covered in black stag silhouettes.

I swallow hard, stepping toward the door. For a brief moment, I consider turning around and running away. Go where, though? Back to the apartment where Brad is probably lounging on furniture I paid for? To a hotel I can't afford?

No, I've made my choice. However bizarre this arrangement is, it's my best option right now. Plus, Alder mentioned he has STI testing kits for us to use.

I raise my hand to knock on the blue door, but before I can, it swings open, revealing not Alder but another enormous blond man.

"Hey, doc," Gunnar Stag booms, grinning widely. "Welcome home."

"You live here, too?"

He steps back, waving me inside with a theatrical flourish. "Nah. But there's a lot of us in this family, and we love each other."

I step into an open-concept living space that's somehow both luxurious and lived-in. Huge windows offer a stunning view of the river and the city across from it, while the kitchen island is cluttered with takeout containers and beer bottles. Three massive men—all versions of Alder with slight variations—are sprawled across couches and armchairs, arguing loudly about something on the television.

Gunnar calls from the arm of the sofa, "Alder! Your dentist is here!"

"She's not *my* dentist," Alder's voice calls from somewhere. "And you know her name is Lena."

The men turn to look at me, and I resist the urge to shrink under their collective gaze. I notice that Tucker's mouth is still slightly swollen. The fourth man—darker blond than the others—stands and approaches with his hand extended.

"Odin Stag," he says. "Oldest and wisest. Despite what Gunnar claims."

"Lena Sinclair," I reply, shaking his enormous hand. "Newest and most confused."

This earns a laugh from all of them, and some tension in my shoulders eases. Before I can say anything else, a blur of fur and stubby limbs comes skittering across the hardwood floor, sliding to a stop at my feet.

I look down at the most charmingly hideous face I've ever seen on a dog. One eye points slightly outward, while its underbite reveals a row of tiny bottom teeth. Its fur—a mix of wiry patches and fluffy tufts—sticks out in unpredictable directions.

"You must be Gordie," I say, crouching down.

The dog's entire body wiggles with the force of his tail wagging. I offer my hand for him to sniff, and he immediately licks my fingers before nuzzling his head under my palm.

"He approves," Alder says, appearing from what I assume is a hallway leading to the bedrooms. He's changed into joggers and a worn Fury t-shirt, his hair damp as if he's just showered. "Which is good because he's the only one whose opinion matters around here."

I squat by the dog, frozen at the sight of this clean-cut Adonis. "You shaved." is what falls out of my mouth.

Alder runs a hand along his chiseled jaw, and I can smell aftershave, soap, and something unique to this beautiful man. "Yeah," he says. "Playoffs are over, so the beard could go, thank god. Those things itch like hell."

"I'm keeping mine," Gunnar yells from across the room, cutting the tension a bit as the brothers argue about their facial hair.

"I think your dog's adorable," I say, trying to regain control of the situation, scratching behind Gordie's ears while he makes snorting noises of pleasure. "So ugly he's cute, you know? Like a little gargoyle with fur."

"That's exactly what I said when Alder brought him home!" Tucker exclaims. "Also, his breath is terrible. Fair warning."

As if on cue, Gordie pants happily in my face, and I'm hit with a wave of doggy halitosis that could wilt flowers. "Oh my," I laugh, turning my face away. "That is... potent."

"I brush his teeth," Alder says defensively. "He just has stomach issues."

"You could bring him to the dental suite sometime," I offer, standing up. "I could check his teeth."

Alder's expression brightens. "You'd do that?"

"Of course. It's literally my job to examine teeth."

Odin snorts. "Yeah, human teeth, not whatever's happening in that dog's mouth."

"Fair point," I concede. "But I think I could identify a problem if there is one, and Alder could go from there."

"See?" Alder says triumphantly. "She's a professional."

I feel myself blushing at his defense of me, which is ridiculous. I am a professional; I just wouldn't normally count smelly mutts among my patients.

"So, Lena," Gunnar says, flopping back onto the couch. "You're moving in..."

Tucker throws an empty water bottle at him. "Chill, man. She and Alder are in a fragile state."

"It's called kindness, moron," Alder interjects before I can respond. "And we're not going into details with you vultures."

"It's fine," I say, surprised by my calmness. "We bonded over our mutual humiliation. Turns out discovering your boyfriend is cheating on you with your new colleague's boyfriend creates a certain... connection."

The brothers exchange glances.

"That tracks," Odin says finally. "Trauma bonding."

"Revenge plot," Gunnar suggests, wiggling his eyebrows.

Alder rolls his eyes. "Can you all please go home now? Lena's had a rough day, and we need to get her settled."

"Fine, fine," Gunnar sighs dramatically. "But Mom wants to know if you're both coming to Sunday dinner."

I freeze. "Sunday dinner?"

"Family tradition," Alder explains. "Nothing formal. Just twenty or thirty Stags eating lasagna and arguing about hockey. Although I guess we're on to soccer spats now that it's summer."

Just twenty or thirty people? I can barely handle the three brothers in front of me. The thought of a houseful of these giant men makes my palms sweat. "You gotta eat, right?" Gunnar holds up his hands. "Might as well eat with great company."

"You are under no obligation to attend," Alder says, clearly reading the panic on my face. "I can tell her you're busy."

"No, that's—" I start, then stop. I've only met Brad's family a handful of times, and here is this hockey family insisting I join in their weekly meal. I'm choked up but manage to say, "I'd like to meet your family."

Odin claps his hands together. "Excellent! They're going to love you. Just don't ask my dad about his veneers." Odin winces, and Gunnar laughs into his beer.

Tucker and Gunnar finally stand up, gathering empty bottles and takeout containers. "We'll get out of your hair," Tucker says. "But we'll see you Sunday."

After a flurry of goodbyes, brotherly insults, and one last check of Tucker's temporary crown, the three brothers finally leave, and I'm alone with Alder and Gordie.

"Sorry about that," he says, running a hand through his damp hair. "I didn't expect them all to be here still."

"It's okay. They seem... nice."

"They're nosy idiots," he says, but his tone is affectionate. "Let me show you around."

The tour is brief but illuminating. The townhouse is massive by my standards—three bedrooms, two bathrooms, a chef's kitchen, and that stunning view. The guest room is larger than my entire first apartment, featuring a king-sized bed.

"This is where you'll sleep," Alder says, setting my suitcase down. "Clean towels in the bathroom, extra blankets in the closet. Wi-Fi password is on the nightstand."

"It's perfect," I say, overwhelmed by the boundless kindness of this near stranger. "Thank you, Alder. Really."

He shrugs, looking embarrassed. "It's nothing. Come on, I'll show you the kitchen."

I follow him back to the main living area, where Gordie has settled on a plush dog bed by the sliding door to the patio. Alder opens the fridge, which is surprisingly well-stocked for a bachelor pad.

"Help yourself to anything," he says. "I usually meal prep on Sundays, but since the season's over, I'm a bit more... flexible."

"I can contribute to groceries," I offer immediately. "And cook sometimes. I'm not great, but I can follow a recipe."

"We'll figure all that out later," he says, waving dismissively. Then, with a slight flush to his cheeks, he points to a wicker basket on top of the fridge. "That's, uh, the safe and satisfied basket."

"The what?"

His blush deepens. "Family thing. Mom insists all of us kids have one. It's just, you know, protection. Condoms, lube, dental dams. STI testing kits. Whatever you might... need."

I stare at him, heat rising in my cheeks. "Oh."

"Not that you'd—I mean, it's not an expectation or anything. Just, it's there if you... if anyone..." He clears his throat. "Anyway, it's there."

I glance at the basket, then back at Alder, who looks like he wants the floor to swallow him whole. "I doubt I'd need anything in there after we do the tests," I say with a self-deprecating laugh. "Not exactly fighting them off, you know? Especially looking like this."

Alder's embarrassment vanishes, replaced by a frown. "Looking like what?"

I gesture vaguely at myself. "You know. Plus-sized. Not exactly the type guys are lining up to—"

"No." He cuts me off sharply. "Don't do that."

"Do what?"

"Put yourself down." His blue eyes are suddenly intense. "There's not a damn thing wrong with how you look."

I blink, startled by his vehemence. "I—it's just a fact, Alder. I'm not society's ideal—"

"Society can go fuck itself," he says firmly. "Brad is an idiot who doesn't deserve you, and his opinions about your body are garbage. Got it?"

Something shifts in my chest—a warm, strange feeling I can't quite name. Alder looks at me as if he genuinely means what he's saying, which makes no sense. He's a professional athlete who could date models and celebrities. Why would he care about my self-image?

"Got it," I say quietly.

He nods once, seemingly satisfied. "Good. Now, are you hungry? I can order something."

As if on cue, my stomach growls loudly, breaking the tension as we both laugh.

"I'll take that as a yes," he says, reaching for his phone. "Pizza okay?"

I frown. "Didn't you all just eat? There were so many food containers."

Alder shakes his head. "Those jagoffs ate. Tucker and Gun are just starting their post-season binge, and Odin has been away from American food for a year. They didn't leave me a single thing, and I could destroy a large pie from Spak Brothers if you're in?"

"Pizza's perfect." As he calls in our order, I find myself studying him—the casual way he leans against the counter, the gentleness with which he scratches Gordie's ears when the dog wanders over, and the fading tension in his shoulders as he jokes with the pizza place he clearly orders from regularly.

There's something undeniably attractive about him, and not just in the obvious way. Yes, he's physically stunning—all the Stag brothers are—but there's something else. A genuineness and an absence of the calculation I'd grown used to with Brad.

When he catches me watching him, I quickly look away, pretending to examine the photographs on his walls. What am I doing? This arrangement is temporary, born of mutual desperation and hurt feelings—a petty revenge scheme.

But as Alder grins at me and asks if I want to sign our exes up for health department mold inspections while we wait, I can't help but smile back. For the first time since the kiss cam disaster, I feel something other than humiliation and anger.

Something perilously close to attraction.

CHAPTER 9
ALDER

LENA'S BEEN LIVING IN MY GUEST ROOM FOR THREE DAYS, AND somehow it already feels like she's always been here. This morning, I found her and Gordie sharing a piece of toast on the patio, watching the sunrise over the river. She didn't know I saw them—I was heading out for an early workout—but the sight lodged somewhere beneath my ribs and hasn't budged since.

Now I'm sprawled on the couch, scrolling through my phone while she showers after her day at work. I've been avoiding social media since the kiss cam disaster, but Brian texted that I should "take the temperature of public opinion." Whatever that means.

I open FaceSpace and instantly regret it.

Fury Defenseman's Love Life Melts Down with Season

Who Is PR Guru Adam Lawson's Mystery Man?

And then, more recently:

Sources Confirm: Fury Team Dentist Also a Victim in Kiss Cam Affair

I'm still staring at the screen when Lena emerges from the

hallway, her hair wrapped in a towel, wearing sweatpants and a faded university T-shirt.

"You look like you've seen a ghost," she says, peering over my shoulder. "Oh."

She snatches the phone from my hands and scrolls through the articles, her expression darkening with each swipe.

"'Sources confirm,'" she reads aloud. "'Insiders say.' Who are these people, and why do they care so much about our private lives?"

"Welcome to professional sports," I say, taking back my phone. "Where your humiliation is just content for the masses."

She sits beside me, maintaining a careful distance between us. We've established an unspoken choreography of proximity over these past few days—close enough for comfortable conversation, yet far enough to avoid accidental touches.

"This is fun, though," I show her my phone. I had a case of dick-shaped pasta delivered to Adam's apartment building and required a signature. The courier took a terrific picture of him looking absolutely horrified.

She grabs the phone again. "Why didn't I think of anything like that?"

"Stick with me, Lena. I'll teach you all the things."

She groans. "Great. So now not only am I the pathetic woman whose boyfriend cheated on her with someone else's man, but I'm also failing at our payback project."

"If it makes you feel any better, I'm the guy who drove his boyfriend into another man's arms," I offer. "The internet has theories about my... abilities."

"That's ridiculous," she says automatically, then flushes when I raise an eyebrow. "I just mean, obviously, that's not why Adam cheated. He's just an asshole."

"Yeah." I stare at the ceiling, thinking. "But maybe we can use this."

"Use what?"

"The speculation." I sit up straighter. "What if we show up somewhere we know Adam will be? Get the media talking even more."

Her eyes narrow thoughtfully. "You mean like our original revenge plan, but with bonus public attention?"

"Exactly." I grab my laptop from the coffee table. "Adam has a big client event tomorrow night—the Hot Metal women's soccer match. He's been posting about it all week on his work account."

"And you want us to... what? Crash it?"

"Not crash. Attend. Very visibly."

Lena bites her lip. "I'm not really cool with the visibly part…"

I nod. "Okay, I can see that. But!" I pull up the Hot Metal schedule. "My cousin's girlfriend plays for them. We were all planning to go anyway before..."

"Before your boyfriend and my boyfriend decided to hook up on national television?" she supplies dryly.

"Local television," I correct with a grin. "The point is, Adam will be working. Schmoozing clients and managing media. And if we show up..."

"It'll throw him off his game." Lena's smile grows slowly. "And create exactly the kind of distraction he hates in a professional setting."

"Plus, I was going to go regardless to support Cara."

She hesitates. "Won't that mess up the game for the women, though? If there's a media circus?"

I hadn't considered that. "I don't want to ruin Cara's match."

"Maybe it wouldn't be so bad," Lena muses, as if she's trying to talk herself into it. "I mean, women's soccer could use more attention, right? More tickets sold, more eyes on the players."

"True." I run a hand through my hair. "And we wouldn't do anything disruptive. Just... exist. Conspicuously."

"How conspicuous are we talking?"

"I'll wear Fury gear, so I'm easy to spot. We get good seats. Maybe we happen to be photographed laughing together." I shrug. "Let people draw their own conclusions."

She considers this and then nods decisively. "Let's do it. Operation Adam Distraction is a go."

"We need a better name than that."

"Operation Soccer Smear?"

I laugh. "Perfect."

On the morning of the match, I wake to the aroma of coffee and the sound of Lena talking on the phone in the kitchen. Her voice is tense in a way I haven't heard before.

"No, Brad, that's not—" A pause. "I'm aware of what people are saying, but—" Another pause, longer this time. "That's really not your concern anymore."

I should go back to my room, give her some privacy. However, something in her tone makes me hesitate.

"I'm not discussing my living arrangements with you," she says firmly. "You gave up the right to opinions about my life when you decided to make out with Adam Lawson on the jumbo screen."

There's a longer silence, and when she speaks again, her voice is ice cold.

"Don't call me again."

I wait a beat before entering the kitchen, giving her time to compose herself. When I round the corner, she's gripping her coffee mug so tightly that her knuckles are white.

"Morning," I say casually, reaching for my mug.

"Morning." She attempts a smile that doesn't reach her eyes. "Sorry if I woke you."

"You didn't." I pour coffee, watching her carefully. "Everything okay?"

"People are trolling Brad online." She sets her mug down with a sharp click. "He's convinced you, and I planned this all somehow. Said we're embarrassing ourselves trying to make *him* jealous."

"Ah, yes. We orchestrated his cheating as part of our master plan to get attention," I deadpan. "Genius."

That brings a genuine smile from her. "He said, and I quote, 'all anyone has to do is look at you to realize why I strayed.'"

Something hot and angry flares in my chest. "He actually said that?"

She shrugs, but I can see the hurt beneath her casual demeanor. "It's fine. It's just Brad being Brad."

"It's not fine. It's bullshit." I lean against the counter, facing her directly. A thought occurs to me. I pull out my phone and make sure she can see as I order a 50-pound bag of organic manure to be delivered to their apartment. "It's a hot day," I tell her. "Let's leave a note that it's fine to drop the package in the doorway." Lena titters and then laughs long and hard. I slide my phone into my pocket and point at her. "For the record, anyone would be lucky to date you."

She rolls her eyes, but there's a hint of color in her cheeks. "You don't have to say that."

"I'm not just saying it." I'm surprised by how strongly I mean it. "You're smart, funny, kind to my weird dog, and you put up with my brothers. That's already more than most people manage."

"Well, when you put it that way," she says with a small laugh. "Clearly, I'm a catch."

"Clearly," I agree, and for a moment, we just look at each other, and something unspoken passes between us. Then Gordie nudges my leg, breaking the spell.

"Someone needs his breakfast," Lena says, turning away quickly.

"Yeah." I clear my throat. "Big day today. Operation Soccer Smear."

"Should we coordinate outfits?" she asks, seemingly grateful for the subject change. "For maximum conspicuousness."

"I'll wear my Fury jersey." I feed Gordie while thinking. "Do you have anything team-related? I might have an extra jersey you could borrow."

"I doubt your clothes would fit me," she says, that familiar self-deprecation creeping in.

"You'd be surprised." I glance at her, suddenly imagining the way my jersey would look draped around her boobs. "But you could wear whatever makes you comfortable. The point is for us to cause chaos, not to dress alike."

She nods, but I can tell she's still thinking about it. "I mostly want to keep my name out of it…but I guess that ship has sailed." Lena releases a groan. "What time should we head over?"

We should aim to arrive around six-thirty. The match starts at seven, which is prime time for Adam to spot us.

"And we just... sit there? Looking happy?"

"We enjoy the match," I correct. "Cheer for the Hot Metal. Eat overpriced nachos. And if photos happen to be taken of us ignoring the gossip…" I shrug. "That's just a bonus."

Lena smiles a mischievous glint in her eye. "I can't wait to see his face."

When we arrive, the stadium is already buzzing. I'm wearing my game-day Fury jersey with a baseball cap pulled low, but it's really just for show. In Pittsburgh, I'm recognized pretty much everywhere, especially during hockey season. I sign a few soccer programs for kids on the way in, and Lena snaps some pics for excited fans.

Lena walks beside me in jeans and a black Hot Metal T-shirt she found at the team store on our way in. "There are a lot of people here," she murmurs as we make our way to our seats.

"Game's been promoted heavily," I explain. "But even though you look damn fine, I think the people are more focused on the field. Hot Metal's having a good season, and Cara's one of their star players."

Lena's lips tip up in a small smile, and I sense her relax after my compliment. "Is Cara really dating your cousin?"

"Yeah, Wes is on the men's team. He's got an away match, though." I guide her through the crowd with a light touch on the small part of her back. "My family's pretty serious about soccer, too. We're athletic overachievers."

"I noticed," she says dryly.

We find our seats—great ones, offering clear views of both the field and the VIP section where Adam will be working. I scan the crowd but don't spot him yet.

"Nervous?" Lena asks, reading my expression.

"No," I lie. "Just looking for familiar faces."

She doesn't call me on it; she just settles into her seat and studies the program. "So, the goal is to kick the ball into the net, right?"

I stare at her for a moment before catching the twinkle in her eye. "Very funny."

"I actually played soccer in high school," she admits. "I wasn't half bad as a defender."

"Why am I not surprised? You strike me as someone who'd be good at blocking people's shots."

She bumps my shoulder with hers. "Was that a compliment or an insult?"

"Definitely a compliment. Defense wins championships."

"Is that why you play defense in hockey?"

"Partly." I consider how to explain it. "I like the strategy of it. Reading the play, anticipating where the puck's going, getting between the opponent and their goal."

"The protector," she says thoughtfully.

"I don't know about that..."

"Well, I do," Lena starts to explain. A roar from the crowd interrupts us as the teams take the field for warm-ups. I point out Cara—Latina, a midfielder with a dark ponytail.

"She's amazing," I tell Lena. "Got recruited right out of college. On the national team, too."

"Your family must be proud."

"We are. Even if she's not technically family yet." I scan the sidelines again and freeze. "Three o'clock. By the media tent."

Lena follows my gaze subtly. "Is that Adam?"

He stands near the press area, clipboard in hand, talking to what appears to be a group of sponsors. He's wearing his professional uniform—slim-cut suit, no tie, trendy glasses—and looks completely in his element.

"That's him," I confirm, my voice tighter than I'd like.

Lena's hand finds mine on the armrest between us. "You, okay?"

"Fine." I force myself to look away from Adam. "Just... it's the first time I've seen him since."

"We can leave," she offers immediately. "This was a stupid idea."

"No." I squeeze her hand, surprised by how much I appreciate the contact. "I'm okay. Really."

"Okay." She doesn't let go of my hand, and I don't pull away. It feels... nice. Grounding.

The match begins, and we settle into watching the action. In the fourteenth minute, Cara makes a brilliant pass that leads to the first goal, and I jump to my feet, cheering. Lena stands, too, laughing at my enthusiasm.

"Your family loyalty extends to girlfriends of cousins?" she teases.

"Women's sports don't get enough credit," I reply. "Plus, Cara's practically a Stag already. Wes is just taking his time proposing."

We're still standing, discussing the goal, when I notice a commotion near the media tent. Adam has spotted us. He's staring, mouth slightly open, distracted enough that one of his clients seems to be repeating a question.

"Mission accomplished," Lena murmurs, following my gaze.

"That was easier than expected."

We sit back down, but I'm acutely aware of Adam's attention throughout the first half. Every time I glance in his direction, he's watching us, his expression growing increasingly agitated.

During halftime, Lena and I hit the concession stand. We're waiting in line when I feel a tap on my shoulder.

"Alder."

I turn to find Adam standing there, professional smile firmly in place, though his eyes are cold.

"Adam," I reply, equally cool. "Working the game?"

"Yes, as you're clearly aware." His gaze shifts to Lena. "Dr. Sinclair, right? I've heard so much about you."

"Wish I could say the same," Lena says sweetly. "But Brad never mentioned you. For obvious reasons."

Adam's smile tightens. "I should apologize for the... awkwardness."

"You mean when you were sucking face with my boyfriend on the jumbo screen?" Lena's voice remains pleasant, but there's steel beneath it. "No apology necessary. You did me a favor."

Adam blinks, clearly not expecting this response. "Well. Good, then." He turns his attention back to me. "Could we speak privately for a moment?"

"No," I say simply. "I'm here to watch soccer with my friend."

"Your friend." He glances between us, skepticism evident. "Does she know what it's like to be in your orbit? With the media everywhere?"

I just glare at him as Adam's face flushes. "We'll leave you to your work," I tell him, placing a hand on Lena's back to guide her forward in the now-moving line.

"This isn't over, Alder," Adam says, low enough that only I can hear. "Call me when you're done playing games."

I don't respond; I just continue forward with Lena. Once we're out of earshot, she exhales dramatically.

"What a douche," she whispers. "I can't believe I was intimidated by the idea of him."

"You were intimidated?"

"A little," she admits. "He's so... polished."

"That's one word for it."

We order nachos and beer, then make our way back to our seats. I'm aware of people watching us. Phones occasionally raised to capture photos. Word has obviously spread about our presence.

"I can see why you fell for him," Lena muses as we sit. "He's very pretty."

"Pretty empty," I mutter, then feel childish. "Sorry. That was petty."

"Hey, petty is what we're here for." She nudges me with her elbow.

I smile, grateful for her lightness. "Right."

The second half begins, and we settle back into watching the match. Adam remains on the sidelines, but I'm less concerned with his presence now. I'm more interested in Cara's footwork and Lena's running commentary, which grows increasingly insightful as the game progresses.

"You really did play, didn't you?" I ask after she correctly predicts a penalty call.

"Told you," she says with a grin. "Four years varsity, thick thighs and all."

"Is there anything you're not good at?"

"Plenty," she laughs. "Relationships, for one."

"Same." I watch as the penalty kick sails into the net, putting Hot Metal up 2-0. "Maybe we should stick to sports."

"Maybe we should."

The rest of the match passes in a blur of good soccer and even better company. Hot Metal wins 3-1, with Cara assisting on the final goal, and the crowd erupts in cheers. As we stand to applaud, I notice several people openly taking photos of us.

"We've been spotted," I murmur to Lena.

"Good." She claps enthusiastically. "Adam looks like he's about to have an aneurysm."

Sure enough, Adam is staring at us from the sideline, his professional composure wavering. One of his clients is trying to get his attention, but his focus is completely on us.

As we exit with the crowd, I feel my phone vibrate with an incoming call. I check the screen and see Brian's name.

"My agent," I explain to Lena. "Should I take it?"

"Go ahead," she says. "I'll wait."

I answer as we step into a quieter area near the exit. "Hey, Brian."

"A-Stag, what the hell are you doing? BuzzTalk is exploding with photos of you and the dentist at the soccer game."

"Watching soccer," I reply innocently. "Cara played great."

"Don't play dumb with me, kid. Is this some kind of revenge date? Because if so, we need to coordinate our messaging."

"It's not a date," I say, though the denial feels strange on my tongue. "Lena's staying at my place temporarily because her ex is fucking mine. We're friends."

"Friends," Brian repeats skeptically. "The kind of friends who hold hands at sporting events?"

I glance at Lena, who's examining a Hot Metal team poster with exaggerated interest, clearly trying not to eavesdrop.

"I was helping her up the stairs," I insist. "But if people want to think otherwise... I'm not going to correct them."

Brian sighs heavily. "Fine. But if this blows up, don't say I didn't warn you. Adam is definitely not chill, and the team has rules about fraternization."

"We're not fraternizing," I argue. "We're... coexisting."

"Whatever you say, A-Stag. Just be careful." He hangs up without saying goodbye, typical Brian style.

I rejoin Lena, who raises a questioning eyebrow. "Everything okay?"

"Fine. Brian's just being Brian."

"Meaning?"

"Meaning he's worried about optics." I guide us toward the exit.

"Mission accomplished then?" she asks as we step into the warm evening air.

"Definitely." I spot Adam across the parking lot, frantically typing on his phone while his clients wait. We walk to my car in comfortable silence, the energy of the evening settling around us. It's not until we're driving home that Lena speaks again.

"Do you think we went too far?" she asks quietly. "With the public appearance thing?"

I consider this. "We didn't actually do anything except watch a soccer match together."

"True, but we knew what people would think. What they'd say."

"Does that bother you?"

She's quiet for a moment. "Not exactly. It's just... I don't want to create more problems. For you, for the team."

"Brian mentioned something about fraternization rules," I

admit. "But they're mostly about coaches and players. I don't think they apply to medical staff and players being friends."

"And if people think we're more than friends?"

It's a fair question and one I don't have a simple answer for, so I just shrug.

We drive the rest of the way home in comfortable silence. I find myself wondering what it would be like to go on a real date with Lena, not just a revenge outing; to hold her hand because I want to, not for show.

It's a dangerous thought, one I push away as soon as it forms. We're roommates. Co-conspirators in a petty revenge plot. Maybe friends. Anything more would complicate an already messy situation.

But as we arrive home and I watch her laughing at Gordie's enthusiastic greeting, I can't help but think that some complications might be worth it.

CHAPTER 10
LENA

GORDIE GREETS US AT THE DOOR LIKE HE THOUGHT WE'D NEVER return, his entire body wiggling with joy. Alder's demeanor softens immediately as he crouches to ruffle the dog's unruly fur.

"Hey, buddy. You miss us?"

Watching them together makes my chest ache in a strange way. For all his imposing physical presence on the ice, there's something gentle about Alder Stag when he's with his dog. My brain flashes to forbidden images of Alder being gentle with me…nope. Not okay, Lena.

"I'm going to turn in," I say, suddenly feeling like an intruder. "It's been a long day."

Alder nods, still focused on Gordie. "Night, Lena."

Inside the guest room, I change into sleep shorts and an oversized t-shirt, before sitting on the edge of the bed, scrolling through the barrage of texts from Brad. Each one oscillates between anger and pleading, following the familiar pattern of our arguments.

How could you do this to me?

We need to talk.

Is this some kind of joke?

I miss you. Please come home.

Home. As if that apartment could ever feel like home again. I think about Alder shipping hot manure to the doorstep and smile, imagining Brad having to deal with it. It's petty, sure, but it does make me feel better to bother Brad like this.

I silence my phone and slip under the covers, but sleep refuses to come. My mind replays the confrontation with Adam, the look on Alder's face when his ex dismissed me, and the way his hand trembled slightly in mine as we walked away.

After an hour of tossing and turning, I give up and get some water. The hallway is dark, but I can see the light spilling from the kitchen. When I round the corner, I freeze.

Alder sits at the kitchen island, shirtless, with a half-empty bottle of whiskey beside him. The overhead lights are off, but the under-cabinet lighting casts an amber glow across his bare shoulders and chest. A tattoo I hadn't noticed before spans his left shoulder blade—a majestic stag leaping over laurel branches, rendered in black ink with incredible detail. His body is a masterpiece. I have to will my heart to begin beating again as I realize I'm truly here in the presence of this beautiful man.

He doesn't notice me at first, lost in the amber liquid in his glass. Without the usual animation in his features, he somehow looks younger. Vulnerable.

I clear my throat, and he startles, turning to face me.

"Sorry," I say quickly. "Couldn't sleep."

"Join the club." His words are a bit slurred like he's been drinking that booze for a long time. He gestures to the stool beside him with his glass. "Water?"

"Please."

As he stands to get me a glass, I can't help but notice the defined muscles of his torso, marred here and there with the bruises and scars of his profession. Being a hockey player isn't just a job—it's written on his body.

"That's a beautiful tattoo," I say as he hands me the water with an unsteady hand. I should suggest he get a glass for himself, but I'm not his mother. I'm not even his girlfriend.

He glances over his shoulder as if he's forgotten it's there. "Family tradition. All the Stags have it. Even my mom and she kept her last name."

I smile at his mention of his mother. "It suits you."

He sits back down, a wry smile curling his lips. "A Stag with a stag."

We sit in silence for a moment, the only sound being the occasional whimper from Gordie's dreams in the living room.

"Adam texted me seven times after we left," Alder says finally, his voice rough. "Kept saying I'm making a fool of myself, called me pathetic."

"Brad sent fifteen," I counter, trying for levity.

His laugh is hollow. "I guess the two of them aren't hitting it off."

I hesitate, then pose the question that's been nagging at me. "Does it bother you? What Adam thinks?"

Alder stares into his glass. "It shouldn't." He takes a long drink. "Six months, Lena. Six months of me chasing after him, making excuses for why he couldn't meet my family, why we could only hang out at my place, why he never introduced me to his friends." He shakes his head. "And he was banging someone else."

"It's not your fault he's a cheating jerk," I say firmly.

"No, but it's my fault I kept accepting the scraps he offered." His gaze finally meets mine, blue eyes clouded with pain and whiskey. "You know why I put up with it? Because I thought he was so much smarter than me. Sophisticated. He works with athletes but has all these opinions about art, politics, and literature."

"And you thought you weren't good enough?" I venture, recognizing the pattern all too well.

"Just a dumb hockey player." He shrugs, the movement rippling across his shoulders. "Why would someone like him want someone like me except for my body?"

The self-deprecation in his voice makes my heart clench. And here I stand, objectifying him as he opens up to me about feeling like a piece of meat. "Alder, that's ridiculous. You're not—"

"Not what? Dumb?" He laughs bitterly. "I left college without a degree. I've spent my entire life learning to check people into boards and stop pucks."

"That's not all you are," I insist, surprised by my vehemence. "And it's not dumb. Do you know how much strategic thinking goes into what you do?"

He looks skeptical, but something in my tone makes him pause.

"You know what I noticed watching your media interviews?" I continue. "You were the one everyone looked at when they had questions about defensive strategy."

"That's just experience," he dismisses.

"No, it's intelligence. Just not the kind Adam values." I can hear the echo of my relationship in his words. "Brad did the same thing to me. Made me feel like my work wasn't important because it wasn't 'intellectual' enough."

Alder snorts. "You're literally a doctor."

"Who fixes teeth, not curing cancer. The 'manual labor' of medicine, he called it." I shake my head at the memory. "He acted like I should be grateful that someone with his brilliant mind would stoop to being with someone so... practical."

"Practical is good," Alder says firmly. "Practical gets shit done."

"Exactly!" I tap my glass against his. "And strategic

thinking on the ice is just as valuable as pontificating about obscure philosophy."

He smiles a genuine one this time. "To practical people getting shit done."

We clink glasses, and something shifts in the air between us—a recognition, perhaps, of kindred wounds.

"I should try to sleep," he says after a moment, pushing the whiskey bottle away.

"You have any plans tomorrow?"

"Just meeting with my trainer. Nothing important." He stretches, wincing slightly. "Might skip it."

"You should go," I say, worried about how much booze he put away tonight and the sadness behind his words. "It would be good to get out of the house."

"Maybe." He stands, gathering his glass and the bottle. "What about you? You've got tooth shit to get done, right?"

I nod, suddenly overwhelmed by the pressures of my job. "I will be making mouth molds until my fingers ache."

"I'll drive you," he interrupts. "Then I'll actually get out of the house."

"You don't have to—"

"Lena." His voice is gentle but firm. "We're friends now, right? Friends help each other out."

Friends. The word feels both comforting and somehow inadequate, but I nod. "Okay. Friends."

He smiles, a shadow of his usual brightness but real. "Goodnight, friend."

As he disappears down the hallway, I'm left wondering how, in just two days, Alder Stag has transformed from a hockey star and convenient ally to... whatever he is becoming to me.

CHAPTER 11
LENA

MORNING BRINGS THE AROMA OF COFFEE AGAIN, BUT THIS TIME, it's my doing. I've beaten Alder to the kitchen and taken the liberty of brewing a pot strong enough to cut through what I assume will be his substantial hangover. I'm midway through making cinnamon toast—a comfort food I discovered he keeps ingredients for—when he stumbles in, looking like death warmed over.

"Morning, sunshine," I say, unable to suppress a grin at his disheveled state. His hair is sticking up at improbable angles, his eyes are bloodshot, and he's squinting against the morning light filtering through the kitchen windows.

"Is it necessary to be so cheerful?" he grumbles, accepting the coffee I push into his hands with obvious gratitude.

"Drink that. Then water. Then more coffee." I slide a plate of cinnamon toast toward him. "And eat something."

He raises an eyebrow. "Bossy."

"Doctor's orders."

"You're a dentist."

"Close enough."

He takes a bite of toast, closing his eyes in apparent appreciation. "This is good."

"It's just cinnamon toast."

"Still good." He takes another bite, then looks at me over the rim of his mug. "God, I miss bread. Where'd you get this?"

I shrug, oddly embarrassed. "Found a loaf in the freezer. I didn't even think about diet restrictions."

He chews and swallows, and I notice again the muscles in his throat. "Well, I don't have any restrictions this summer." He nods, then winces at the movement. "Sorry about last night. I don't usually drink like that."

"Don't apologize." I sit across from him with my coffee. "We've both had a rough couple of days."

"Still planning on going in today?" He looks dubious about his ability to function.

"Absolutely. And so are you." I stand, retrieving a bottle of ibuprofen from my purse. "Take two of these, shower, and you'll feel semi-human again."

He accepts the pills with a look of amused resignation. "You're not going to let me wallow, are you?"

"Nope. Wallowing is for tomorrow. Today, we're being productive adults."

"Why tomorrow?"

"Because I have a fitting scheduled for Tucker, I'll be too busy to stop you from feeling sorry for yourself."

This earns me a genuine laugh, followed by a grimace as the sound apparently reverberates through his aching head. "Fair enough."

I watch him shuffle off to shower, struck by how different this morning routine feels from any I shared with Brad. There's no tension, no walking on eggshells, no subtle digs about my appearance or habits—just easy companionship and mutual support.

It's nice. Dangerous, but nice.

• • •

The Pittsburgh Fury training facility is state-of-the-art, a gleaming testament to the city's dedication to its hockey team. Looking remarkably better after a shower and more coffee, Alder guides me through security with the effortless confidence of someone who belongs.

The facility buzzes with activity despite the season being over. Support staff, trainers, and a handful of players mill about, some nodding to Alder as we pass. I notice how he straightens slightly, his public persona slipping back into place—confident, easygoing, professional.

He glances at his watch. "I should head to my meeting. Text me when you're done for the day?"

"Will do. Thanks for the ride."

He flashes me a grin, already looking more like himself than he did at breakfast. "What are friends for?"

The morning flies by in a flurry of paperwork, equipment checks, and introductions to the staff. By noon, I've established my clinic protocols, reviewed patient files, and scheduled several players for procedures during the off-season. Experiencing this level of autonomy and resources after the emergency room's constant scramble is exhilarating.

I know that as soon as these guys are back to full contact, I'll be looking at some gory situations. But this summer is all about temporary crowns, deep cleanings, and a few fillings.

I'm organizing supplies when a knock at my door interrupts my thoughts. I expect it to be one of the administrative staff, but instead, Alder stands there, holding a paper bag that smells tantalizingly of garlic.

"Lunch?" he offers. "I brought Italian."

I typically avoid smelly food if I'm going to be breathing near people's faces, but I'm not seeing patients today… "You're a lifesaver, " I say as I clear space on my desk as he unpacks containers of pasta. "How was your meeting?"

"Boring. End-of-season review, preliminary plans for next year." He shrugs, handing me a fork. "The usual."

"Sounds thrilling."

"About as thrilling as cataloging dental supplies." He nods toward the cabinet I'd been organizing.

I laugh, acknowledging the point. "So this is the glamorous life of professional athletes. Meetings and medical check-ups."

"The parts they don't show in commercials." He twirls pasta on his fork. "How's your day going?"

"Good. Busy. Your brother is scheduled for his flipper fitting tomorrow."

Alder groans. "Great. He'll be whining all evening."

"Big baby about all dental work, huh?"

"The biggest. Mom had to bribe him with ice cream well into high school."

I laugh at the image of towering Tucker Stag being bribed like a child. "Speaking of your family... about Sunday dinner."

Alder's expression softens. "You don't have to go if you're not comfortable. I can make excuses."

"No, I want to." I'm surprised to realize I mean it. "I just... what should I expect? Are they going to interrogate me? Should I bring something?"

"Just yourself." He hesitates. "And maybe prepare for questions. They're nosy but well-meaning."

"How many people are we talking about?"

"Depends. Core family—my parents, brothers, probably Odin's girlfriend, Gunnar's fiancée." He counts on his fingers. "Then there's the extended crew—trio of uncles, their kids, maybe some family friends."

"So, twenty people is a conservative estimate?"

He chuckles. "Pretty much. We're a big herd."

"And they all play hockey?"

"And pro soccer. It's the family business." He says it lightly, but something in his tone catches my attention.

"Is that hard? The family legacy thing?"

He considers this, setting down his fork. "Sometimes. Dad played for the Fury, and now three of his kids play, too. Hockey's in our blood."

"But?"

"But sometimes I wonder..." He trails off, then shakes his head. "It's stupid."

"I doubt that."

He meets my eyes, and for a moment, I glimpse the vulnerability from last night. "Sometimes I wonder if anyone would notice if I just... stopped. Quit hockey. Did something else." He laughs self-consciously. "They'd still have Tucker and Gunnar carrying the torch."

"You don't enjoy playing anymore?" I ask carefully.

"I do. Most days." He sighs. "But it's like... it's so tied up with who I am to them. Alder Stag, defenseman. Take that away... What's left?"

The question hangs between us, heavy with meaning. Before I can respond, his phone buzzes. He glances at it and then stands abruptly.

"Trainer's looking for me. I should go." He gathers the remnants of our lunch. "Thanks for listening to me whine."

"That wasn't whining," I say firmly. "That was being human."

Something flickers across his face—surprise, maybe, or gratitude. "I'll meet you in the lobby at five? For the ride home?"

Home. The word catches me off guard—his home, not ours. Yet, in less than a week, it already feels more like home than anywhere I've lived in years—such a contrast to my reaction to Brad's message.

"Perfect," I say and watch him go, wondering what else there is to learn about Alder Stag beneath the surface he shows the world.

• • •

I'm mentally exhausted but satisfied with the day's progress by quitting time. As promised, Alder is waiting in the lobby, deep in conversation with the head coach. He spots me and waves me over.

Coach Thompson's face shifts when Alder stoops to pick up my bag. Coach turns to Alder. "Been meaning to talk to you about all the hubbub, A-Stag."

I wince, but Alder keeps a warm palm on my arm. He says, "My agent has a lot of wheels turning. Doc here is working with me to make lemonade from all this."

Coach Thompson nods, staring, licking his teeth. Eventually, he says, "You did a good job with T-Stag and his pretty face." Curiosity evident, he glances between Alder and me, but he's professional enough not to pry. "A-Stag, we'll talk soon." Coach claps him on the shoulder. "Keep feeling free to share your strategy ideas with me, with or without your brother."

Alder looks genuinely startled by the suggestion. "Thanks, Coach."

As we head to the parking lot, I can't resist saying, "Just a dumb hockey player, huh?"

He rolls his eyes, but I catch the small smile tugging at his lips. "One good idea doesn't make me a genius."

"No, but it does prove my point from last night. Your kind of intelligence counts, too."

He's silent as we approach his car, but as he opens my door, he says quietly, "Thanks for that."

CHAPTER 12
ALDER

I open Lena's car door, the simple "Thanks for that" still hanging in the air between us. Her point about my hockey intelligence has settled deep in my chest, a small warmth I'm not ready to examine too closely.

The drive home is comfortable, the silence broken only by Lena's occasional comments about her day or my observations about traffic. This commute together feels strangely domestic as if we've been doing it for years instead of one day.

Her phone rings as we pull into the townhouse complex. I glance over and see her face tighten as Brad's name flashes on the screen.

"It's him," she says unnecessarily, voice suddenly small.

I shift the car into park and turn toward her. "You don't have to answer."

"I know." The phone continues its insistent buzzing. "But if I don't, he'll just keep calling."

"Want me to take it?" I offer before I can stop myself. The idea of this asshole harassing her makes something protective flare in my chest.

"No, I should handle this." She takes a deep breath and accepts the call. "Hello?"

"Finally!" Brad's voice is loud enough to hear every word. "I've been trying to reach you for two days, Lena. What the hell is going on?"

"I needed space after seeing you kiss someone else on the jumbo screen at my new job." Her voice trembles slightly, and I resist the urge to grab the phone.

"That was... I can explain that. If you'd just come home—"

"I'm not coming home, Brad."

"You're being ridiculous. Where are you even staying? A hotel? You can't afford that on top of our rent."

Our rent. The entitled tone in his voice makes my jaw clench. From our conversations, I know that he never paid a cent toward their living expenses.

"I'm staying with a friend." Lena glances at me, and I try to project steadiness and support.

"What friend? You don't have friends here." The casual cruelty twists my stomach. "Is it him? That hockey player? Adam thinks you're dating him. Lena, be serious. Look at yourself. Why would someone like him want someone like you except as some kind of revenge?"

The words land like a sucker punch, echoing my insecurities about Adam so precisely that I raise an eyebrow at Lena, who looks equally shocked by the parallel.

"You don't get to tell me what I'm worth anymore, Brad," she says, a steel entering her voice that I haven't heard before. "I'm not coming home. I'll get my things another time when you're not there."

"You're making a huge mistake," Brad warns. "You think you can do better than me? That he wants more than just a quick revenge fuck? You're delusional. You're going to end up alone and begging me to take you back."

"Goodbye, Brad." She hangs up, her hands visibly shaking.

The car fills with tense silence. I search for something profound to say, but what comes out is, "He sounds nice."

It startles a laugh out of her, breaking the tension. "I can't believe I didn't see it before."

"Charming fucker." I hesitate, studying her face. "You okay?"

"Not really," she admits. "But I will be."

I nod, understanding the need for space after emotional confrontation. "Want to walk Gordie with me? River path's pretty at sunset."

Relief crosses her features. "I'd like that."

Inside, Gordie nearly trips Lena in his enthusiasm, which makes us both laugh. I grab his leash, and we head out to the river path that runs through our townhouse community. The evening light turns everything golden, softening the edges of what's been a hard few days.

"He said basically the same thing about me that everyone says," Lena notes after we've walked in silence for a while. "That nobody would take me seriously as a girlfriend because of how I look."

A burst of rage hammers into my ribs, but I force myself to suppress it. "Makes you wonder what we saw in them, doesn't it?"

"I've been asking myself that a lot lately."

I pause on the path, watching Gordie sniff intently at a shrub. "I think... I was so focused on being accepted for being bi that I ignored all the other ways he wasn't accepting me."

The admission costs more than I expected, leaving me feeling exposed. However, Lena's understanding nod eases the discomfort.

"I get that," she says. "I was so grateful Brad 'saw past' my size that I didn't notice he was using it as a weapon to keep me believing I couldn't do better."

"You're fucking gorgeous," I say, meaning it more than I expected to. "For what it's worth."

Our eyes meet, and something passes between us that tightens my chest—maybe understanding or recognition—something that makes this friendship forged from outrage feel suddenly complicated.

The moment breaks when Gordie, impatient with our stillness, tugs on his leash.

We continue walking, shifting to safer topics—her new office, my off-season training plans, and whether Gordie would like to go to the dog park this weekend. By the time we loop back to the townhouse, I'm somehow both more settled and unsettled than when we left.

I order takeout—more carbs—and we eat on the couch while I pull up game recordings. I find myself pointing out defensive strategies and explaining plays more intensely than I usually would. It's a reflex after her earlier comment about my hockey intelligence, a need to prove something I shouldn't have to prove.

But Lena watches with genuine interest, asking insightful questions that make me see the game through fresh eyes. She's probably primarily interested in how all of it impacts the guys' teeth, but there's something affirming about explaining my craft to someone who wants to understand it. It feels like, in addition to that, she might care about something that matters to me.

When she finally heads to bed, pausing in the hallway to turn back to me, I expect a simple "goodnight."

Instead, she says, "For what it's worth... I think everyone would notice if you stopped playing hockey. Not because of the family legacy or the Stag name, but because you bring something to the game that's uniquely you."

I stare at her, momentarily speechless. No one—not coaches, not teammates, not even family—has ever articulated my value to the game quite like that. Not as a Stag, not as an enforcer, but as me. I've always been half of a twin pair…valuable because of what I share with my brother.

"Thanks, Lena," I manage finally, my voice rougher than intended.

After her door closes, I lower the TV volume and reach for the whiskey bottle. Not to drown the day like last night, but to sit with this unfamiliar feeling of being truly seen.

I pour a single finger and sip it slowly as Gordie settles on my lap with a contented sigh. I stroke his fur absently, thoughts circling back to Lena—her quiet strength on the phone with Brad, how easily she's slipped into my life as if she's always belonged here.

This wasn't the plan. The plan was revenge. Petty pranks to show Adam and Brad exactly what they'd lost. Simple. Straightforward. Temporary.

But as I finish my whiskey and head to bed, Gordie padding beside me, I realize there's nothing simple about what's happening between Lena and me. We're becoming friends, genuine friends, with the kind of honesty I never had with Adam.

The question gnawing at me as I slide under the covers is whether friendship will be enough when I'm starting to feel the pull of something more.

"I swear if I have to look at one more mouth mold, I'll scream," I announce as I enter the townhouse the next afternoon, bracing myself to be mauled by Gordie.

Tucker Stag's removable denture fitting went remarkably well, considering his anxiety about all things dental. This is probably because I prescribed him a Valium, and Gunnar dropped him into my chair half-high. But it was the fifth fitting I'd done today, and my fingers ache from the precision work.

My roommate glances up from his perch on the couch, pocketing his phone. "How was Tucker?"

"Brave as a four-year-old getting his first filling, but we made it through."

Alder laughs. "So, he cried the whole time?"

I set my bag down and squat to greet Gordie. "Only on the inside." "How was your workout?"

"Brutal. My trainer's determined to rebuild my entire left side this summer." He rubs his shoulder with a wince. "I'm going to shower," Alder announces, disappearing down the hall.

I take the opportunity to change into leggings and a loose T-shirt, then head to the kitchen to assess dinner options. By the time Alder emerges, hair damp, wearing sweatpants and a faded Fury T-shirt, I've determined that takeout is our best option.

"Thai or pizza?" I ask, looking up from my phone.

"Neither." He flops onto the couch with a groan. "My body is one giant knot. What I really need is to just... not think for a while."

I set my phone down. "Bad day?"

"Not bad. Just..." He rubs a hand over his face. "Between the training and fielding calls from Brian about media shit and dodging questions about us... I'm fried."

"Want me to order dinner while you nap?"

He looks at me thoughtfully. "You know what I want? To get high. Just zone out completely."

The statement surprises me, though I'm not sure why. "I didn't know you smoked."

"I don't. It never seemed like a good idea. But now?" He shrugs. "League doesn't test for it. But I have no idea how to get drugs. Is that pathetic?"

I let out a laugh before I can stop myself. "Of course, you're not pathetic. And actually, I do."

"You do what?"

"I know where to get some ganja."

Alder sits up, eyebrows raised. "Dr. Sinclair, you naughty girl. Where?"

I absolutely cannot believe the rush of heat I feel at the sound of Alder forming the words "naughty" and "girl" in regards to me. I clear my throat. "Brad keeps a stash in his desk drawer. Top quality stuff, apparently. Medical grade."

"And you never partook?"

"Once or twice." I shrug. "Not really my thing."

"So, where's this desk drawer?"

"In the apartment. In his 'office.'" I make air quotes around the word.

Alder's eyes light up. "The apartment you still need to get your stuff from?"

"Yeah, that's—" I stop as his meaning becomes clear. "Oh. You're suggesting we—"

He grins, and there's something mischievous in it that makes my stomach flip. "You need your things, and I need to unwind. Might as well liberate some of Brad's finest while we're there."

"That's... petty theft."

"You think he'll report it to the cops?" The blinding smile Alder sends my way includes dimples.

I try not to stare and consider his question. "Hell, I probably paid for it to begin with."

"There you go. Just retrieving your property." He leans forward. "Come on, when did you last do something just because it felt good? Something a little reckless?"

The question catches me off guard. Does moving in with a hockey-playing stranger count? When was the last time otherwise? Before Brad, certainly. Perhaps even before dental school.

"Alright," I say, surprising myself. "Let's do it."

Alder's grin widens. "That's my girl."

The phrase sends another surge of warmth through me, which I immediately try to squash. I'm not his girl.

But as we plan our "heist," as Alder insists on calling it, I can't help but relish the conspiratorial energy between us.

"It would be great if he were out tonight," Alder says, pulling takeout menus from a drawer. "I'd rather not have a confrontation if we can avoid it. Although I also don't want to think about him and Adam fucking…"

I pull out my phone and open the shared calendar app Brad insisted we use. "Looks like he has a department mixer tonight until 9."

"Perfect. We'll go at 7:30, be out by 8:30."

"We should probably eat first," I suggest. "And maybe get some snacks for... after."

Alder glances up from the menus, a slow smile spreading across his face. "Planning to join me, Dr. Sinclair?"

"I'm keeping my options open."

He laughs with a deep, genuine sound that makes me smile in return. "I like this rebellious side of you."

We decide on burgers, and while waiting for delivery, I make a list of essentials I need to retrieve from the apartment: clothes, toiletries, important documents, and my framed diploma… It's surprisingly little, considering I lived there for four years.

"You should unlink yourself from that shared calendar, you know," Alder says, watching me scroll through my phone. "Cut those digital ties."

"You're right." I delete the app entirely. "One less way for him to track me."

The burgers arrive, and we eat at the kitchen island, finalizing our plan. Alder will provide the muscle. I'll go straight for the essentials. In and out, there is minimal conversation if Brad happens to be there.

"What if he asks where I'm staying?" I ask, suddenly nervous.

"Tell him the truth," Alder says simply. "You're staying with me. Let him think we fuck all the time."

I cross my legs and purse my lips, shaking my head at his candor. This plan awakens Alder's mischievous side, which borders on manic. But he's more animated than I've seen and it's adorable.

By the time we finish eating and load empty laundry baskets into Alder's car, my nervousness has transformed into something akin to excitement. There's something liberating about taking control like this, about having someone like Alder supporting me.

"Ready?" he asks as we pull up outside my old apartment building.

I take a deep breath. "Ready."

The apartment feels smaller than I remember, or maybe it's just that I'm seeing it through new eyes. The furniture I paid for, cheap though it may be. The decor I chose, create a home that now looks strange and unwelcoming.

"Nice place," Alder comments, looking around.

"It served its purpose." I head straight for the bedroom, pulling out the suitcases. "I'll start with clothes."

Alder follows, leaning against the doorframe as I start emptying my side of the closet. "Want me to help?"

"Sure. Dresser over there—top two drawers are mine."

We work in comfortable silence for a while, with me packing clothes as Alder empties my dresser drawers. It's strangely intimate, him handling my things, but not uncomfortable.

When we've filled the first basket, he asks, "Where's this office with the good stuff?"

"Second bedroom is down the hall."

While I continue to pack clothes and toiletries, Alder disappears to find Brad's stash. He returns a few minutes later, triumphantly holding up a small wooden box.

"Jackpot," he says with a grin. "And bonus—found these." He holds up a bag of gourmet chocolate-covered espresso beans. "Perfect for munchies."

I laugh, feeling lighter than I have in days.

He tucks the wooden box and the chocolates into his pocket. "How are we doing on time?"

I check my phone. "It's a little after eight. We should wrap up soon."

I'm just tucking my underwear and bras into the second basket when we hear it—keys in the front door lock.

"Shit," Alder whispers. "I thought you said he'd be out until nine."

"That's what the calendar said." My heart rate skyrockets. "He must have left early."

We freeze, listening to Brad as he enters the apartment. His voice carries down the hall—he's on the phone.

"No, babe, I told you it's fine. She's not an issue." A pause. "Yeah, staying with your hockey player, apparently. Ridiculous, right?" Alder's face darkens at Brad's dismissive tone. "I just need to grab some papers, and I'll head over," Brad continues, his voice getting closer.

Alder looks at me, then at the bedroom door, then back at me. Before I can process what's happening, he moves toward me in two long strides.

"Trust me," he whispers, pressing me against the wall beside the bedroom door.

And then his lips meet mine.

The kiss starts as a performance—I'm aware enough to recognize that. A distraction, a strategy. But then his hand comes up to cup my face, and something shifts. His lips are soft yet insistent, and despite myself, I respond. My hands find his waist, fingers curling into the fabric of his T-shirt.

I hear Brad's footsteps in the hallway, but they seem distant and unimportant compared to the feeling of Alder's body pressed against mine, the gentle stroke of his thumb along my jaw, and the heat spreading through me like wildfire.

The bedroom door swings open. "What the hell are you doing in here?"

For a moment, Alder continues to kiss me as if Brad's interruption is merely an annoyance. When he finally pulls back, his eyes meet mine briefly, and what I see there makes my breath catch—confusion, fire, something unplanned.

Then he turns to Brad, keeping his body partially in front of mine. "We can do what we want in Lena's bedroom. Or anywhere else."

Brad stands in the doorway, phone still in hand, his face

contorted with indignation. His gaze flicks from Alder to me, then to the baskets full of my things.

"You're actually leaving? For him?" The disbelief in his voice would be comical if it weren't so insulting.

I find my voice, though it comes out slightly breathless. "Yes, I'm leaving. Not for him. For me."

LENA AND I RUSH FROM THE BEDROOM, BRAD'S WORDS STILL echoing in my ears. Her face is flushed, and her breathing uneven—though whether from the kiss or the confrontation, I can't tell. Maybe both.

"Don't forget your diploma," I say, grabbing the framed certificate from the wall. Not because I'm thinking clearly, but because I need something to do with my hands that isn't touching her again.

Brad scurries ahead and blocks the doorway, his skinny frame somehow managing to occupy the entire space. "So that's how it is? You're actually with this... meathead?"

I feel Lena tense beside me. Before she can respond, I step forward, holding Lena's diploma in one hand and a laundry basket full of her clothes in the other.

"Move," I say simply.

"Or what?" Brad sneers, looking me up and down. "You'll hit me? Prove what a big tough guy you are?"

"Brad, just let us leave," Lena says, her voice steadier than I expected.

He ignores her completely. "What's your type exactly, Stag? Men, women, whatever's convenient for your image?"

His gaze shifts to Lena. "Or is it just desperate people with low standards?"

Something hot and dangerous flares in my chest. I set down the basket slowly and deliberately.

"Alder, don't," Lena murmurs, her hand on my arm. "He's not worth it."

She's right. But I'm not about to let this asshole have the last word. I step closer to Brad, enjoying the brief flash of fear in his eyes as he realizes just how much bigger I am.

"My type," I say quietly, "is people who aren't self-absorbed parasites. Now move, or I'll move you."

For a moment, I think Brad might actually try something. Then, his survival instinct kicks in, and he steps aside.

"This is a mistake, Lena," he calls after us as we head for the door. "Don't come crawling back when he gets bored of slumming it!"

I feel rather than see Lena's wince; it takes everything in me not to turn around and shove Brad through a wall. Instead, I guide her out with a hand at the small of her back, laundry basket balanced on my hip.

We make it to the car in silence, loading her things into the hatch. It's not until we're three blocks away that the tension finally breaks.

Lena lets out a strangled laugh. "Oh my god."

I glance at her, a smile tugging at my lips despite the adrenaline still surging through me. "You okay?"

"That was..." She shakes her head, laughing again. "I can't believe we just did that."

"The great weed heist," I agree, feeling my laughter bubbling up. "Complete with dramatic confrontation."

"And unexpected kissing," she adds, then immediately looks away out the passenger window.

Right. The kiss. The completely-for-show, totally-not-real kiss that's still burning on my lips.

"Yeah, sorry about that," I say, focusing intently on the road. "Seemed like a good distraction."

"It worked."

"Right. Good."

We lapse into silence for the rest of the drive, the wooden box of stolen weed sitting between us like a promise.

Gordie is vibrating with delight at our return. His enthusiasm breaks whatever awkwardness had settled between us in the car.

"Yes, we missed you too, sir," Lena laughs, scratching behind his ears. "Even though we were only gone for an hour."

"Want me to help bring the rest of your stuff in?" I offer.

"Could you? I'll take this little monster outside."

We work in tandem—me carrying in baskets, her walking Gordie—until all her belongings are stacked neatly in her room. It already feels like hers, no longer the "guest room."

"We can deal with unpacking tomorrow," I say, eyeing the stuff I've set by her dresser. "Right now, I think we've earned a celebration."

Lena follows my gaze, a small smile playing on her lips. "Are we really doing this?"

I open the box, revealing several neatly rolled joints and a small bag of loose marijuana. "Unless you've changed your mind?"

"No, but..." She looks at me curiously. "Have you ever actually done this before?"

"Nope." I shrug, trying to seem nonchalant. "Hockey's been my life since I was three. Never wanted to risk it."

"But now you do?"

"Now I'm off-season, recently humiliated, and living with a gorgeous woman who steals drugs from her ex. So yeah, my risk assessment has shifted slightly."

She laughs, reaching for the box. "Well, fortunately for you, I know what I'm doing. More or less."

I watch, fascinated, as she selects a joint and examines it critically. "Brad's dealer must have rolled these. They're decent."

"How do we, you know...?" I make a vague gesture.

"We need a lighter. Or matches."

"Hmm." I tap my chin, thinking. "Oh! The safe and satisfied basket."

"Seriously?"

"You thought I was joking about it? There's probably matches in there for the massage candles."

Lena raises an eyebrow. "Massage candles?"

"Those would be for the satisfied portion of the basket," I explain, reaching for the wicker basket. Sure enough, buried among the condoms and lube packets are tinned candles and a book of matches. I hold it up triumphantly.

"Perfect." Lena grabs a throw blanket from the couch. "Let's go outside. It's a nice night."

We settle on to the patio furniture, the river a dark ribbon below us, the city lights shimmering across its surface. For Pride month, the bridges spanning the Allegheny are lit up in rainbow colors, casting multicolored reflections on the water.

"It's beautiful out here," Lena says, wrapping the blanket around her shoulders against the slight chill.

"One of the reasons I chose this place." I sit beside her, close but not touching. "Watch the fireworks after home baseball games. See the seasons change."

She places the joint between her lips—a sight that does unexpectedly distracting things to my pulse—and strikes a match. The flame illuminates her face in the gathering dusk as she inhales, the tip of the joint glowing red.

She holds the smoke for a moment before exhaling and then offers it to me. "Your turn."

I take it, our fingers brushing in the exchange. "Do I just...?"

"Inhale, but not too deep for your first time. Hold it a second, then exhale."

I follow her instructions, immediately dissolving into a coughing fit that makes her laugh.

"Easy, tiger," she says, patting my back. "Small puffs."

My second attempt is going better. We pass the joint back and forth in comfortable silence, watching the lights of the city blur and grow more vibrant as the drug begins to take effect.

"Oh," I say after about fifteen minutes. "I get it now."

Lena grins. "Getting there?"

"Everything feels... slower. But in a good way." I lean back in my chair, looking up at the sky. The city lights wash out most of the stars, but the bridges' rainbow illumination seems to pulse with new significance. "Those are really pretty."

"They are." She follows my gaze to the bridges. "I forgot it was Pride month."

"I never forget." I take another small hit, feeling bolder. "Though I'm not feeling very proud right now, given how spectacularly I failed at my last relationship."

"You didn't fail. Adam did."

"Maybe." I pass the joint back to her. "But I chose him, you know? I kept making excuses."

"I get that." She takes a hit, the ember briefly illuminating her face. "Four years with Brad. Four years I'll never get back."

"Why'd you stay so long?"

She shrugs, a small, vulnerable gesture. "He made me believe no one else would want me. That I was lucky to have him. And I believed it."

"That's such bullshit," I say, the words coming out more forcefully than intended. "You're amazing."

She laughs, but it doesn't sound happy. "You don't have to say that."

"I'm not just saying it." I turn to face her fully. "You're

smart and kind, and you fixed my brother's tooth without murdering him, which automatically makes you a saint."

This gets a genuine laugh. "The bar is pretty low there."

"Plus, you're gorgeous." The marijuana seems to have disconnected my brain-to-mouth filter, but I can't bring myself to care. "Brad's an idiot."

She studies me for a long moment, her expression unreadable in the dim light. "You're high."

"Doesn't make it less true."

We lapse into silence again, finishing the joint and watching the lights on the water. I wonder if she's thinking about Brad's weird comments on my sexual preferences as if he weren't jumping from one gendered person to another. The marijuana has relaxed me completely, melting away the aches from training and the tension from our confrontation with Brad. My thoughts drift pleasantly, occasionally circling back to the kiss we're both pretending was just for show.

"I'm hungry," Lena announces eventually. "Did we get those chocolate espresso beans?"

"Nachos," I declare, standing up too quickly and feeling the world tilt slightly. "We need nachos."

I pull out tortilla chips, cheese, jalapeños, and salsa in the kitchen. Lena perches on a barstool, watching me with amusement as I layer ingredients into a baking dish.

"I thought you'd be more precious about food," she comments. "Being a professional athlete and all."

"Off-season," I remind her, sliding the nachos into the microwave. "Two glorious months where I can eat like a normal person."

She opens the bag of chocolate-covered espresso beans, popping one into her mouth. "These are so good. Want one?"

I lean across the counter, and instead of taking the bean she offers, I eat it directly from her fingers. Her eyes widen slightly, and I immediately wonder if I've crossed a line. But then she smiles a slow, beautiful thing that makes my stomach flip.

"You know what I love about you?" I say, the words tumbling out before I can stop them. "You actually eat. Like real food."

She raises an eyebrow. "As opposed to...?"

"I've dated women who would only order salads, no dressing, and wouldn't even eat those. It was as if food was the enemy. Hell, Adam hasn't eaten a grain in years."

"Well, food and I have a very loving relationship," she says, eating another chocolate bean.

"It's refreshing." I check on the nachos, which are starting to bubble. "I like a woman who enjoys things."

"What else do you like in a woman?" she asks, her tone casual but something in her eyes making me think the question isn't.

The weed has thoroughly dismantled my filters, so I answer honestly. "Intelligence. Kindness. A sense of humor." I pull the nachos from the oven and set them on the counter between us. "Physically? I like women like you."

"Like me, how?" She's not looking at me but is suddenly very interested in selecting the perfect nacho.

"Curves." The word comes out lower than I intended. "Soft. Strong. Thighs I could sink my teeth into."

Her head snaps up, eyes wide.

Shit. Did I actually say that out loud?

"That's, uh, the weed talking," I backpedal, shoving a too-hot nacho into my mouth and immediately regretting it. "Sorry."

"Don't be." She selects her nacho, carefully avoiding my gaze. "It's... nice to hear."

We eat in silence for a while, the high making the food taste impossibly good. I try to avoid staring at her lips as she licks salsa from her fingers, but I'm not completely successful.

"I should probably get to bed," she says eventually, stifling a yawn. "It's been a long day."

"Of course," I nod, simultaneously relieved and disappointed. "I'll clean this up."

She stands, stretching in a way that makes her shirt ride up slightly, revealing a strip of soft skin to which my eyes are immediately drawn.

"Thanks for tonight," she says. "The heist. The... everything."

"Anytime."

She hesitates momentarily, wanting to say something else, then simply nods. "Goodnight, Alder."

"Night, Lena."

After she disappears down the hall, I collapse onto a barstool, my head in my hands. What the hell am I doing? Thighs I could sink my teeth into? Jesus Christ, A-Stag.

The weed has made my thoughts sluggish but intensely focused, and all I can think about is that kiss. The softness of her lips. The slight sound she made when I touched her face. The way her body felt pressed against mine. Did she feel the rock-hard length of my dick pressed against her soft belly? Did she like it if yes?

This is dangerous territory. We're roommates. Payback partners. Friends, maybe. However, anything more would complicate an already messy situation. She's fresh out of a four-year relationship with an asshole who didn't appreciate her, and I'm still raw from Adam's betrayal. We're using each other for revenge and convenience.

And yet.

And yet, I can't remember the last time I felt this comfortable with someone. Can't remember laughing this freely or feeling this... seen. Even high, with my defenses down, I don't feel like I need to be anyone but myself with her.

My phone buzzes with a text. Adam's name appears on the screen, and I feel nothing but mild annoyance for the first time in days. I delete the message without reading it, then turn my phone off completely.

I head back to the patio, taking in the rainbow bridges and the dark river below. My thoughts drift from hockey to family to the woman sleeping down the hall from me. For the first time in longer than I can remember, neither Adam nor hockey occupies the center of my mind.

Just Lena.

CHAPTER 15
LENA

I stare into my drawers at the limited wardrobe I managed to grab from Brad's apartment. Sunday dinner with the Stag family. What does one wear to meet an entire family of superstars?

I could ask my roommate, but we've barely spoken since we kissed and got high together the other day.

The kiss.

I finally settle on dark jeans and a forest green tank that doesn't make me look like I'm trying too hard. Maybe, I hope.

A knock on my door makes me jump. "Almost ready?" Alder calls through the wood.

"Five minutes," I reply, reaching for my makeup bag.

"No rush."

I hear him hesitate outside the door as if there's more he wants to say. But then his footsteps retreat down the hall, and I exhale.

I finish getting ready, trying to tamp down my nerves. It's just dinner, I tell myself, with about twenty professional athletes and their closest relatives. No pressure.

When I emerge, Alder is waiting by the door, car keys in hand. He's wearing mesh shorts and a navy Pittsburgh

University shirt, making his eyes appear impossibly bluer. Gordie sits at his feet, looking forlorn at being left behind.

"You look nice," Alder says, his gaze flickering over me before quickly returning to Gordie.

"Thanks. So do you." I fidget with my purse strap. "I feel like I should bring something. Wine? Dessert?"

"Just yourself," he assures me. "There will be an ocean of food."

I swallow. "Should I be nervous?"

"Absolutely not," he says, then immediately undermines this with: "Well, maybe a little. Uncle Tim will be there."

"Your lawyer uncle?"

"Yeah, he's kind of intense. Very nice on the inside, though." Alder hesitates. "I haven't really told them anything about..." He gestures vaguely between us.

"About our arrangement?" I supply.

"About any of it." He runs a hand through his hair. "They know you're staying here."

A moment of awkward silence stretches between us, both of us carefully, not to mention the kiss that's been hanging unspoken in the air since that night at Brad's.

"We should probably have some kind of story," I suggest.

"It's fine. They're just my family." He waves a hand dismissively, already opening the door. "They'll be too busy arguing about Gunnar's wedding menu to interrogate us."

His confidence is not remotely reassuring.

The Stag family home is a sprawling Craftsman-style house in Squirrel Hill, not far from the universities. When we arrive, the driveway is already filled with cars, forcing Alder to park halfway down the block.

"Last chance to bail," he jokes as we walk up the sidewalk.

"Would we be ordering pizza instead?"

"God. No. Mom would hunt us down and force-feed us her lasagna."

As if on cue, the front door swings open, revealing a statuesque woman with silver-streaked dark hair and Alder's jawline.

"You're late," she announces, though her smile is warm. "And you must be Lena." She opens her arms. "I'm Juniper."

Before I can extend a handshake, I'm enveloped in a hug that smells of basil and expensive shampoo.

"It's lovely to meet you, Mrs. Stag," I say when she releases me.

"Juniper, please," she corrects, ushering us inside. "I kept my name, you know. Couldn't bear to give up the alliteration."

The house is a beautiful chaos of noise and activity. I count at least fifteen people in the open living and dining areas, many of them tall, blond, and unmistakably related to Alder. Gunnar spots us first, waving from where he sits with a curvy brunette who must be his fiancée, Emerson.

"The baby returns," he calls. "And he's brought the tooth fairy."

I feel Alder tense beside me, but Juniper swats Gunnar's arm as we approach.

"Behave," she warns, then gently pushes me toward Emerson. "Lena, meet the bride-to-be. Em, this is Lena, Alder's friend."

I catch the careful phrasing and wonder how much Juniper actually knows or suspects.

Emerson stands to greet me, and I'm struck by how she's built similarly to me—curved hips, full chest, soft arms. She's wearing a sundress that highlights rather than hides her figure and carries herself with easy confidence.

"So, you're the infamous new team dentist," she says with a grin. "And Alder's mystery woman from the soccer match."

I flush. "I don't know about infamous..."

"Are you kidding? The photo of you two was all over social media. Cara's been complaining about how you stole her thunder after that assist." Despite her words, Emerson's tone is friendly. "Come sit with me. I need a break from floral arrangements."

I glance at Alder, who nods encouragingly. "Go ahead. I'll get us drinks."

I join Emerson on the couch, where she immediately pulls out her phone to show me wedding food options. It's a surprisingly effective icebreaker, and I find myself relaxing as we discuss the merits of various Pittsburgh traditions like cookie tables and pierogis.

"You have to understand," Emerson explains, "marrying into this family means incorporating hockey somehow. Juniper's already suggested an ice sculpture."

"Of hockey sticks?"

"Of stags. Like, actual deer. On ice." She rolls her eyes, but her affection is obvious. "This family takes their name very seriously."

"I noticed the tattoo," I admit. "On Alder's shoulder."

"The family tat? They all have it. Even Cara's talking about getting one, and she's just dating Wes." Emerson leans closer. "Between us, I'm holding out until the wedding. Gives Gunnar something to look forward to."

I laugh, genuinely enjoying her company. Across the room, I spot a slim woman with an athlete's posture who must be Cara. She's watching us with thoughtful eyes, reminding me that she saw Alder and me at her game and how we used her match for our petty revenge.

Alder returns with drinks, handing me a glass of white wine. "Mom's interrogating Tucker about his removable tooth," he explains. "I barely escaped."

"Tucker's here?" I scan the room, looking for Alder's twin.

"He's in the kitchen, trying to escape mom," Alder says. "Food's almost ready."

A tall, distinguished-looking man approaches us, his expression unreadable. "Alder," he says, extending his hand. "Good to see you."

"Uncle Tim." Alder's smile tightens slightly. "This is Lena Sinclair, the new team dentist. Lena, this is my uncle, Tim Stag, attorney at law and family nuisance."

Tim's handshake is firm, his assessment of me is unmistakable. "Dr. Sinclair. I've heard a great deal about you." His gaze flicks between Alder and me. Before I can respond, Juniper calls everyone to dinner.

Alder places a hand on the small of my back, guiding me to the dining room. "Ignore him," he whispers. "He's always looking for problems to solve."

The Stag dining table could easily seat thirty, and it's nearly full tonight. I find myself seated between Alder and Gunnar, with Tucker across from us.

"Hi, Tucker," I say. "How's the tooth?"

His eyebrows rise in surprise, and he spits his partial denture into his hand. "Good. You think I should be worried?"

I laugh. "I think you're just fine."

Dinner commences with a flurry of passed dishes and overlapping conversations. Juniper's lasagna is indeed magnificent, and I find myself genuinely enjoying the chaotic Stag family dynamic. It's so different from meals with my mom and whichever boyfriend of hers we were living with, which were often silent affairs punctuated by critiques of my appearance or eating habits.

As the meal progresses, I notice Uncle Tim watching Alder and me with calculating eyes. Eventually, he clears his throat during a pause in conversation.

"So, Alder," he says, his voice carrying down the table. "I've been seeing quite a lot about you in the press lately."

Conversations quiet as attention shifts to us. Alder's fork pauses halfway to his mouth. "Have you?"

"Indeed. You and Dr. Sinclair seem to be generating quite a bit of attention." Tim's tone is casual, but his eyes are sharp. "Particularly at Cara's match the other night."

Cara, seated next to Juniper, looks up. "Yeah, thanks for bringing your drama to my game, by the way. Very subtle."

"We were there to support you," Alder protests.

"Please," Cara says. "You were there to stir up gossip and fan flames."

I feel heat rising in my cheeks as all eyes turn to us. Wes drapes his arm protectively around Cara's shoulders and frowns at Alder.

"I'm curious," Tim continues, "if either of you have considered the professional implications of your... friendship. The team has strict policies about fraternization. I know because I wrote them."

I open my mouth to explain that we're just roommates, just friends, but Alder speaks first.

"We're having a summer fling, Uncle Tim. That's all."

The words hit me like a bucket of ice water. I stare at him, my mouth slightly open, as he continues. Gunnar must have dropped his fork because I hear a clatter from his direction.

Somehow, Alder keeps on talking. "Besides, the season's over. It's not fraternization if we're not actively working together, right?"

I can feel my eyes widening and my cheeks burning. A summer fling? That's what he's calling this? That's what he's telling his family about me?

Around the table, reactions vary from concern to amusement. Juniper appears troubled, while Gunnar barely suppresses a laugh. Tucker watches me closely, his expression unreadable.

"I'm not sure the organization would see it that way," Tim says carefully. "There are optics to consider, especially after the unfortunate end to the season."

"I think what Tim's trying to say," Juniper interjects, "is

that we're concerned about the timing. For both of you." Her kind eyes meet mine. "Rebounds can be... complicated."

"It's not a rebound," Alder insists as I sit frozen beside him, still processing his 'summer fling' declaration. "It's just... uncomplicated fun."

Cara snorts. "Is that what you call using my match as your coming out party?"

"We weren't—"

"Save it," she interrupts. "Half the stadium was talking about you two instead of the game."

An uncomfortable silence falls over the table. I stare at my half-eaten lasagna, wishing I could disappear. This isn't what I signed up for. We never agreed to tell his family we were having a "fling." We never agreed to any of this.

"Well," Juniper says brightly, "who's ready for dessert?"

As the conversation reluctantly shifts to safer topics, I excuse myself to use the restroom. Instead, I find myself wandering onto the back porch, in need of air and distance. The sun is setting over the treetops, painting the sky in shades of orange and pink.

I consider calling a ride, just leaving without a word. But that would only add to the spectacle. Despite my anger and embarrassment, I can't quite bring myself to abandon Alder.

The door opens behind me, and I brace myself for an awkward conversation with my housemate. However, it's his mom who joins me, two glasses of wine in hand.

"Thought you might need this," she says, offering me one.

I blink in surprise and then accept the glass gratefully. "Thank you." I take a long sip, letting the cool wine soothe my frayed nerves.

Juniper stands beside me at the railing, looking out into the backyard, which is sliced in two by a metal ramp. Juniper notices me pondering it and says, "We installed that last year when Odin was badly injured and using a scooter." She smiles. "We always want it to be easy for our kids to come to us."

The sentiment triggers a wave of emotion that shimmers up my spine. "That's … really lovely."

"Thank you," she says, taking her glug of wine. "It doesn't always translate to the boys actually bringing us their problems…" She makes a face that implies we are changing the subject to Alder. "I think you know that my son doesn't always think before he speaks."

I cough out a laugh. "I'm learning that."

Juniper takes our glasses and sets them on a table on the deck. Then, she takes my hand in hers. "Did you know I was the Fury's legal counsel when I first met Alder's dad?"

I shake my head. "You were?"

She tips her head. "We were having a bit of a summer fling…and I suffered quietly in fear that I'd get disbarred when people found out I was dating a player." Juniper releases my hand and twists her wedding band, contemplating. "I wrestled with it for months. Put my career first, tried to ignore how I felt." Her gaze is distant, remembering. "And I was utterly miserable."

My throat tightens. "But you obviously figured it out."

"I did." She turns to me, her expression serious. "There was a little more flexibility…I worked for Tim's firm, and it was easy enough to reassign me. So, it's not quite the same thing."

We're both quiet for a moment as I struggle to form a response to what she's confided in me. Eventually, she squeezes my arm. "Whatever is happening with you and my son, you always have a place at our table. You can always come to me."

With that, she leaves me alone on the porch, her words echoing in my mind. The simple assertion of acceptance touches something profound within me, a longing I hadn't fully acknowledged, even to myself. The door opens again; this time, it is Alder, looking uncertain and slightly lost.

"There you are," he says. "I was wondering where you'd disappeared to."

"Just talking to your mom," I reply.

He looks surprised. "My mom?" His expression turns wary. "What did she say?"

I sigh, not ready to share before I've fully processed Juniper's words. "She told me you don't always think before you speak."

He winces and scratches at the back of his neck. "I'm sorry," Alder says. "I shouldn't have said that. About the fling."

"No," I agree. "You shouldn't have."

"Uncle Tim was pushing, and I panicked." He runs a hand through his hair. "He's always been like a second father to me, and he's also my lawyer, so he's hyperaware of things that could affect my career."

"So, you told him we're having a casual summer hookup? Is that what you want?"

"No! I mean, I don't know what this is." Alder gestures helplessly between us. "We never really defined it."

"Because we've been avoiding talking about the kiss," I say, finally addressing the elephant in the room.

He visibly flinches. "Yeah."

"Look, Alder." I grip the porch railing. "I appreciate you letting me stay with you. I even appreciate the idea of making our exes jealous. But if we're going to do this—whatever 'this' is—we need to be on the same page."

"You're right." He steps closer. "I'm sorry. I should have talked to you before saying anything."

"Yes, you should have." I cross my arms. "So, what are we doing here, exactly? Are we roommates? Friends? A summer fling? What's the story we're telling people?"

He hesitates. "What do you want it to be?"

It's a frustrating response—answering a question with a question. Yet, as I look at him, standing in the fading light, I realize I'm not entirely sure what I want anymore. The lines have blurred somewhere between the revenge plot and the real connection.

"I want honesty," I say finally. "With each other, at least, even if we're not completely honest with the world."

Alder nods, relief evident in his expression. "I can do that."

"And I want boundaries," I continue. "Clear ones that we both agree on."

"Absolutely."

"And I don't want to be blindsided again." I fix him with a firm look, surprising myself by how easily I'm expressing a need to this man. "No more improvising major relationship declarations without consulting me first. And no telling your family we're sleeping together when I'm not prepared to respond to that."

"Deal." He extends his hand, a small smile playing on his lips. "Partners?"

I eye his hand, remembering the last time we made an agreement. How quickly things changed. How complicated they became.

But I take it anyway, feeling the now-familiar warmth of his palm against mine. "Partners."

His expression shifts, and he leans closer. "And just so you know, I'm fine with people thinking we're fucking."

The door opens again before I can process this revelation, and Tucker pokes his head out. "Dessert's almost gone, you two. And bro, Uncle Tim wants to talk to you about something."

Alder groans. "We'll be right there."

As his twin disappears back inside, Alder looks at me uncertainly. His hand finds the small of my back again as we step into the kitchen, a gesture that's becoming familiar— comforting, even. I should probably establish that as one of our boundaries—what kinds of touches are acceptable in our "arrangement."

But not tonight. Tonight, I'll allow myself to enjoy the warmth of his hand through my shirt, the solidarity of facing his family together, the strange new feeling of belonging that has nothing to do with revenge, and everything to do with the man beside me.

It's certainly a dangerous feeling. However, as we rejoin the chaos of the Stag family, I find that I can't quite summon the desire to care.

CHAPTER 16
ALDER

A TEXT FROM TUCKER ARRIVES AT 6:03 AM:

> 5-mile loop. 20 min. Don't be late.

I stare at my phone, tempted to ignore it. After last night's disaster at family dinner, the last thing I want is Tucker's opinions on my life choices. However, turning down a run with my twin would mean admitting something's wrong, and I'm not ready to give him that satisfaction.

I slip out of bed, careful not to wake Gordie, who's sprawled across the foot of my mattress. As I pull on my running shorts and lace up my shoes, I glance at Lena's closed door. Is she angry? Probably. I would be.

"*Summer Fling.*" What the hell was I thinking?

I scribble a quick note—

Out for a run with T. Back by 8

—and leave it on the kitchen counter before heading out. Not that she should care why I'm gone or even notice. We're friends. We're not having a fling. We're both hurting from big breakups. Whatever.

The morning air is thick with humidity, promising a scorcher later. Tucker is waiting at our usual spot by the Schenley Park trailhead, stretching his quads against a bench. Since college, we've been running this loop, a five-mile circuit through the park that ends with a brutal uphill slog. Our dad and his brothers prefer to run the paved roads and flatter options in Highland Park. We always felt like we were tougher or something, tackling the hills in a different park.

"You're late," he says without looking up.

"By two minutes."

"Still late."

I don't argue; I just start my warm-up stretches. We fall into our familiar routine, mirror images performing identical movements. It used to freak our coaches out.

We start running in silence, finding our rhythm side by side. Tucker has always been slightly faster on the straight-aways, but I have better endurance on the hills. After decades of competing, we've settled into a pace that challenges us both equally.

Two miles in, Tucker finally breaks the silence.

"So, a summer fling."

I keep my eyes on the path ahead. "Don't start."

"Too late." He matches my stride effortlessly. "What were you thinking, A?"

"It just came out, okay? Uncle Tim was pushing, and I panicked."

"Yeah, but 'summer fling'? You basically told Mom you're using our new team dentist for sex."

I wince. "That's not what I meant."

"Sure, sounded like it. Poor Doc looked like she wanted to crawl under the table and die."

We reach the frog pond at the halfway point, and I'm grateful for the excuse to stop talking as a flock of geese waddles across the path. Tucker waits until we're running again before continuing his lecture.

"So, what is going on with you two? Because something's definitely going on."

"I don't know," I admit. "We haven't really defined it."

Tucker snorts. "Classic Alder."

"Fuck you, Fucker. This isn't like with Adam, if that's what you're implying. We're just... helping each other through a shitty situation."

"By sucking face?"

I stumble slightly, catching myself before I faceplant on the trail. "How did you—"

"I heard you and Lena whisper-fighting. Something about 'the kiss' you've both been avoiding talking about."

Great. Just great. Not only did I humiliate Lena in front of my family, but now my fat mouth just set off another avalanche of shit.

"It was a distraction," I say. "Her ex walked in while we were getting her stuff. I kissed her to throw him off."

"And how'd that work out for you?"

I think about Lena's soft lips, the small sound she made when I touched her face, and how right it felt to hold her against me. "It worked fine."

Tucker gives me a knowing look but mercifully drops that line of questioning. We run in silence for another quarter mile before he speaks again.

"You know, the fam never liked how you let Adam treat you."

I tense. "Adam has nothing to do with this."

"Doesn't he? Six months of you chasing someone who wouldn't even acknowledge you in public, and now you're suddenly in a 'summer fling' with the first person who shows interest after he dumps you?"

"Adam didn't dump me. He cheated on me. There's a difference."

"The point is," Tucker continues, undeterred, "you deserve better than that. Better than Adam and better than whatever half-assed arrangement you're trying to set up with Lena."

We hit the hill that marks the final stretch of our run, and I push the pace, partly to punish Tucker and partly to channel my growing frustration. He keeps up because, of course, he does.

"I'm just saying," he pants, "you're worth someone being excited to be with you. Worth more than some weird payback plan."

"You don't know what you're talking about."

"Don't I?"

He gives me a pointed look, and I frown. "Care to share, Fucker?"

He claps me on the shoulder, and I take a small joy in knowing I'm slimy with sweat and sunscreen. "I'm just saying it sucks being with someone under ... shady circumstances." With that mysterious truth bomb, Tucker pulls slightly ahead as we crest the hill. I can see the wildflowers and benches near the row of parked cars. "It starts to feel bad all the time, and you internalize that shit. You know?"

I hate that I do.

"Lena's not like that," I say, though I'm unsure why I'm defending her in this context. We're not actually dating.

"No, she's not." Tucker slows as we approach the end of our route. "Which is why you need to figure out what you're doing. Before someone gets hurt, and I mean that both emotionally and professionally, bro."

We stop at the park entrance, both of us breathing hard. Tucker takes a long drink from his water bottle, then fixes me with a serious look.

"Just don't fuck this up, A. She seems cool. Too cool to be your 'summer fling.' And she fixed my tooth." He flaps his fake tooth up and down for emphasis.

"I got it, okay? Message received." I'm sweaty, tired, and in no mood for more twin wisdom. "I'll talk to her."

Tucker nods, apparently satisfied. "Good." He checks his watch. "Gotta go. Breakfast with my summer fling."

I flip him off as he jogs backward down the street, laughing at his joke. Asshole.

The drive back to the townhouse gives me time to think, though I'm not sure it helps. Tucker's right about one thing—I need to figure out what I'm doing with Lena. The problem is that I have no idea what I want from her or this arrangement.

I shouldn't be looking for anything like this when I'm raw. I should be focused on hockey.

But when I walk through the door, Lena is pouring coffee into a travel mug in the kitchen. She's dressed for work, hair pulled back, looking impossibly put-together and really fucking hot, even in scrubs.

"Morning," she says, her tone carefully neutral. "Coffee's fresh."

"Thanks." I hover awkwardly by the counter. "About last night—"

"We don't have to talk about it right now." She glances at her watch. "I need to get to the facility. Banksy is coming in this morning for scans."

"Right." I shift from one foot to the other, suddenly acutely aware that I'm sweaty and she's immaculate. "I'll see you later? Maybe I can cook dinner?"

She hesitates, then nods. "Sure. That sounds nice."

As she grabs her bag and heads for the door, I'm struck by how much I want to reach out, stop her, say... something. But what? *Sorry, I told my family we're having a meaningless fling? Sorry, I kissed you and pretended it didn't matter? Sorry, I have no idea what I'm doing?*

The door closes behind her, and I'm left alone with my coffee and confusion.

MY DRIVE TO WORK IS FRAUGHT THIS MORNING. PART OF ME wants to clear the air after last night, but another part is grateful for the breathing room. Our conversation on the porch settled some things but left others deliberately vague.

Partners. That's what we'd agreed to be. But partners in what, exactly? We aren't even really doing anything to get revenge on our exes. And I've made absolutely zero progress freeing myself from my lease.

My phone rings in the distinctive tone I've assigned to my mother. For a moment, I consider putting it to voicemail, but that would only delay the inevitable.

"Hello, Mom."

"Lena! I was beginning to think you were avoiding me." Her voice has the artificial brightness she uses when building up to criticism.

"Just busy with the new job." I cradle the phone between ear and shoulder, taking a swig of my coffee.

"Yes, the new job." A pause. "And the new boyfriend."

My stomach drops. "What?"

"Don't play innocent, Lena-bear. You're all over the internet. 'Hockey Star and New Team Dentist: Hockey's Hottest New Couple.' There's a picture of you at some game."

I close my eyes. Of course, she's seen it. "It's not what it looks like."

"Oh?" The skepticism drips from her voice. "What is it, then?"

"It's complicated."

"Mmm." She makes that little hum of disapproval I know so well. "Well, at least they got your good side in the photo. Though that shirt wasn't doing you any favors."

And there it is—the inevitable comment about my appearance.

"The shirt was fine, Mom."

"If you say so, dear." Another pause. "So you've moved on from Brad already? To a professional athlete?"

The edge in her voice makes me bristle. "Yes, I have. Alder is hotter and nicer than Brad ever was."

The words fly out before I can stop them. On the other end, my mother makes a sound of surprised delight.

"Well, well! So it is serious. Do tell me, what does a hockey player see in a dentist? Besides the obvious financial benefits."

"What's that supposed to mean?"

"Nothing, nothing." Her tone suggests the opposite. "It's just that these athletes often look for... stability. A comfortable place to land. A sugar daddy arrangement, but with the genders reversed."

"That's—that's not—" I sputter, outraged. "Alder makes more money in a month than I'll make in a year!"

"Then he must really like you." She says it with such disbelief that it feels like a slap. "Just be careful, Lena. I don't want to see you sad and alone. Or worse, unemployed. These kinds of workplace romances can get complicated."

She's right about that, at least. "My job is fine, Mom."

"I should hope so. With those student loans of yours..." She trails off meaningfully. "How much is it now? Three hundred thousand?"

"Three twenty-five," I mutter. The number that haunts my

dreams. At least I wasn't duped into paying for Brad's degree. How pathetic that that feels like a silver lining right now.

"Well. Good thing you have that fancy new job."

The rest of the call is mercifully brief, just updates about her garden and complaints about the neighbors. I feel emotionally wrung out when I finally hang up like I've run a marathon.

In my office, I pull up my student loan account on my phone, staring at the numbers as if they might have magically decreased. They haven't. The balance is $325,742.16, with interest accruing daily. My emergency room dentistry job barely covered the minimum payments. The Fury position is a lifeline, offering enough income actually to make progress on the principal.

If I lose this job...

I can't lose this job.

Which means I need to be more careful about this thing with Alder. Whatever it is—partnership, fake relationship, summer fling—it doesn't matter what we call it. I can't afford to pursue it if it threatens my professional standing.

———

The Fury facility is quieter than usual this morning. My first appointment isn't until ten, which gives me time to organize patient files and prepare for the day.

Just as I'm settling in, a knock sounds at my door. Ryan Banks—Banksy, as the team calls him—stands in the doorway with an easy smile.

"Morning, Doc. I hear you're the person to see about a new mouthguard?"

"That's me," I confirm, gesturing to him. "And I believe you're scheduled for a scan too."

"Unfortunately." He grimaces as he sits in the examination chair. "No offense, but I hate these things."

"Most people do," I assure him, preparing the scanning equipment. "But it's quick and painless."

As I work, Banksy makes casual conversation. He's charismatic and friendly, lacking the apprehension that Tucker displayed during his appointment.

"So," he says while I adjust the scanner, "you and Alder, huh?"

I keep my face carefully neutral. "We're friends."

"Right." His tone is knowing but not unkind. "How's he doing with all this? The Adam thing, I mean."

The question catches me off guard. I hadn't considered that as one of the few openly LGBTQ+ players, Banksy might feel a certain solidarity with Alder.

"He's... coping," I say carefully. "It's been a tough week."

Banksy nods. "I bet. The media can be brutal, especially with this kind of thing. When I came out, they dissected every aspect of my life for months."

"How did you handle it?" I ask, genuinely curious.

He shrugs. "Kept my head down. Played hockey. Let my game speak for itself." He grins. "And I had a great support system. Sounds like Alder does, too."

Something pointed in his gaze that makes me wonder if he's trying to tell me something.

"Open wide," I say instead of responding, and he complies, effectively ending that line of conversation.

After finishing Banksy's scan for his new mouthguard, I walk him to the door. He pauses before leaving.

"Tell Alder the guys have his back, would you? Whatever's going on with you two—" he holds up a hand when I start to protest, "—is your business. But he should know the team supports him. And we should get the dogs together soon." He grins.

"I'll tell him," I promise, touched by his concern.

After Banksy leaves, my office phone rings. The receptionist informs me that Charles Sutton, the team owner, and Coach Thompson would like to see me in the conference room.

My stomach drops. This can't be good.

———

The conference room feels overly spacious for just three people. Mr. Sutton occupies the head of the table, with Coach Thompson seated to his right. They both rise when I enter, a courtesy that fails to alleviate my nerves.

"Dr. Sinclair," Sutton says, extending his hand. "Thank you for joining us. Please, have a seat."

I settle into a chair, keeping my back straight and my hands folded on the table. I project a calm professionalism while internally screaming.

Sutton asks, "How are you finding your position with the Fury so far?"

"Very well, thank you," I reply. "Everyone has been extremely welcoming."

"Good, good." He nods, glancing at Coach Thompson. "We pride ourselves on being a family organization."

Something about the way he says "family" makes my skin prickle.

"Now," Sutton continues, "we wanted to touch base about a few organizational matters. As you know, the off-season is a critical time for planning and preparation."

What follows is a seemingly innocuous discussion about facility protocols, player treatment schedules, and equipment needs. My contract is probationary for 90 days, which is all things I knew already. But threaded through it all is an undercurrent I can't quite name.

Until Coach Thompson clears his throat and says, "We also wanted to discuss *team culture*."

There it is.

"Of course," I say, keeping my voice steady.

"The Fury organization has certain... expectations regarding staff-player interactions," Sutton explains. "While we encourage a collaborative environment, we also believe in maintaining appropriate professional distance."

My cheeks burn, but I nod as if this is a perfectly normal conversation to be having.

"I completely agree," I say. "Professional boundaries are essential in medical practice."

"Excellent." Sutton smiles, though it doesn't reach his eyes. "We've had some... unfortunate media attention recently. Nothing directly concerning your department, of course, but it's important that all staff understand our policies regarding public representation of the team."

Coach Thompson slides a folder across the table. "Our media guidelines and fraternization policies. Standard for all staff. But you probably know we spent the first half of last season tied up in media nonsense with our goalie. We want to get ahead of anything if you take my meaning."

I take the folder, fingers numb. "Thank you."

"We have high hopes for you, Dr. Sinclair," Sutton says, his tone warmer now that the message has been delivered. "Dr. Bowman spoke very highly of your skills, and the players already seem comfortable with you."

"That's very kind," I manage. "How is he feeling?"

Sutton shakes his head. "Hates forced retirement. His wife and mine are friends. He'll probably stop by sometime to check in on you."

Thompson nods. "We just want to ensure nothing... complicates your ability to do your job effectively."

The meeting wraps up shortly after, with reassurances that this was just a routine check-in, the same one all new staff receive. But as I walk back to my office, folder clutched to my chest, I know better.

They're warning me about Alder.

————

Back in my office, I close the door and sink into my chair, finally allowing the mask of professionalism to slip. My hands shake as I open the folder, scanning the fraternization policy.

"Personal relationships between team medical staff and players are strongly discouraged due to potential conflicts of interest and impacts on team dynamics. Staff found to be in violation of this policy may be subject to disciplinary action, up to and including termination."

Termination. The word seems to pulse on the page.

I think about my student loans. About my mother's voice, dripping with doubt. About the apartment, I need to find. About the career I've worked so hard to build.

My phone buzzes with a text from Alder:

> Any preferences for dinner tonight? Also, had a revenge idea that wanted to run by you.

Our plan. Our "summer fling" plan. The plan that might cost me everything.

I type a quick response:

> Can't tonight. Swamped with patient files. Will catch up later.

It's not entirely a lie. I do have files to review. And I need space to think and figure out how to navigate this impossible situation.

Because the truth is becoming painfully clear: What began as a petty revenge scheme has evolved into something I can't afford—professionally or emotionally.

I need to find my own place and establish clear boundaries with Alder. I need to protect my job.

What I don't need is to fall for a patient, even one with kind eyes, a gentle touch, and a weird dog I've grown far too attached to.

I pull up apartment listings on my computer, determined to take control of at least one aspect of my increasingly complicated life. Ditching the idea of revenge against Brad, I come up with a new plan—one that's just for me.

Step one: Find a place of my own.

Step two: Establish professional boundaries with Alder.

Step three: Somehow ignore the fact that I'm already halfway to falling for him.

"Focus, A! Where's your head today?" Tucker snaps his fingers in front of my face, pulling me back to the present moment—his living room, now transformed into a makeshift gym with kettlebells scattered across expensive rubber mats.

"I'm focused," I growl, but it's a lie, and everyone knows it. Even our trainer, Marco, exchanges a knowing look with Gunnar from where they're working on lunges.

Tucker snorts and shoves a medicine ball into my chest. "Yeah, right. You've missed every throw in the last five minutes. Stop checking your phone and get your head in the game."

I reluctantly tuck my phone back into my pocket. No new messages from Lena anyway. My third text today—and it's not even noon—has gone unanswered like the others this week since she noped out of eating dinner with me. I hate that she's busy trying to move out of my house, and I hate that it's the right thing for her job security.

"Maybe your boy's got lady troubles," Gunnar calls from across the room. "How's the dentist, A?"

"She's got a name," I snap, hurling the medicine ball back at Tucker with unnecessary force. He catches it with a grunt. "And she's fine."

Tucker gives me a pointed look. "Sounds totally fine. You've been moping around all week."

"I'm not moping." I reach for a towel, wiping sweat from my brow. "I'm just... a little tired."

Marco claps his hands. "Alright, circuit change. Twins on the battle ropes, Gunnar on box jumps. Three minutes each, then rotate."

We move to our stations, but not before I check my phone one more time. Nothing. I shove the phone back in my pocket, ignoring the twist in my stomach.

"Trouble in paradise?" Tucker mutters as we position ourselves at the heavy ropes.

"There is no paradise," I grunt, gripping the heavy ropes. "We're just roommates."

"Right." Tucker's eyebrows lift skeptically. "That's why you've been checking your phone every thirty seconds."

"And three, two, one—go!" Marco starts the timer before I can respond, and we begin slamming the ropes against the floor, creating waves that travel between our hands.

The physical exertion helps distract me, but not entirely. It's been a week since the disaster at Sunday dinner, and Lena has been avoiding me ever since. That's not fair. She's been focused on her to-do list and trying to get out of her lease, and she's not letting me help. Then she got upset that I was trying to sic my uncle on her landlord to grease the wheels of her real estate issues. The few times we've been in the same room, the conversation has been painfully polite and brief.

I thought we reached an understanding on my parents' porch. Partners, we'd agreed. But partners in what, exactly? This question keeps me up at night, along with memories of that kiss at Brad's apartment. And the worst part is I'm being a total dick about it because Lena is keeping things profesh and being a roommate while I'm hanging around like a sad puppy.

"Time!" Marco calls, and we drop the ropes, breathing heavily. Gunnar steps over, sweat dripping from his face.

"So, you and the Doc are going through a rough patch," he says casually, as if commenting on the weather.

I glare at him. "There's nothing to gossip about," I insist, though my chest tightens at the idea that other people are discussing us. "And we're not going through anything because we're not together."

Both my brothers exchange skeptical looks that make me want to throw something.

"What?" I demand.

"Nothing." Tucker grabs his water bottle. "Just wondering why you're so pissy about someone you're supposedly not with."

I open my mouth to argue, but Marco claps his hands again. "Less talking, more sweating! Gunnar on ropes with me, Tucker on box jumps, Alder on push-up holds. Let's go!"

As I drop into plank position, my mind drifts back to Lena. I understand she wants to solve her problems, but is it really so bad if she leans on legitimate connections she's made? Like my lawyer uncle…

Maybe she doesn't quite trust me yet since her fucker ex messed with her head so much. It's been a minute since I made any progress on our revenge plans. What if pulling the lever on that barbershop quartet to humiliate Brad at work helps Lena see that I mean what I say?

I walk through the front door of my townhouse, immediately greeted by the sound of the shower running and Gordie's enthusiastic slobber. At least someone in this house is still happy to see me.

"Hey, buddy," I ruffle his fur, dropping my gym bag by the door. "Where's our roommate hiding today?"

I hear singing from the shower, and Gordie yelps in response.

I settle at the kitchen island with my laptop, Gordie curled near my feet on his fancy bed. Time to get back on top of the petty revenge situation. Something to remind Lena why we teamed up in the first place.

The barbershop quartet idea had been her suggestion—having singers interrupt Brad's class to shame him publicly. I remember how her dark eyes had lit up at the thought, one of the few times I'd seen her genuinely excited.

I type "singing telegram Pittsburgh" into the search bar. Several options pop up, but one catches my eye: "The Four Flats: Specializing in Personalized Musical Embarrassment Since 1996." Their website features photos of four middle-aged dudes of varying races in striped vests and boater hats, apparently delighting in making people squirm at office birthdays and retirement parties.

Perfect.

Next, I search for Brad Reid at Pittsburgh University. His faculty assistant page appears, complete with a smug-looking headshot and a list of his summer courses. I click through to the department schedule, and—bingo—he's giving a lecture on "Ethics in Modern Philosophy" tomorrow afternoon at 2 p.m. The irony is almost too perfect.

I dial the number from the quartet's website, explaining my request as Gordie watches me with his head tilted curiously.

"So let me get this straight," says the quartet leader, who introduces himself as Barney. "You want us to interrupt a university philosophy lecture to sing about what a cheating mooch this professor is?"

"Exactly." I grin, imagining Brad's face. "How much?" I give him the details—classroom location, time, Brad's description—and suggest "No Scrubs" by TLC as the song.

"Classic choice," Barney approves. "We'll prepare something special for the occasion."

I hang up just as the shower turns off. A few minutes later, Lena emerges in her bathrobe, her hair wrapped in a towel. She startles slightly when she sees me.

"Oh! I didn't hear you come in."

"Just got back," I say casually, closing my laptop. "How was work?"

"Fine." She doesn't quite meet my eyes. "Busy."

"Too busy for dinner tonight?" I try to keep my tone light.

She tightens the belt of her robe. I resist the urge to step into her space and pull it off her. My god, I am a sleaze. Lena says, "I really need to catch up on patient files. Rain check?"

There it is again—the same excuse. No wonder.

"Sure," I say, unable to keep the edge from my voice. "Maybe tomorrow night instead? We could order from that Thai place you like."

"Maybe." She shifts uncomfortably. "I should get dressed."

Before I can say anything else, she disappears down the hall, leaving me with Gordie and the increasing certainty that something is very wrong.

The next day, I'm practically vibrating with anticipation. I've arranged to "coincidentally" run into Lena at the training facility around 1:30, giving us just enough time to "spontaneously" decide to visit Brad's lecture. It's the perfect plan.

Except Lena doesn't show up for our "coincidental" meeting, despite my careful timing based on her schedule. By 1:40, I'm pacing the lobby, sending increasingly desperate texts.

> Are you still at the facility?

> I'm in the lobby if you want to grab coffee

> Lena?

Finally, at 1:45, I get a response:

> In a meeting with management. Can't
> talk now.

My heart sinks. The quartet is already en route. In fifteen minutes, they'll burst into Brad's classroom and deliver a musical humiliation that was supposed to be for both of us to witness.

For a brief moment, I consider calling them to cancel. But the thought of Brad's smug face stops me. No, this is happening, with or without Lena.

I race to my car and speed toward campus, hoping to at least document the moment for her. I park in someone's reserved spot, leave my blinkers on, and manage to slip into the lecture hall just as the clock hits 2 PM. Brad is at the front, gesturing dramatically as he discusses something about categorical imperatives. The room is about half full, with students typing on laptops or staring vacantly at their phones.

And then, right on cue, the doors on the opposite side of the lecture hall swing open. Four men in matching striped vests and straw boater hats stride in, humming in perfect harmony.

Brad stops mid-sentence, confusion spreading across his face. "Excuse me, what is—"

"Brad Reid?" the lead singer interrupts cheerfully.

"Yes, but I'm in the middle of—"

"We have a special musical message for you!"

What follows is three minutes of exquisitely crafted public humiliation. The quartet launches into a barbershop version of "No Scrubs," with lyrics modified to address Brad's specific offenses—living off his girlfriend, cheating with another man, and claiming to be an ethics expert while displaying none. Students are recording on their phones, some laughing openly.

Brad's face cycles through confusion, shock, anger, and then a sickly kind of resignation as he realizes resistance is futile. He stands frozen at the podium, knuckles white against the wood.

I sink lower in my seat, filming the whole thing while trying not to draw attention to myself. I created a fake account on one of those video apps and am live-streaming this with all kinds of hashtags. This is everything I hoped it would be, except for one crucial detail—Lena isn't here to enjoy it.

As the quartet finishes with a flourishing harmony on "No, we don't want no scrubs," followed by a cheerful "Message delivered courtesy of Dr. Lena Sinclair," I slip out the back door, already composing a text to share the video with her.

But when I get to my car, I find three missed calls and twice as many texts from Lena.

> Did you hire a barbershop quartet to humiliate Brad????

> ALDER. Answer your phone.

> WHAT DID YOU DO???

My stomach drops. This is not the reaction I was expecting.

I call her immediately, but it goes straight to voicemail. I send a quick text:

> Heading home now. Can explain everything.

When I walk through the door twenty minutes later, Lena waits in the living room, arms crossed and expression stormy. Gordie senses the tension and scurries to his bed, watching us warily.

"Before you say anything," I begin, "I have a video I think you'll want to see."

"I've already seen it." Her voice is ice. "It's all over social media. #ProfessorRoast is trending."

"Good!" I throw my hands up. "Isn't that what we wanted? Public humiliation for the guy who humiliated you? It was your idea!"

"My idea that I didn't ask you to execute without consulting me!" She paces the living room. "Do you have any idea what you've done?"

"Uh, delivered perfect karmic justice to your cheating ex?"

"You've potentially destroyed my professional reputation!" Her voice rises. "I had a meeting with management this week. About professional boundaries. About the fraternization policy that could get me fired if I'm seen to be in a relationship with a player!"

I blink, taken aback. "What does humiliating Brad have to do with me? How would management link those two things?"

"Oh, gee." She taps a sturdy finger against her red, pouty lip. "They called me in for a discussion after we were spotted at Cara's match. They weren't exactly subtle, reminding me that I could lose my job if I was unprofessional. And what's more unprofessional than sending a singing quartet to humiliate a university professor in front of his students publicly?"

Understanding dawns, cold, and sickening. "Lena, I didn't know—"

"No, you didn't know because you didn't ask!" She runs a hand through her hair in frustration. "You just decided to take matters into your own hands. Without talking to me first!"

"I was trying to surprise you!" I protest. "You've been avoiding me all week. I thought you were disappointed that we weren't making more progress on our revenge plans."

"I wasn't avoiding you because of the revenge plans. I was trying to create distance because I can't afford to lose this job!"

She drops onto the couch, deflated. "Do you know how much student debt I have? This position with the Fury is the only way I can make payments and still afford to live."

I sink down beside her, keeping a careful distance. "I'm sorry. I really didn't think—"

"That's the problem, isn't it? You didn't think." She looks at me, and I see genuine hurt beneath the anger. "You just went ahead and made decisions for both of us. Just like at your family dinner, announcing we're having a 'summer fling' without consulting me first."

Her words hit uncomfortably close to home. How the hell do I keep doing this–running my mouth until I fuck over everyone I care about? "I said I was sorry about that."

"And yet here we are again." She sighs, the fight draining out of her.

"We can be more careful. I can be more thoughtful. Keep things professional." It's not like me to be impulsive like this, not really. I'm usually more strategic. This situation with Adam has me fucked in the head.

"It's not just that." She looks away. "I think I need space to figure things out. On my own."

"Is this because of the quartet?" I'm scrambling now, feeling something important slipping away. "Because I can fix that. I'll call my agent. I'll talk to management and explain that you had nothing to do with it."

"It's not just the quartet." She finally meets my eyes again. "It's everything—the kiss at Brad's apartment. Your family thinking we're a couple. The media attention. It's too much."

I feel a hollowness spreading in my chest. "So you're just going to leave? Just like that?"

"Not right away," she concedes. "I haven't found a place yet. But I did get the lease transferred out of my name." She shrugs and smiles, a small victory. I want to hug her or at least give her a high five, but I'm not sure how to *be* around her right now.

We sit in silence for a moment, the distance between us on the couch feeling suddenly vast. Gordie whines softly from his bed, sensing the tension.

"I've come to rely on you," I finally admit, my voice quieter than intended. "These past couple weeks, having you here... it's made everything better." I swallow hard. "You're a good friend, Lena. Probably the best friend I have right now outside of my brothers."

Her expression softens slightly. "You've been a good friend to me, too, Alder. But that's why this is so hard. I can't risk my career, even for a good friend."

"What about Gunnar's wedding?" The question seems trivial in the face of everything else, but it bursts out of me anyway. "It's next week. The whole team will be there. I need... I was hoping you'd be my plus one."

She hesitates, and for a moment, I think she's going to refuse because of the optics. "I'll think about the plus-one status," she says finally. "But no promises."

It's not much, but it's not a no, either. I'll take it.

"I'm sorry about the quartet," I say again. "I really was just trying to make you happy."

"I know." A ghost of a smile flickers across her face. "For what it's worth, the video was pretty satisfying. Brad looked like he was going to dissolve into the floor."

"So, mission accomplished, at least partially?"

She shakes her head, but the slight curve of her lips betrays her. "You're impossible."

"Part of my charm," I attempt, but the joke falls flat in the still-tense atmosphere.

We lapse into silence again. There's so much more I want to say, but I'm unsure how, or if I should. I miss our easy conversations. The townhouse feels wrong when she's not in it.

But those aren't things you say to someone who's already got one foot out the door.

"I should get some work done," Lena says finally, standing up. "Real work this time, not just an excuse."

"Right." I nod, staying seated. "I'll make dinner. If you want some."

"Maybe." She pauses at the edge of the living room. "Alder? No more surprises, okay?"

"No more surprises," I agree. "I swear on my best pair of Bauers."

After she disappears down the hall, I slump back against the couch. Gordie takes this as permission to approach, jumping up beside me and resting his head on my lap with a sympathetic whine.

"I really screwed up, didn't I?" I murmur, scratching behind his ears. He truly does stink. I'll have to find a groomer who can see him regularly.

My phone buzzes with a text. For a hopeful moment, I think it might be Lena, already forgiving me. But Adam's name appears on the screen.

Can we talk?

I stare at the message for a long moment before deleting it without replying. Whatever twisted game Adam is playing, I want no part of it.

I STARE AT MY PHONE IN DISMAY. THE REALTOR HAS CANCELED the eighth—eighth!—apartment showing this week. "Unit was just rented. I'm so sorry. I will call with other options," reads the text. I slump back in my office chair, tossing my phone onto the desk with more force than necessary.

Finding a new place is proving to be impossible. Everything in my price range is either forty minutes from work or has serious issues. The one decent apartment I toured had a lease ready for me to sign until the landlord "remembered" their no-pet policy when I mentioned occasionally dog-sitting for friends.

I have no idea why I would mention Gordie to a potential landlord. He's not even my dog. And Alder isn't going to call *me* when he goes out of town and needs help with the smelly mutt.

The lunch hour is nearly over, and I've accomplished nothing except increased frustration. I should be reviewing hockey teeth, not scrolling through rental listings I can't afford. I force myself to open Tucker Stag's chart, focusing on his upcoming fitting, but my thoughts keep drifting back to his twin.

Things have been strained at the townhouse since the

barbershop quartet incident four days ago. We've been polite —excruciatingly so—as if we're careful houseguests instead of the friends we'd become. I find myself missing our easy banter and scheming. I still haven't talked to him about our strategy for Gunnar's wedding.

I should be there as a member of the Fury staff. However, I seriously doubt my ability to keep my hands off Alder when he's in fancy clothes, especially if he smells like aftershave again.

My phone buzzes. My first instinct is to ignore it, assuming it's another cancellation. But when I glance down, I see Alder's name.

> Weather's supposed to be perfect tomorrow.
> Let's get out of our heads for a day.

I hesitate, my fingers hovering over the screen. I should decline, maintain boundaries, and focus on apartment hunting.

But the thought of another day spent calling realtors and looking at dingy studios tightens my chest. Beneath my professional concerns lies a simpler truth I'm reluctant to admit: I miss him.

> What did you have in mind?

I type before I can talk myself out of it.

> Kayaking on the river. Pittsburgh rite of
> passage. No pressure.

My stomach immediately clenches. Kayaking? With my body? The image of trying to wedge myself into a tiny plastic boat while athletic people look on in judgment makes me want to curl into a ball.

> Not sure if that's my thing.

I respond, which is the understatement of the year. His reply comes quickly:

> Have you ever tried it?

> No, but...

I stop typing, recognizing the familiar pattern. How many experiences have I avoided because of fear? How many times have I let Brad's voice in my head—or my mother's—dictate what I should and shouldn't attempt with this body?

Before I can overthink it, I delete my hesitant message and type:

> Never tried it, but I'm willing to give it a shot. What time?

> 9 am? I'll drive. Bring sunscreen.

I set my phone down, a mixture of excitement and anxiety swirling in my stomach. It's just kayaking, I tell myself. It's not a date. It's two friends spending time together. Yet, that feels like a big, fat lie.

Friday morning dawns clear and bright, just as Alder predicted. I emerge out of my room in swim shorts and a t-shirt, having agonized over my outfit choice for far too long. Alder is already in the kitchen, packing a small cooler.

"Morning," he says with cautious cheerfulness. I'm probably imagining him staring at my legs. But then, maybe he's blinded by the miles of white skin that haven't seen the sun yet this summer. He clears his throat. "Coffee?"

"Please." I accept the mug he offers, noticing he's wearing

swim trunks and a faded college t-shirt that stretches across his broad shoulders. "Where are we going exactly?"

"Aspinwall. There's a kayak rental place up there that's a bit off the beaten path." He closes the cooler. "Less crowded than the downtown spots. Figured you'd prefer that."

The thoughtfulness of this choice catches me off guard. "Yeah, that's... thanks. That's perfect."

He shrugs, but I can see he's pleased by my reaction. "Ready whenever you are."

The drive to Aspinwall is quiet but not uncomfortable. Alder lets me control the music, and I settle on a playlist of indie folk that seems to fit the morning. As we leave the city behind, the knot of tension in my chest begins to loosen.

When we arrive at the kayak rental place—little more than a shed near a boat launch—there are only a few cars in the small gravel lot. The Allegheny River stretches before us, glinting in the morning sun.

"It's beautiful here," I say, surprised by how peaceful it feels despite being so close to the city.

"One of Pittsburgh's best-kept secrets," Alder agrees. "My brothers and I used to come up here in high school when we weren't on the ice. You know, our mom is an Olympic rower."

My eyes widen. "I didn't know that, but I guess I'm not surprised. Is rowing the same as kayaking?"

Alder laughs, a warm, low sound that sends sparks dancing in my belly. "Not the same thing at all, Lena. But we're going to have fun, I promise."

As we approach the rental shed, my anxiety returns full force. The attendant, a college-aged white guy with a deep tan, greets us with practiced enthusiasm.

"Morning, folks! Looking to get out on the water today?"

"Two singles, please," Alder says, handing over his credit card before I can reach for my wallet. "For a few hours."

"You got it. Need any instruction, or have you done this before?"

"I've been out a few times," Alder says. "My friend's a first-timer."

The attendant nods. "No problem. I'll give you both a quick rundown. What size life jackets do you need?"

My cheeks burn at the question. I open my mouth, unsure how to answer without drawing attention to my size, but before I can speak, Alder says casually, "We'll both need XLs."

The attendant doesn't bat an eye. He just reaches behind him and pulls two orange life jackets from hooks. Like it's nothing. Like size makes no difference, and the only concern is safety. "These should work. Try 'em on to be sure."

I take the offered jacket with trembling fingers, surprised when it unfolds to a size that looks like it might actually fit. I slip it on over my t-shirt and find that, while snug, it closes without issue.

"All good?" Alder asks, already buckled into his vest.

"Yeah," I say, a little stunned. "It fits."

He raises an eyebrow. "What, did you think they wouldn't have our size? I'm big too, Lena."

His matter-of-fact tone makes me laugh despite myself. "I guess I didn't think about it that way."

"That's what I'm here for. To provide perspective." He grins, the first genuine smile I've seen from him in days, and something warm unfurls in my chest.

The attendant shows us the basics—how to hold the paddle, how to get in and out of the kayak, and simple steering techniques—before helping us launch. I wobble precariously as I settle into the plastic seat, certain I'm about to capsize before even leaving the dock.

"You've got it," Alder encourages from his own kayak. "Just breathe and find your center. The boat wants to stay upright, I promise."

Somehow, I manage to push off from the metal dock without tipping over. The kayak feels surprisingly stable once

I'm actually moving, and after a few tentative strokes with the paddle, I start to get the hang of it.

"This isn't so bad," I call to Alder, who's paddling alongside me with practiced ease.

"Told you!" He grins again. "Let's head upriver a bit. There's a nice stretch with less boat traffic."

We paddle in companionable silence for a while, finding a rhythm that carries us smoothly through the water. This physical activity clears my mind in a way that nothing has in weeks. I'm not thinking about fraternization policies, student loans, or apartment hunting—just the next stroke of the paddle, the sun warming my shoulders, and the quiet splash of water.

And, while Alder is a professional athlete, he's not zooming ahead or making this into a workout by any means. We're just cruising, and it's really, really nice.

"So," Alder says after we've been on the water for maybe twenty minutes, "I've been meaning to ask. Did Brad ever respond to his musical serenade?"

I can't help but laugh. "Not directly. However, one of the dental assistants at the facility has a daughter in his department. Apparently, he tried to finish the lecture as if nothing happened, but then dismissed the class early. He canceled his office hours for the rest of the week."

"Mission accomplished, then." He looks pleased with himself.

"I suppose so." I navigate around a partially submerged log. "I'm sorry I overreacted that day. It was just... the timing couldn't have been worse with the management meeting."

"No, you were right to be upset." Alder's voice is more serious now. "I should have talked to you first. I just thought..." He trails off, focusing on his paddling.

"Thought what?"

He shrugs. "That you were avoiding me because you were

disappointed. Maybe if I showed some initiative with the revenge plan, things would return to how they were."

His honesty catches me off guard. "I wasn't disappointed in you, Alder. I was trying to protect my job." I pause, considering how much to reveal. "And maybe protect myself a little too."

"From me?" He sounds genuinely confused.

"From this whole situation." I gesture vaguely between us, nearly losing my balance in the process. "It's complicated, and I'm not good at complicated."

"Seems like we're both pretty bad at it," he admits with a small smile. "Maybe we should stick to simple today."

"Simple sounds perfect."

We continue upriver, pointing out red hawks swooping above the water and laughing at a dog that barks frantically at us from the riverbank. The conversation flows as easily as the current, touching on childhood memories of summer, favorite water activities, and Gordie's hilarious fear of the neighbor's garden hose.

After about an hour, Alder suggests we head back. "There's a little café near the rental place. Best bagels in Pittsburgh."

"Lead the way," I say, surprised by how reluctant I am for our time on the water to end.

The return journey is even easier, as we're now moving with the current. By the time we reach the boat launch, I feel more relaxed than I have in weeks. The attendant helps us out of our kayaks, and I'm pleased to find that I'm not even embarrassed when he steadies me as I climb out.

"How're your arms feeling?" Alder asks as we return our life jackets.

I rotate my shoulders, noticing the pleasant burn of muscles used in new ways. "I'll be sore tomorrow, but the good kind of sore."

"Nothing a hot shower won't fix." He takes a long pull from his water bottle, and I try unsuccessfully to look away from his throat as he swallows. He wipes his mouth with the back of his hand, and I realize I'm almost drooling. "Ready for lunch? It's just a short walk."

Farmer x Baker is a café built into a repurposed shipping container at the edge of Aspinwall Riverfront Park. The line stretches outside the container, but Alder assures me it moves quickly.

"Trust me, it's worth the wait," he says, and twenty minutes later, when I'm biting into the most perfect avocado toast I've ever tasted, I have to agree.

We sit at a small table outside the café, watching families with children and people walking dogs enjoy the park.

"Gunnar's wedding … tomorrow," Alder says suddenly. "I know things have been weird, but... I'd still really like it if you'd come *with* me."

I take a sip of my iced coffee, buying time to organize my thoughts. "I haven't changed my mind about finding my place," I say finally. "I still think it's for the best."

"I know." He looks down at his plate. "The invitation stands regardless. It would mean a lot to have you there."

I pat his hand. "I'm going to the wedding regardless. But the question is how much time I can safely spend with you while we're there."

He shakes his head. "You're the only one who gets it. What I've been through with Adam. And..." he hesitates, "because I like spending time with you. Today has been the best day I've had in weeks."

The simple honesty in his voice makes my chest tighten. "Mine too," I admit.

"So? Wedding date?" He gives me a hopeful look.

"Okay," I say, surprising myself with how easily the agreement comes. "I'll be your very casual, friendly plus one."

His smile is like the sun breaking through clouds. "Perfect. Now finish your fancy toast so I can show you the rest of the park."

After eating, we wander through the green space, eventually finding ourselves at a small playground. There are a few children climbing on the equipment, but the swings are empty.

"Race you," Alder says suddenly, and before I can respond, he's jogging toward the swing set.

I follow, laughing despite myself. "Are you five years old?"

"Sometimes," he admits, dropping onto one of the swings. "Come on, when's the last time you let yourself just play?"

I can't remember, which is probably answer enough. I sit on the swing beside him, feeling slightly ridiculous but also strangely free.

"Bet I can go higher," he challenges, already pumping his legs.

"You're on."

We swing side by side, trying to outdo each other, laughing like children. The fact that we're two grown adults —one a professional athlete, one a dentist with a doctorate— makes it all the more absurd and extraordinary.

"Jump on three!" Alder calls when we're both swinging high. "One, two, three!"

My first instinct is fear, but something about Alder and our morning together snuffs out that hesitation. I let go of the chains and sail through the air. I feel free as if I'm flying—an actual bird. With a soft thud, I squeal before landing in the mulch, momentum carrying me forward onto my knees. Alder lands beside me, both of us laughing too hard to care about the mulch now stuck to our clothes.

"I can't believe we just did that," I gasp between laughs, brushing wood chips from my palms.

"I can," he says, sitting up beside me. "You're fun, Lena Sinclair."

He reaches over, and for a moment, I think he's going to take my hand. Instead, he gently plucks a piece of mulch from my hair. His fingers linger for just a second.

"And you're really beautiful, you know that?" he says, his voice softer than before. "Especially like this, with your cheeks all rosy and your eyes bright."

My breath catches. No clever response comes to mind, no deflection or self-deprecating joke. All I can do is meet his gaze as something electric passes between us.

"Alder," I begin, not sure what I'm going to say next.

"Mom! Mom! Look at me!" A child's voice breaks the moment as a little boy races past us to the climbing structure.

Alder withdraws his hand, but his eyes remain fixed on mine. "We should probably head back," he says, though he doesn't sound particularly convinced.

He stands and offers his hand, effortlessly pulling me to my feet. We brush ourselves off as best we can and begin walking back toward the parking lot, a newfound awareness humming between us.

"Thanks for today," I say as we reach his car. "I needed this more than I realized."

"Me too." He opens my door for me. "We should do it again sometime. Before you..." He trails off.

"Before I find a new place," I finish for him. "That might be a while at the rate I'm going. Everything decent is either too expensive or already taken."

"No rush," he says, and I can hear both relief and caution in his voice. "The guest room is yours for as long as you need it."

As we drive back to the city, windows down and music playing, I find myself relaxing into the moment, letting go of the constant fretting about the future. For today, at least, I can simply enjoy this—the warm breeze, the music, the comfortable presence of the man beside me.

Maybe just for this weekend, I can stop overthinking everything and simply enjoy this strange, unexpected connection we've found.

THE LATE AFTERNOON SUN SLANTS THROUGH OUR TOWNHOUSE windows as I rummage through the fridge, searching for something to offer Lena. *My* townhouse. Shit. After our day at the river, I'm not ready for it to end. I want to preserve this new easiness between us, this return to something that feels remarkably like friendship.

Or maybe something more.

I can't stop thinking about how she looked today—cheeks flushed with exertion, hair wild from the river breeze, that genuine laugh when she jumped from the swing. She'd seemed so free, so different from the guarded woman who's been avoiding me all week.

"You hungry?" I call toward the hallway where she disappeared to change out of her damp clothes. "We've got leftover chicken, or I could throw together some pasta."

No response, but I hear her footsteps, then a strange sound that makes me straighten up and close the fridge.

"Alder? Can you come here?" Lena's voice has an edge I haven't heard before.

I find her kneeling beside Gordon, who's lying on his side in the hallway. My dog's eyes are half-closed, his usual manic energy completely absent.

"What's wrong with him?" I ask, dropping to my knees next to them.

"I'm not sure, but something's definitely off." Lena gently strokes Gordie's head. "He was pawing at his mouth when I walked past. Has he been eating and drinking normally?"

I try to think. I've been so wrapped up in my issues that I haven't paid close attention. "He didn't finish his breakfast this morning, but I figured he was just being picky. He does that sometimes."

Lena frowns, her hand moving to Gordie's jaw. "I'd like to look in his mouth. Can you hold him still for me?"

I nod, cradling Gordie's head in my lap. He whimpers slightly but doesn't resist as Lena carefully pries his jaws apart.

"Shit," she mutters, peering inside. "Alder, his gums are severely swollen. There's—" She shifts position to get a better look. "I think there's an abscess on the left side of his back. It's pretty bad."

"What does that mean? He just needs antibiotics or something, right?" I try to keep my voice steady, but there's a rising note of panic I can't quite suppress.

Lena meets my eyes, her expression grave. "Dental abscesses in dogs can be serious. They can spread the infection to other parts of the body very quickly. We need to get him to an emergency vet. Now."

"He's just a smelly dog," I protest weakly. "Everyone always says he's smelly."

"Alder." Lena's voice is firm but gentle. "This isn't normal smelly dog stuff. This is a serious infection. Trust me on this. Teeth matter."

The certainty in her voice galvanizes me into action. I scoop Gordie into my arms, surprised at how limp he feels, and head for the door. "There's an emergency clinic in Shadyside, about fifteen minutes from here."

"Give me your keys," Lena says, following close behind. "I'll drive. You sit with him."

I hesitate for only a moment before tossing her my keys. We hurry to the car, Gordie making small, pitiful sounds against my chest that twist something deep inside me.

"It's okay, buddy," I murmur, sliding into the back seat with him still cradled in my arms. "We're going to get you fixed up."

Lena navigates through early evening traffic with calm efficiency, occasionally glancing over with concern etched on her face. "Keep talking to him," she suggests. It'll help keep him calm."

So, I do. I tell Gordie about the birds we saw on the river today, about the swings, about how I'm going to buy him the fancy organic treats once he feels better. My voice catches occasionally, but I keep talking, as much for myself as for him.

By the time we pull into the emergency vet clinic's parking lot, my shirt is damp with sweat, Gordie's drool, and my arms ache from holding him. But I refuse to let him go until a vet tech meets us at the door with a gurney.

"What happened?" she asks, helping me transfer Gordie onto the small wheeled cart.

"Dental abscess," Lena answers before I can speak. "Severe swelling in the lower left quadrant, likely affecting the back molars. He's lethargic and showing signs of pain when touched near the jaw."

The tech gives Lena an appraising glance. "Medical background?"

"Dentist," Lena says. "Human teeth, but the principles are similar."

"Got it." The tech nods and begins wheeling Gordie through a set of double doors. "The doctor will examine him. You can wait in the reception area, and someone will come out to collect your information."

"Can't I go with him?" The words burst out of me, desperate and raw.

"I'm sorry, sir. Hospital protocol. We'll update you as soon as possible."

I stand frozen, watching the doors swing shut behind Gordie, my arms suddenly aching with emptiness. Lena's hand finds my elbow, gently guiding me toward the waiting area.

"He's in good hands," she says softly. "Come on. Let's get the paperwork started."

I nod silently, allowing her to lead me to the reception desk. Lena mutters under her breath about the cost, but I will pay any amount for that mutt to be healthy. He's been my rock through some tough shit. I throw my credit card on the counter.

The next thirty minutes pass in a blur of forms and pet insurance questions. I sign whatever's put in front of me, grateful that Lena seems to know what information they need when my brain simply won't cooperate.

The waiting room is quiet, with just an elderly couple holding a cat carrier and a woman scrolling through her phone while her small dog sleeps at her feet. I slump into an uncomfortable plastic chair, elbows resting on my knees, staring at the industrial carpeting.

"What if—" I begin, but can't bring myself to finish the thought.

Lena sits next to me, close enough that our shoulders touch. "Don't go there," she says. "One step at a time."

I nod, trying to focus on her steady presence rather than the swirling fears in my head. But as the minutes tick by, it becomes harder to maintain my composure. Needing a distraction, I pull out my phone and see a text from Gunnar.

Tomorrow's the best day ever! I'm so pumped, guys.

Reality crashes in on me all at once. Gunnar's wedding. Tomorrow. How could I have forgotten?

"Fuck," I mutter, dropping my phone into my lap. "Gunnar's getting married tomorrow."

"I know," Lena says. "We'll make it. Gordie will be okay, and we'll make it to the wedding."

Before I can respond, the elderly couple across from us starts whispering and pointing. The woman nudges her husband and gestures toward me with poorly concealed excitement.

Not now. Please, not now. I tug at my hair, wishing I'd shoved a hat on my head. Wishing for one moment that I possessed a forgettable face.

Lena shifts slightly, angling her body to block their view of me. "Do you want some water?" she asks loudly enough for them to hear. "I saw a vending machine down the hall."

"No, I'm—" My voice breaks embarrassingly. "I'm okay."

She reaches for my hand, interlacing our fingers in a gesture that feels both casual and intimate. "He's going to be fine," she says, and I realize she's still performing for our audience, giving me the cover of a private moment.

"Mr. Stag?" A different vet tech appears at the door. "The doctor would like to speak with you."

I stand on unsteady legs, and Lena rises with me, still holding my hand. The tech leads us to a small consultation room where a middle-aged Asian woman in scrubs waits with Gordie's chart in her hands.

"I'm Dr. Wei," she says, gesturing for us to sit. "Your dog has a severe abscess that's causing significant infection. We've given him pain medication and started antibiotics, but he's going to need surgery to extract the affected teeth and drain the abscess."

"Surgery?" My mouth goes dry. "When?"

"As soon as possible," Dr. Wei says, her expression serious. "The infection is quite advanced. We'd like to keep him overnight for monitoring and do the procedure tomorrow afternoon."

Tomorrow. Wedding day.

"Will he be okay?" It's the only question that matters right now.

"With prompt treatment, the prognosis is good. Dental infections can be serious, but he's young and otherwise healthy." She glances between Lena and me. "The surgery should take about two hours, and then he'll need to recover here for at least 4-6 hours afterward. You could likely take him home tomorrow evening, but he'll need careful monitoring and medication for several days."

I nod, trying to absorb the information through the fog of panic. "Whatever he needs. Just... fix him."

Dr. Wei's expression softens. "We'll take good care of him, Mr. Stag. The receptionist can go over the costs and paperwork with you."

I tug on my hair. "Can I stay here overnight with him? This feels really shitty. Sorry."

Lena pats my hand and looks at Dr. Wei, whose lips are pressed in a tight line. "Dr. Wei, I'm a trauma dentist and have experience with injected medications and monitoring vital signs. Do you think we could take Gordon home to wait for his surgery call?"

The vet taps her hands on the table, sighs, and pulls out a notepad. "We're pretty full here, so I'm going to say yes. Here is the recommended antibiotic and pain medication schedule." She scribbles some notes that all seem like gibberish to me, but Lena knows what's happening. She meets my eye and says, "I promise, Alder, we can handle this back home."

When Dr. Wei leaves in a rush, staring blankly at the wall. Gunnar's wedding is at 4 PM tomorrow. Even if Gordie's surgery is first thing in the morning, there's no way I can leave him alone while he recovers. Not for something as trivial as a wedding.

Even if it is my brother's.

"Alder," Lena says gently. "Talk to me."

"I can't go to the wedding," I say flatly. "I can't leave him."

"Yes, you can. We'll figure something out." She leans forward, forcing me to meet her eyes. "Is there anyone who could stay with Gordie after his surgery? Someone you trust?"

I think for a moment. "My neighbor, LeMarcus. He dog-sits when I'm on the road. But this is different. This is medical."

"The vet staff will handle the medical part. LeMarcus just needs to be with him, right? Keep him company while he recovers?"

"Maybe." I scrub a hand over my face. "I could ask him."

"Good. Do that." She squeezes my knee. "Let's finish the paperwork and go home."

Somehow, Lena manages to handle everything. She's calm and assertive, and I stare in wonder as they teach her how to give my dog his pain medication.

He wags his tail weakly and licks her hand, and I almost pass out from relief. I press my forehead against his, whispering promises I intend to keep about toys and treats and never ignoring him again.

It's nearly ten by the time we leave the clinic. I text LeMarcus on the drive home, and he immediately responds that he'll be happy to Gordie-sit tomorrow. Small mercies.

I cradle Gordie in my arms like a baby after Lena parks. She unlocks the door and smiles at me as I pass, walking directly to my room and placing Gordie on my bed where he belongs.

When I stand to take off my shirt and prepare to climb into bed with my dog, I see Lena in the doorway. She studies a bag of pre-filled syringes and arranges them up on my dresser.

I stare at her, this woman who spent her day off paddling rivers and swinging on playgrounds with me, who recognized Gordie's distress when I dismissed it, who drove us to the emergency vet and handled the paperwork when I could barely function.

"Stay with me," I beg, the words escaping before I can second-guess them. "In my room, I mean. The bed's plenty big enough, and—" I falter, unsure how to express the hollow ache in my chest that I know will expand the moment I'm alone.

Lena studies my face for a long moment. "Okay," she says finally. "But just sleeping. I'm not taking advantage of your emotional state."

A startled laugh escapes me. "Wasn't planning to seduce you while worrying about my dog's surgery, but thanks for clarifying."

She smiles, the tension breaking slightly. "Just setting boundaries. Something we're supposedly getting better at."

"Supposedly," I agree, climbing beneath the sheets, shirt on.

Lena disappears to change and brush her teeth, returning in sleep shorts and an oversized t-shirt. She smiles and climbs into the bed on the other side of Gordie, the two of us flanking him.

I turn off the light, and we both lie there, stroking his fur as he snores.

"Thank you," I say finally. "For today. All of it."

"Anyone would have done the same."

"No, they wouldn't." I look at her silhouette in the darkness. "Most people would have just told me to calm down and call a vet in the morning. You recognized it was serious. You took charge when I couldn't."

She's quiet for a moment. "I care about Gordie too, you know."

"I know." And I do know, suddenly and with complete certainty. "That's kind of amazing."

We lapse into silence again, but it's more comfortable now.

The knot of tension in my chest slowly unravels as exhaustion takes over. Just as I'm drifting off, Lena's hand finds mine under the covers, her fingers tangling with mine in a loose hold.

"He's going to be okay," she murmurs, her voice thick with approaching sleep.

"Yeah," I whisper back. "Yeah, he is."

My phone rings at 4:17 AM, jolting me from sleep. Disoriented, I fumble for it and nearly drop it in my haste to answer when I see the vet clinic's number.

"Hello? This is Alder Stag."

"Mr. Stag, this is Amanda from Pittsburgh Emergency Veterinary Clinic. We've had a schedule change and have an opening for Gordie's surgery at 6:30 this morning. Can you come in by 5 to complete the pre-surgical paperwork?"

"Yes," I say immediately, sitting up. "Yes, we'll be there."

I end the call and turn to find Lena already awake and watching me with concern.

"They can take Gordie at 6:30," I explain, already climbing out of bed. "We need to be there by 5."

She glances at the clock and immediately pushes back the covers. "I'll be ready in ten minutes."

We move with urgent efficiency, brushing teeth and throwing on clothes, checking on Gordie with choreographed precision as if we've been sharing mornings for years instead of weeks. Lena gives him a shot of something like it's no big deal and then showers my dog with kisses. I'm profoundly grateful for her silent understanding of the situation and the way she matches my pace without question.

"I texted LeMarcus," I tell her as we head for her car. "He'll meet us at the clinic around noon after the surgery."

She nods, sliding into the passenger seat this time. "Perfect. That should give us plenty of time to get ready for the wedding."

I start the car, then pause, turning to look at her. Her hair is pulled into a messy bun, she's wearing yesterday's clothes, and there are pillow creases on her cheek. She looks exhausted, worried, and utterly beautiful.

"You really don't have to come to the wedding," I say. "After all this, I'd understand if you'd rather skip it."

She gives me a look that's equal parts exasperation and affection. "Alder Stag, I'm going to your brother's wedding. Now drive, or we're going to be late for Gordie's surgery."

I drive, trying to focus on the road rather than the strange, wonderful feeling expanding in my chest—a feeling that has nothing to do with relief about Gordie's care and everything to do with the woman beside me.

The woman who, against all probability and maybe good sense, has become essential to my life in ways I'm only beginning to understand.

OVER THE PAST FEW HOURS, THE WAITING ROOM CHAIR HAS become a torture device. No matter how I shift, I can't find a comfortable position. At least there aren't arms on it to dig into my thighs. But my back aches, my neck is stiff, and the endless loop of daytime television is steadily eroding my sanity.

Yet these physical discomforts are nothing compared to the weight of waiting. I've spent years on the other side of this equation—the professional behind the door, performing procedures while families wait in rooms exactly like this one. But being the person waiting is a new experience altogether, and it's giving me a fresh perspective on how my patients' families must feel.

Alder paces the waiting area, checking his phone obsessively as if willing it to ring with news. He's barely sat down since they took Gordie into surgery two hours ago. I watch him move, the coiled tension in his shoulders, the way he periodically runs both hands through his hair until it stands at alarming angles.

"Sit down," I say for the third time. "You're making me dizzy."

He glances at me, then drops heavily into the chair beside

mine. "What's taking so long? They said two hours. It's been two hours and seven minutes."

I place my hand on his knee, which is bouncing rapidly. "Surgeries don't run on exact timetables. Dr. Wei will come out when she's finished. Gordie's in good hands."

He covers my hand with his own, squeezing with more pressure than he probably realizes. "I know. I just—" He exhales sharply. "I hate not being able to do anything."

"Yeah," I say softly. "I get that."

And I do. The helplessness of waiting is a uniquely miserable feeling, especially for someone like Alder, who's accustomed to solving problems through sheer physical will. Watching him navigate this vulnerability has revealed layers I hadn't fully appreciated before. The professional athlete, the charming brother, the revenge conspirator—all these versions of Alder Stag are now joined by this worried dog dad who spent the night whispering reassurances to his pet between fitful stretches of sleep.

I find myself unexpectedly drawn to this version. The realization hits me with startling clarity as I sit in this uncomfortable chair, surrounded by outdated magazines and the faint antiseptic smell: I care about this man. Not as part of our revenge plan, not as my roommate or the owner of the dog I've grown attached to, but as himself—as Alder.

The thought should frighten me, but after the past twenty-four hours, it simply feels like acknowledging something that's been true for a while now.

"Mr. Stag?" Dr. Wei appears in the doorway, still wearing her surgical mask. "Gordon's surgery went well. We removed the infected teeth and drained the abscess. He's in recovery now."

Alder springs to his feet, pulling me up with him since he's still holding my hand. "Can we see him?"

"In a few minutes. He's still coming out of anesthesia, but his vitals are stable, and his prognosis is excellent."

The relief on Alder's face is so profound I can almost feel it radiating from him. He turns to me with a brilliant smile, making my chest ache.

"He's okay," he says as if I hadn't just heard the same news.

"He's okay," I confirm, returning his smile.

Dr. Wei discusses aftercare instructions, medication schedules, and follow-up appointments. I find myself instinctively taking mental notes, falling into my professional habit of cataloging medical information, while Alder is surprisingly attentive to every detail.

Just as Dr. Wei finishes, the waiting room door opens to reveal a lanky Black teenager with a backpack slung over one shoulder.

"What's good, A-Stag? How's my man Gordie?"

"LeMarcus." Alder's relief is palpable as he clasps the boy's hand in a complicated handshake. "Thanks for coming. Gordie just got out of surgery. He's going to be fine."

"That's what's up." LeMarcus nods, then turns curious eyes to me. "You must be the dentist. My ma said you moved in."

I feel the heat creep into my cheeks. "Lena Sinclair. Nice to meet you."

"LeMarcus Washington, dog-whisperer." He grins, revealing a set of perfectly aligned teeth. "Braces," he explains, catching my professional assessment.

"I can tell," I say. "Beautiful occlusion."

LeMarcus laughs. "Yo, A-Stag, she really is a dentist. I thought maybe that was some kind of code."

Alder rolls his eyes. "Why would I need a code for her profession?"

"I dunno, man. You hockey dudes are weird."

While we wait to see Gordie, Alder goes over the plan with LeMarcus, who listens with surprising attentiveness for a college-aged kid. I observe their easy rapport, the way

LeMarcus teases Alder without hesitation, and the obvious affection beneath their banter.

"So, I'll stay here with G-man til he's released and then drive him home in your Escalade," LeMarcus says, ticking points off on his fingers. "You two go to the wedding, get your fancy on, and I'll text updates so you don't stress the whole time."

"Message me Gordie pics every hour," Alder says seriously, and LeMarcus snorts.

"Every hour? Nah, that's excessive. How about every twenty minutes?"

They burst into laughter, and I smile despite my exhaustion. There's something deeply endearing about seeing this side of Alder—the one who inspires such loyalty from his young neighbor, who worries about his rescue dog, and who notices when I'm uncomfortable at parties or self-conscious about fitting into a kayak.

When they finally walk us back to see Gordie—groggy, with a cone of shame and stitches in his gum—Alder kneels beside the crate, whispering to him through the grate. The tenderness in his expression makes my throat tight. For just a moment, I allow myself to indulge in the dangerous thought that Alder Stag might be someone I could actually fall for if circumstances were different.

If we weren't conspiring for revenge on our exes.

If he weren't technically my patient.

If I weren't planning to move out.

"We're going to make it," I say, glancing at the dashboard clock as Alder drives us back to the townhouse in my Honda.

Alder clenches his jaw and weaves through traffic with the confident precision of someone who's spent a lifetime navigating Pittsburgh's labyrinthine roads. Still, his white knuckles on the steering wheel suggest he's feeling anxious.

"I feel like no matter what I do today, I'm letting someone down." He doesn't look at me as he says this, swerving onto the 9th Street bridge and veering toward our…his townhouse complex.

"Hey," I try to sound soothing. "You are keeping Gordie safe. You responded immediately when you knew something was wrong. And you said your brother's wedding is casual. We'll pound some coffee, throw on our fancy clothes, and zoom back across the river."

My words seem to calm him a bit, even as anxiety blooms in my chest at the thought of facing Alder's entire family—plus his teammates and coaches—after our emotionally charged night.

As if reading my mind, Alder says, "We should probably keep our hands to ourselves at the wedding. Uncle Tim will be watching, and he's already suspicious about the fraternization policy."

"That won't be a problem," I assure him, staring out the window at passing houses. "Coach and half the team will be there. I'll be on my best professional behavior."

"Right." Something in his tone makes me glance over, but his expression is unreadable as he navigates a turn. "Professional."

We lapse into silence, the unspoken implications of our conversation hovering between us. What are we, exactly? Roommates who shared a bed last night because of a crisis? Something more complicated that neither of us can define?

By the time we arrive at the townhouse, it's nearly 1:30, giving us just over two hours before the ceremony. We part awkwardly in the hallway, each heading to separate bathrooms to shower away the hospital smell and exhaustion.

"I, uh, put fresh towels in the guest bath yesterday," Alder says, running a hand through his hair. "And I peeked at your shampoo brand and stocked up when I was at the store."

The fact that he noticed which products I prefer sends a

slight tremor through me. "Thanks," I manage before escaping to the bathroom.

Under the hot spray of the shower, I try to sort through the tangle of emotions the past day has created. Concern for Gordie. Sympathy for Alder. The strange intimacy of sharing his bed and the even stranger realization that I slept better next to him than I have in months. The way his hand sought mine in the night, our fingers interlacing like it was the most natural thing in the world. My thoughts slip to the kiss, to the press of his hard length against my soft belly. Nope, I cannot allow myself to go there. Especially not today.

I emerge from the bathroom wrapped in a towel, padding down the hall to my room with damp hair and racing thoughts. My most immediate concern is what to wear to this wedding. In my hasty packing when leaving Brad's apartment, I didn't exactly prioritize dressy clothes.

I rifle through my drawers, growing increasingly frustrated as I discard option after option. Too casual. Too professional. Too summery. Too worn.

Underlying it all is the familiar anxiety: Will I look out of place among all these athletes and their conventionally attractive partners? Will people wonder what Alder is doing with someone who looks like me?

Brad's voice slithers into my mind: *All anyone has to do is look at you to realize why I strayed.*

I push the thought away fiercely. No. I refuse to let him in my head today.

Just as I'm about to give up and text Alder that I need to make an emergency shopping run, my hand brushes against something silky at the back of the closet. I pull out a navy blue dress I'd forgotten I owned—a splurge from my final year of dental school that I wore exactly once before Brad commented that it was "a bit much" for my figure.

I hold it up skeptically. The fabric is beautiful, a rich midnight blue with a subtle shimmer. The neckline is more daring than I usually go for, and the cut is designed to emphasize curves rather than minimize them.

With a deep breath, I slip it on, steeling myself for disappointment. But when I turn to the mirror, I'm startled by my reflection. The dress fits—more than fits—it looks good. The color brings out the warmth in my skin, and the cut accentuates my waist while skimming over my hips.

For the first time in longer than I can remember, I look at my body without immediately cataloging its flaws. Instead, I see strength in my arms that paddled a kayak yesterday, compassion in the hands that helped comfort Gordie, and confidence in the set of my shoulders after navigating a crisis with calm professionalism.

I slide the dress back off so I can lotion up.

I blow-dry my hair into loose waves, apply makeup with more care than usual, and locate the low heels I'd tossed into my suitcase as an afterthought. The woman in the mirror looks like me, but somehow more—more confident, more present, more alive.

Looking at this version of myself, I can almost believe what Alder said on the riverbank yesterday: *You're really beautiful, you know that?*

The dress is laid out on the bed as I finish my makeup in my underwear and bra, still debating whether I'm truly brave enough to wear something so fitted to mingle with Alder's family and my colleagues. I lean toward the mirror, applying mascara with careful precision when I hear the door open behind me.

"Lena, have you seen my—"

Alder's voice cuts off abruptly. I freeze, the mascara wand still raised, and meet his eyes in the mirror.

He stands motionless in the doorway, one hand resting on the knob. His gaze travels slowly from my face down to my lace-trimmed bra, over the curve of my waist, lingering on my hips in the matching navy underwear, and then down my bare legs.

I should say something. Move. Cover myself. React in any way at all. But the look on his face has paralyzed me—a raw, unguarded hunger that sends heat cascading through my body.

When his eyes finally return to mine, their intensity steals my breath. There's no artifice in his face, no calculation—just pure, honest desire.

"Lena," he says, his voice rough and low. "You're so fucking sexy."

CHAPTER 22
ALDER

I STAND FROZEN IN THE DOORWAY, THE WORDS STILL HANGING IN the air between us. *You're so fucking sexy.* Did I really say that out loud?

Lena stares at me through the mirror, mascara wand suspended mid-air, her eyes wide. Neither of us moves. Neither of us speaks. My gaze travels over her again, helplessly drawn to the curve of her waist, the soft swell of her breasts in that lace bra, the matching panties hugging her rounded hips.

Blood rushes in my ears, and I know I should apologize, back out of the room, and close the door. But my feet won't move, and my mouth has apparently lost all connection to my brain.

"I..." I finally manage, my voice rough. "I should have knocked."

Lena slowly lowers the mascara wand, carefully setting it on the vanity. She doesn't grab a towel or try to cover herself. Instead, she turns to face me directly, and the motion sends a jolt of heat straight through my core.

"Yes," she says, her voice steadier than I would have expected.

Our eyes lock, and something electric passes between us.

I'm acutely aware of my racing pulse, the dryness in my mouth, the way my jeans have suddenly become uncomfortably tight.

The silence stretches, taut and charged, until my phone buzzes in my pocket. The sound breaks whatever spell has held us in place, and I fumble to check the message—a photo of Gordie in his cone from LeMarcus, with the caption:

> Patient resting comfortably. Doc says no twerking for two weeks.

Under normal circumstances, this would make me laugh. Right now, I can barely process the words on the screen.

"I'll let you finish getting ready," I say, backing out of the room without ever remembering what I came to ask for in the first place. "We should probably leave in ten minutes."

I close the door and lean against the wall in the hallway, running a hand over my face. What the hell just happened? After weeks of careful boundaries and trying my best to protect her while being a friend, I've completely shattered the illusion with one unfiltered comment.

The drive to my brother's neighborhood is short, though every minute feels like an eternity. Lena sits beside me in the passenger seat of her car since we left mine with LeMarcus, her dress now covering the body I can't stop thinking about. Her scent fills the car, something light and floral that makes me want to bury my face in her neck.

Keep it together, A-Stag.

"You look beautiful," I say, keeping my eyes firmly on the road. It's a massive understatement, but it's the most appropriate thing I can manage right now.

"Thank you." She smooths a hand over the silky fabric of her dress. "You clean up pretty well yourself."

I'm wearing a light blue button-down with the sleeves rolled up, dark jeans, and a navy tie that I'm suddenly aware matches her dress almost perfectly. We look like a real couple who coordinated their outfits, which will only fuel the speculation I'm supposedly trying to avoid.

"Sorry about earlier," I say, unable to let it go. "I shouldn't have just walked in like that."

"It's fine." Her voice is casual, but I catch the slight hitch in her breath. "We're roommates. These things happen."

Do they? Do roommates usually tell each other they're sexy while staring at them in their underwear? After I previously told her I want to bite her thighs? And now I really, really want to bite those thighs...

I want to pursue this to clear the air, but we're already pulling up to the small parking area near Gunnar and Emerson's place. Above the hum of city traffic, I hear the sounds of laughter and music as I help Lena out of the car.

Gunnar and Emerson chose an easy venue—the riverside patio behind their apartment building, decorated with strands of lights and glass bulbs that catch the late afternoon sun. Simple wooden tables dot the grass, laden with comfort food. I spot a fully tricked-out cookie table with a zillion different varieties and a huge ice chest full of milk to go with it.

"This is lovely," Lena says, taking in the scene. "So relaxed."

"That's Gun and Em for you. They care about the marriage, not the wedding." I rest my hand on the small of her back without thinking, then quickly pull away when I remember our agreement to keep our distance today.

My thumb tingles where it brushed against the silk of her dress. It's going to be a long evening.

We make our way through the gathering, with Lena greeting various family members and teammates. Each time I say her name, each time I watch her smile and shake hands, I remember the curve of those hips and the soft skin I haven't touched. Keeping my hands to myself is becoming an exercise in willpower I wasn't prepared for.

Uncle Tim nods at us from across the patio, his calculating gaze tracking our movements. Coach Thompson is here as well, raising an eyebrow when he spots us but offering a small nod of acknowledgment. The fraternization policy hangs over us like a cloud, but it's increasingly difficult to care when Lena looks the way she does tonight.

"A-Stag!" Tucker materializes beside us, clapping me on the shoulder. "And Dr. Sinclair, looking absolutely stunning." He gives me a knowing smirk. "You two just missed Gun's mini-meltdown when he couldn't find his bow tie."

"Is he okay now?" I ask, scanning the crowd for my brother.

"Yeah, he's fine. Odin found it in the bathroom." Tucker's gaze shifts between Lena and me, his smirk widening. "You two seem... tense. Everything good?"

Heat creeps up my neck. Is it that obvious? "Everything's fine. Just been a long day with Gordie's surgery."

"Riiiight. Gordie." Tucker winks at Lena. "How's the patient doing?"

"He's recovering well," she says smoothly. "LeMarcus is sending regular updates." She holds up her phone, and they smile at the latest pic with Gordie licking a frozen strawberry.

Tucker seems to want to say more, but a small string ensemble begins to tune up, signaling the ceremony is about to start. We make our way to the seats facing the river, where Gunnar already stands, looking nervous but happy in jeans and a blue bow tie.

I find myself stealing glances at Lena as we sit side by side. The sunlight catches the golden undertones in her skin, making her practically glow. The neckline of her dress reveals a tempting expanse of collarbone and the gentle swell of her cleavage. I force my gaze forward, focusing on my brother instead.

The music changes, and everyone turns to see Emerson appear from the apartment building. She's radiant in flowing blue silk that clings to her curves, her dark curls crowned with wildflowers. The look on Gunnar's face is one I've never seen before—pure, undiluted joy and certainty.

Something twists in my chest as I watch them. What makes Gunnar so different from me? How is he able to find someone who looks at him the way Emerson does now? Someone who chooses him, solely him, without hesitation or qualification?

I was there when he first saw her in Vegas. They knew immediately they were forever.

Adam never looked at me like that. He kept me hidden, comfortable with the scraps of his attention. And before him, there was a series of relationships that never quite clicked, never felt complete.

What's wrong with me that makes me so hard to love?

The ceremony is brief, with Gunnar and Emerson exchanging simple vows about choosing each other, fighting for their love, and supporting dreams. When Gunnar turns to the crowd and announces, "That's it! We're married!" the kids in the string ensemble hit a slightly off note that somehow makes the moment perfect.

I try to shake off my pity party and glance at Lena, finding her eyes shining with unshed tears and a small smile playing on her lips. Without thinking, I reach for her hand, our fingers tangling together on the seat between us. She looks down at our joined hands, then back at me, her smile deepening.

For a moment, I allow myself imagine what it would be like if this were real. If Lena were genuinely my date for this wedding, not my fake girlfriend, my roommate, or my team's dentist. Just a woman I was falling for, free from all the complications.

The thought is so appealing that it's almost painful.

The reception begins immediately after the ceremony, with caterers bringing out additional food to complement the dishes already on the tables. I grab two glasses of champagne from a passing tray and hand one to Lena.

"To marriage," I toast, clinking my glass against hers.

"To happiness," she counters, taking a sip. A small drop of champagne lingers on her lower lip, and I have to physically restrain myself from leaning in to taste it.

"There you are." Odin approaches us, looking far more relaxed than when I last saw him at family dinner. "So good to see you again, Dr. Sinclair."

"Please, call me Lena." She smiles warmly at my oldest brother. "And congratulations on your masters. Tucker told me you're job hunting?"

He nods and downs the rest of his champagne. "We can't all work for the Fury, but we can try, right?" Odin laughs and turns to me. "Can I steal you for a minute, A?"

I glance at Lena, who nods. "Go ahead. I want to congratulate the bride anyway."

As she walks away, Odin follows my gaze, noting how my eyes track her movements across the patio. Behind him, I notice Tucker checking his phone, frowning, and quickly excusing himself from a conversation with our uncle. He heads toward a quiet corner of the yard, phone pressed to his ear, his posture tense.

"She seems great," Odin says casually, pulling my attention back from whatever Tucker's dealing with.

"She is," I agree, too quickly.

"How are you doing with everything? The Adam situation?"

I shrug, watching as Lena reaches Emerson. The two of

them immediately fall into an animated conversation. "It's fine. Ancient history."

"Is it?" Odin raises an eyebrow. "Because you look at her like she's much more than a 'summer fling' or a rebound."

"I don't know what she is," I admit. "It's complicated."

"Because of the team policy?"

"That, and... everything else." I take a long sip of champagne. "We're roommates. She works for the team. We're both coming off bad breakups."

Odin follows my gaze to where Lena is now laughing at something Emerson has said. "You deserve someone who looks at you like that," he says quietly.

"Like what?"

"Like you're the only person in the room worth looking at." He claps me on the shoulder. "Don't overthink it, little brother. Sometimes, the best things in life don't make sense on paper. You can trust me because I'm a psychologist now."

I shove his hand off my arm. "You've had your degree for about five minutes, ass-hat."

He pulls me into a hug and then wanders off to find his girlfriend. I find myself drawn into conversations with various family members and teammates, listening to everyone's vacation plans and summer training strategies. Through it all, I'm hyper-aware of Lena's presence. The way she throws her head back when she laughs. How gracefully she navigates conversations with my family. The slight sway of her generous hips when she walks.

As the evening progresses, keeping my hands to myself with each passing hour grows more difficult. All the adrenaline and exhaustion piles up in my system until I'm throbbing with the need to be with Lena. Especially when a real band called String Fury takes over from the kids' ensemble, filling the riverside patio with music that demands dancing.

Gunnar and Emerson take the floor first, swaying together in their own world. Lena stands at the edge of the makeshift dance floor, watching Dad dip Mom with a small smile. The lights strung above catch in her hair, giving her an almost ethereal glow. I approach her from behind, close enough to catch the scent of her perfume but not quite touching.

"Dance with me," I say quietly, the words escaping before I can stop them.

She turns, surprise flitting across her face. "What happened to keeping our hands to ourselves?"

"One dance," I say. "Professional colleagues can dance at a wedding without violating any policies."

Her gaze searches mine, then drops to my extended hand. "One dance," she agrees, placing her palm against mine.

I lead her onto the dance floor, resting my hand on her waist as hers settles on my shoulder. The contact, even through layers of fabric, sends electricity through me. My hand curves automatically around the swell of her body. Like it fucking belongs there, touching her. We begin to move in time with the music, our bodies finding an easy rhythm together.

"You're a good dancer," she says, looking surprised.

"Hockey players need balance and coordination." I guide her through a gentle turn. "Dad had us in ballet a few off-seasons."

She smiles. "It shows."

We move together, the space between us gradually shrinking as the song progresses. I'm hyper-conscious of every point of contact—my hand on her waist, her fingers on my shoulder, our clasped hands. The scent of her perfume surrounds me, making it hard to focus on anything but how much I want to pull her closer. I want my thigh in between hers, pressing into that space where I hope she's burning as hot as me.

"I'm not sorry about what I said earlier," I say, my voice low after a moment.

Her eyes widen slightly, and I watch her throat work as

she swallows. "I... I've been fighting this," she admits. "Whatever this is between us."

"Me too." I tighten my grip on her waist slightly, feeling her respond by pressing incrementally closer. "Not very successfully, apparently."

"No," she agrees, her lips curving into a small smile. "Not very."

The music shifts, the tempo slowing further. Lena's body sways against mine, and I have to bite back a groan at the subtle friction. Images from earlier flood my mind—Lena in that lingerie, the softness of her belly, the fullness of her breasts. I wonder what she'd feel like bare under my hands, how her skin would taste...

"A-Stag." Coach Thompson's voice cuts through my thoughts like a bucket of ice water. He stands at the edge of the dance floor, expression carefully neutral. "Mind if I steal the good doctor for a dance? I've been meaning to discuss the new dental protocols for next season."

I release Lena immediately, taking a step back. "Of course, Coach."

As Thompson leads Lena away, I catch her glancing back at me, her eyes dark with the same desire I'm fighting to control. The knowledge that she wants this too—wants me— is both exhilarating and maddening.

I make my way to the bar, suddenly in desperate need of something more substantial than champagne.

The night progresses, a blur of food, music, and conversation, but my attention remains fixed on Lena. After her dance with Coach, she's careful to maintain a respectable distance, but our eyes keep finding each other across the patio.

I watch Gunnar and Emerson together, so obviously in love that it's almost painful to witness. They move as a unit, finishing each other's sentences and communicating with glances and small touches. Whatever they have, it's real and solid in a way I've never experienced.

But maybe I don't need what they have. Not right now. Maybe what I need—what Lena and I both need—is simpler. More elemental.

The realization hits me as I watch her laugh at something Tucker says. We've been overthinking this entire situation. Everyone already thinks we're having a summer fling. Maybe we should stop fighting it and just... have one.

There is no pressure, no expectations beyond mutual pleasure and comfort. We can address this attraction, enjoy each other for a few weeks, and then move on when pre-season starts and Lena finds her own place. It is clean, uncomplicated, and honest.

I feel relieved by this solution. We don't need to analyze it to death or worry about fraternization policies. We just need to be discreet and understand that this isn't forever. It's just for now, and it's going to be hot.

I make my way to where Lena stands near the river, a slight breeze lifting tendrils of hair from her shoulders. The sun has set, painting the water in shades of deep blue and purple, mirroring the color of her dress.

"Hey," I say, coming to stand beside her. "How's your night going?"

"Good." She smiles up at me. "Your family is wonderful. And the wedding was beautiful."

"It was." I hesitate, then decide to be direct. "I've been thinking."

"Dangerous," she teases, but I can hear the slight catch in her voice.

"Maybe we've been making this more complicated than it needs to be."

"How so?" She turns to face me fully, her eyes searching mine.

"Everyone already thinks we're having a summer fling." I move closer, lowering my voice. "Maybe we should stop fighting it."

Her breath hitches almost imperceptibly. "Alder..."

"No pressure," I continue quickly. "No expectations. Just... this." I run a hand lightly down her side, feeling her shiver under my touch. "For as long as it makes sense."

Lena's eyes darken, her lips parting slightly.

"We'll be discreet." I move closer still, nearly closing the gap between us. "It's not like we're planning forever here. Just... addressing what's already happening."

She studies my face, and I can practically see the wheels turning in her mind as she weighs options and considers the consequences. Then, something in her expression shifts, softening.

Hope surges through me as she leans in, her lips brushing my ear as she whispers, "Take me home, Alder."

CHAPTER 23
LENA

The rideshare pulls away from Gunnar and Emerson's building, leaving no evidence of our hasty departure. We didn't say goodbye to anyone—not to Alder's brothers, not to Coach, not even to the bride and groom. One moment, we were standing by the river, Alder's hand trailing down my side as he suggested we stop fighting our attraction, and the next, we were slipping through the crowd and out to the street, his phone already summoning a car since we'd been drinking.

The air between us in the backseat crackles, electric. Alder sits close enough that his thigh presses against mine, the heat of him burning through the thin fabric of my dress. Neither of us speaks. What is there to say when we've finally acknowledged what's been building for weeks? I can't bring myself to worry about work right now.

Alder's phone buzzes, and he checks it. The blue glow of the screen illuminates his profile.

"LeMarcus," he explains, his voice low and rough. "Gordie's settled in my room. He had some chicken and took his meds."

"That's good," I manage, though at this moment, Gordie is the furthest thing from my mind. My entire body thrums with anticipation, need, and the knowledge that soon—finally—Alder's hands will be on me.

Alder types a quick response, then tucks his phone away. "I told him we're on our way and to feel free to head home."

"Good," I say again, unable to summon more eloquent words. I hope LeMarcus takes the hint and doesn't linger. As much as I appreciate his care for Gordie, I need Alder with a ferocity that surprises me. It's really all I can do right now to keep my hands out of my underwear in the back seat of this car.

A small, rational part of my brain tries to remind me of all the complicated reasons—the team's fraternization policy, my desperate fiscal need for this job, and the fact that we're both on the rebound. But that voice is drowned out by the insistent pulse between my legs, the memory of Alder's eyes darkening as he looked at me in my underwear, the way his hands felt on my waist as we danced.

We're not promising each other forever. We're not even promising each other tomorrow. This is about tonight, about finally giving in to the attraction that's been building since that kiss in Brad's apartment—if I'm being honest since the first day I moved into Alder's townhouse.

The car stops in front of our building, and Alder helps me out, his hand lingering at the small of my back as we walk to the door. The simple touch feels different now—possessive, intentional. My skin tingles beneath his palm.

LeMarcus is in the living room when we enter, his backpack already slung over one shoulder. "Hey, there's the party people," he says with a grin that suggests he knows exactly what's going on. "Gordo's all tucked in and comfy."

"Thanks, man," Alder says, his voice admirably steady. "You're a lifesaver."

"No worries." LeMarcus's eyes flick between us, taking in our tense postures as we're both slightly flushed. "Well, I'll head out. My ma's expecting me."

"Let me get you some cash," Alder says, already pulling out his wallet.

I shift impatiently as they handle the transaction, eager for LeMarcus to leave so we can be alone. Finally, finally, he heads for the door.

"Take care of that dog," LeMarcus says, then adds with a smirk, "and yourselves."

The door closes behind him, and suddenly, we're standing in the entryway, the air thick with anticipation.

"We should check on Gordie," Alder says, though his eyes never leave mine.

"Of course," I agree.

We move down the hallway to Alder's bedroom, where Gordie is indeed settled on the bed, cone around his neck, eyes half-closed with medication. He wags his tail weakly when he sees us.

"Hey, buddy," Alder murmurs, gently petting his head. "You feeling better?"

The tenderness in his voice and the care he shows his pet stir something deep inside me. Alder might present himself as a tough hockey player, but there's a gentleness to him that continues to surprise me.

Gordon seems comfortable, already drifting back to sleep, and Alder straightens up. When he turns to face me, the gentleness is gone, replaced by something darker, more primal. His posture shifts, shoulders squaring, jaw tightening.

He's no longer the worried dog dad or the dutiful brother attending a wedding. This Alder is all predator, and I'm his chosen prey.

He steps toward me, deliberate and slow, backing me into the hallway. I retreat instinctively, pulse racing, as he leaves the bedroom door open for Gordie if needed.

"Lena," he says, my name like a declaration on his lips.

And then he moves, closing the distance between us in two long strides. Before I can react, his arms wrap around me, lifting me effortlessly. I gasp, my arms instinctively circling his neck as he carries me down the hall toward my bedroom.

I've never been carried like this before—like I weigh nothing like I'm precious cargo. His strength is both intimidating and thrilling, the solid muscle of his chest pressed against me as he moves purposefully through the doorway to my room.

He lays me on the bed with surprising gentleness, then follows me down, his body covering mine. We stare at each other for a heartbeat, the final moment of hesitation before crossing a threshold we can't uncross.

Then his mouth is on mine, and any remaining doubts evaporate. His kiss is nothing like the brief press of lips we shared in Brad's apartment. This is hungry, demanding, his tongue seeking entrance, which I readily grant.

His hands roam my body with the same urgency, mapping the curves he'd only glimpsed earlier. This is usually the part where I worry about how my body feels to my partner, but Alder has made it clear that he is deeply turned on. And that alone almost sends me over the edge.

My hands explore the broad planes of his back and the solid strength of his shoulders. His mouth travels from my lips to my jaw, then down the column of my throat, drawing a moan from deep in my chest.

"God, Lena," he murmurs against my skin. "You have no idea how long I've wanted this."

"I think I have some idea," I manage, arching into him as his hand cups my breast through my dress.

He pulls back slightly, and I whimper at the loss of contact. His eyes are dark, pupils blown wide with desire.

"I need to tell you," he says, his voice strained. "I sent in the test kit. After Adam. Everything's healthy."

The abrupt shift to practical matters catches me off guard, but I appreciate his honesty. "Me too," I say. "All clear."

Relief crosses his features. "Good," he says. "Still, we should use protection."

"Yes," I agree, touched by his responsibility even in this heated moment.

He rolls off me, and I make a small sound of protest. "I have condoms in the basket," he explains. "Above the fridge."

"The safe and satisfied basket?" I ask with a small smile.

He responds with a serious expression. His voice is nearly a growl when he orders, "Be naked when I get back."

The command in his voice sends a thrill through me. I've never been with someone who speaks to me this way—not demanding, exactly, but confident, expectant. It's intoxicating.

"Yes, sir," I reply, the teasing honorific feeling right on my tongue.

He groans, leaning down for one more searing kiss before striding out of the room. The moment he's gone, I sit up, reaching for the zipper of my dress with trembling fingers that suddenly quiver.

This is happening. I'm about to have sex with Alder Stag. And something tells me it's going to ruin me for sex with anyone else.

I slip the dress off my shoulders, letting it pool around my waist before stepping out of it completely. My bra and panties follow until I'm standing naked in the soft light filtering through the curtains.

For the briefest moment, old insecurities threaten to surface— in my head, Brad's voice criticizing my body, reminding me of all the ways I don't measure up to conventional beauty standards. But I push those thoughts away, remembering the raw desire in Alder's eyes when he saw me in my underwear earlier, the way he called me sexy without hesitation or qualification.

I position myself on the bed, leaning back against the pillows, feeling strangely powerful in my nakedness. I've seen glimpses of Alder's body over the weeks we've lived together—shirtless in the kitchen making coffee, coming in from a run in shorts that cling to his muscular thighs. But I've never seen all of him, and anticipation coils low in my belly at the thought.

I hear his footsteps in the hallway, approaching the bedroom, and my heart rate quickens another notch. He pauses in the doorway, his eyes widening as he takes me in, sprawled across the bed.

"Fuck, Lena," he breathes, and the reverence in his voice makes me feel beautiful, desirable, perfect exactly as I am.

He moves into the room, tossing a condom onto the nightstand. His hands move to his tie, loosening it before pulling it over his head and dropping it to the floor. His fingers work on the buttons of his shirt, revealing more skin with each one that he opens.

I watch, mesmerized, as he shrugs off the shirt, exposing the broad expanse of his chest, the definition of muscle earned through years of training. My hand drops to my nipple, the skin taut and sensitive as I trail a finger while observing Alder undress.

His hands move to his belt next, and I hold my breath as he unbuckles it, the soft clink of metal loud in the quiet room. He unzips his jeans and lets them fall to the floor, revealing black boxer briefs that do little to hide his arousal. My breath leaves me in a low moan as Alder hooks his thumbs in the waistband of his underwear, eyes never leaving mine as he pushes them down, finally standing before me completely naked.

He's magnificent—all lean muscle and golden skin, his erection jutting proudly from a nest of darker blond curls. He wraps a hand around the thick length, giving a slow stroke that makes my mouth water.

"You're so fucking beautiful," he says, echoing my thoughts back to me. "I can't believe you're looking at me like that."

"Like what?" I ask, my voice breathy and wanting.

"Like you want to devour me." He moves toward the bed, his eyes wild and hungry. "That's how I'm looking at you, too."

He joins me on the mattress, his weight making it dip as he crawls over me, all controlled power and lethal grace. His skin is hot against mine, his body covering me like a living blanket as he settles between my thighs.

"I need to taste you," he murmurs, his mouth finding the sensitive spot just below my ear. "All of you."

"Please," is all I can say as all coherent thought flees while his hands and lips begin their exploration.

He takes his time, mapping my body with reverent attention. His mouth leaves a trail of fire down my neck, across my collarbone, dipping to capture a nipple in the wet heat of his mouth.

I gasp, arching into the sensation as his tongue flicks across the sensitive peak. His hand finds my other breast, kneading gently before rolling the nipple between his fingers.

"You're so responsive," he says against my skin, sounding pleased. "Just for me."

His praise washes over me, heightening every sensation as he continues his journey downward, tongue tracing patterns across my ribs and my stomach, dipping into my navel.

When he reaches the apex of my thighs, he pauses, looking up at me with a question in his eyes.

"Yes," I breathe, answering before he can ask. "Please, Alder."

He smiles, a predatory flash of teeth, before settling between my legs, hooking my knees over his broad shoulders. The first touch of his tongue against my center has me crying out, fingers clutching at the sheets.

He groans, the vibration adding to the sensation as he explores me with lips and tongue. He seems to delight in discovering what makes me gasp, what makes me moan, what makes my hips lift, seeking more.

I'm lost when he slides a finger inside me, curling it to find the spot that makes stars burst behind my eyelids. My release builds with shocking speed, coiling tighter and tighter until I shatter, his name on my lips as waves of pleasure crash through me.

He works me through it, gentling his touch as I come down before pressing a kiss to my inner thigh and crawling back up my body.

"I love watching you come," he says, his voice rough with desire. "So fucking beautiful."

He reaches for the condom on the nightstand, tearing the packet open with his teeth. I watch, still dazed with pleasure, as he rolls it on.

Then he's positioning himself between my thighs again, the blunt head of him nudging at my entrance.

"Okay?" he asks, one last check.

I nod beyond words and reach up to pull him down to me. He kisses me deeply as he pushes forward, my taste on his lips, entering me in one slow, controlled thrust that has us both moaning into each other's mouths.

He stills once fully seated, his forehead pressed against mine, our breath mingling. "You feel incredible," he whispers. "So good, Lena."

"Move," I urge, my hands finding his hips. "Please."

He obeys, withdrawing almost completely before sinking back in, setting a rhythm that has me climbing toward another peak. His strokes are deep and measured, his eyes never leaving mine, creating an almost too much intimacy to bear.

I wrap my legs around his waist, changing the angle, drawing him deeper still. He groans, his pace faltering slightly before he catches himself.

"Not going to last," he warns, his voice strained. "You feel too good."

"It's okay," I assure him, my pleasure building once more. "I'm close, too."

He slips a hand between us, finding where we're joined, his thumb circling the bundle of nerves that sends lightning through my veins. The dual sensation of him inside me and his skilled fingers on my clit is overwhelming.

"Come for me again," he commands his voice a growl that reverberates through me. "Let me feel you."

His words push me over the edge, my second orgasm crashing through me. My inner muscles clench around him, and he follows me over with a hoarse cry, his hips jerking erratically as he finds his release.

For a long moment, we stay locked together, sweat-slicked skin against skin, heartbeats thundering in counterpoint. Then he carefully withdraws, pressing a soft kiss to my lips before rolling to the side to dispose of the condom.

When he returns, he gathers me against his chest, his heartbeat strong beneath my ear. Neither of us speaks right away, content to simply exist in the afterglow, our bodies cooling in the night air.

"Hey, Lena?" His fingers trace lazy patterns on my back as I snuggle my cheek against his chest.

"Mm?"

"Is it okay if we go sleep with Gordie?"

I untangle from his arms, sitting up. "Of course. You should go to him."

He shakes his head. "I want you there. With me." His eyes are vulnerable, and I tamp down the small voice that whispers this feels like much more than a fling.

"Lead the way," I tell him, my mouth tipping into a smile. "I'm going to use the bathroom and be right in."

He nods and plants a kiss on my forehead, walking naked

down the hall like a man on a mission. And it's this–the care he feels for this helpless dog–that tells me there's no way I can go back to not having sex with him after he just exploded my world.

But that's a complication for tomorrow. I hurry to clean up and make my way to Alder's room, where I'm content to lie in his arms, my body pleasantly exhausted, my heart full of something I'm not ready to name.

And I'm not sure I'll ever be the same.

CHAPTER 24
ALDER

I WAKE TO EARLY MORNING SUNLIGHT FILTERING THROUGH MY blinds, and a woman's unfamiliar but perfect weight curled against my side. For a moment, I just breathe, taking in the scent of Lena's lotion mingled with the lingering traces of sex and sleep. Gordie is stretched out at our feet, the cone still firmly in place, but his tail thumps gently against the mattress when he notices I'm awake.

Lena's head rests on my chest, her brown hair spilling across my skin. One arm is thrown across my stomach, her leg tangled with mine. I love the contrast of her soft skin against my hairy hockey thighs. She looks peaceful in sleep, all the careful composure she maintains during the day softened and melted away.

Last night replays in my mind—the heated rush from the wedding to our townhouse, the way she looked spread across her bed waiting for me, the sounds she made when I touched her. I've had my share of hookups, but nothing has ever felt like that. Like finding something I didn't know I'd been missing.

Gordie whines softly, drawing my attention. He's squirming in a way that suggests he needs to go outside soon.

His energy seems better than yesterday, which is a good sign for his recovery.

Beside me, Lena stirs, her eyelashes fluttering against her cheeks before she opens her eyes. For a brief second, confusion crosses her features, then recognition and warmth.

"Hi," she says, voice husky with sleep.

"Morning," I reply, brushing a strand of hair from her face. "How'd you sleep?"

"So well, despite a dog fighting me for space on the mattress." She stretches, her body pressing against mine in ways that immediately reawaken my desire. "How's our patient?"

Our patient. I like the sound of that. "Seems more energetic this morning. I think he needs to go out, though."

As if understanding, Gordie gives another soft whine and walks up to the bed, his cone bumping awkwardly against the headboard.

Lena laughs, sitting up and reaching for him. "Careful, buddy. You're going to hurt yourself."

The sheet falls away as she moves, exposing her breasts to the morning light. I'm momentarily distracted by the sight, my mouth going dry. She catches my gaze and smiles, a slow, knowing curve of her lips.

"See something you like, Stag?"

"Everything," I admit, unfiltered honesty coming easily in the quiet intimacy of the morning.

Her cheeks flush prettily, and for a moment, I think we might not be getting out of bed anytime soon. Then Gordie whines again, more insistently.

"I think someone has different priorities," she says, laughing.

We both climb out of bed, finding the minimum clothes needed for decency—sweatpants for me, one of my T-shirts, and her underwear for me. The sight of Lena in my shirt, legs bare, hair tousled from sleep and sex, makes my chest tighten with something deeper than just desire.

Together, we navigate Gordie's leash with his cone and head outside into the humid morning air. The river gleams in the near distance, and a few neighbors are already out, walking dogs or jogging along the path. Kim waves at us from her patio with a knowing smile as she takes in our disheveled appearance.

"Morning, you two," she calls. "Gordie feeling better?"

"Much better," Lena replies easily, as if we do this daily as if she's been part of this routine for years instead of hours.

We stroll along the grass, letting Gordie sniff and do his business. I find myself stealing glances at Lena in the golden morning light. There's something surreal about this moment —this woman I was determined to keep at a professional distance now walking beside me in my clothes, fresh from my bed, caring for my dog.

Our hands brush as we walk, and I capture hers in mine, our fingers intertwining naturally. Her hand is strong from the work she does, and I love that she doesn't bristle at my rough palm. We don't speak much, but the silence is comfortable. When Gordie finishes his morning duties, we head back to the townhouse, our shoulders gently bumping as we walk.

"Hungry?" I ask as we enter.

"Starving," she admits. "But Gordie probably needs his medicine first."

She's right, and the fact that she remembers, that she cares enough to prioritize him, affects me deeply.

"The pills are in my bathroom," I tell her. "I'll wrap them in cheese from the fridge."

We move around each other with surprising ease as we prepare Gordie's medicine and help him settle in. I find myself wondering how we've developed such effortless coordination after just one night together.

Once Gordie is medicated and resting comfortably on his

bed in the living room, Lena turns to me, her posture slightly awkward.

"I should probably shower," she says. "I'm still a bit... sticky."

Images from last night flash through my mind—Lena coming apart under my touch, the taste of her lingering on my tongue, the wet heat enveloping me. My body responds instantly to the memories.

"Need help with that?" I ask, the words coming out more hopeful than suggestive.

She bites her lip and then nods. "If you're offering."

I take her hand again, leading her toward my bathroom with its larger shower. "Definitely offering."

There's a brief, awkward moment as we both strip, but then Lena drops my T-shirt to the floor, standing before me in just her panties, and any hesitation evaporates. I hook my thumbs in the waistband of my sweatpants and push them down, never taking my eyes off her.

The shower warms quickly, steam filling the bathroom as we step under the spray together. Water cascades over Lena's curves, accentuating the places I explored with my hands and mouth just hours ago. I reach for the shampoo, but she stops me, taking it from my hands.

"Let me," she says, pouring a dollop into her palm.

I duck my head, allowing her to work the shampoo into my hair. Her fingers massage my scalp, and I groan at the simple pleasure of it. When she's finished, I return the favor, watching as her eyes close in contentment.

As I rinse the suds from her hair, my hands slide down her body, tracing the curves of her breasts and the softness of her stomach. She shivers despite the warm water pressing closer.

"You're so beautiful," I murmur against her wet skin, meaning it more than I've ever meant those words before.

She makes a small, disbelieving sound, and I'm determined to prove it to her. I drop to my knees on the shower floor, ignoring the hard tile against my skin as I press kisses to her stomach, her hips, and the soft insides of her thighs. And finally, like a man starved, I sink my teeth into those legs I've been fantasizing about since the day I met her.

"Alder," she gasps as I move closer to where she wants me.

I look at her through the spray, with water dripping from my eyelashes. "Yes?"

"You don't have to—"

"I want to," I tell her, my hands sliding up the backs of her legs. "Let me taste you again."

Her answer is to widen her stance slightly, one hand bracing against the shower wall, the other tangling in my wet hair. I take her invitation eagerly, my tongue finding her center with renewed purpose.

The shower adds a new dimension to the experience—the constant flow of water washing away and replenishing her arousal, the steam intensifying her scent. I lose myself in the task, cataloging every gasp and moan, learning what makes her thighs tremble and her grip tighten in my hair.

When she comes, it's with a sharp cry that echoes off the tiled walls, her body shuddering against my mouth. I steady her with my hands on her hips, guiding her through the aftershocks until she gently pushes me away, oversensitive.

She pulls me to my feet, her eyes dark with satisfaction and renewed desire. "Your turn," she says, reaching between us to wrap her hand around my length.

I groan, my forehead dropping to her shoulder as she strokes me. Her touch is perfect—firm yet gentle, finding a rhythm that has me teetering on the edge embarrassingly quickly.

"Lena," I warn, feeling the familiar tightening at the base of my spine.

"It's okay," she murmurs, speeding her movements, eyes glued to my cock. "Let go for me."

Her permission is all I need. I come, muffling my groan

against her neck, my release spurting over her hand and stomach before being carried away by the shower spray. We stand wrapped in each other for a moment, my breathing harsh in my ears.

When I regain my senses, I reach for the body wash, gently re-cleaning us both. There's something intensely intimate about this—more so, somehow, than the sex itself. Lena seems to feel it too, her expression soft and a little vulnerable as I run soapy hands over her skin.

"I like taking care of you," I admit, surprising myself with the confession.

Her smile is radiant. "I like it too."

After that, we finish our shower quickly, and the hot water begins to run cool. As we dry off, the easy silence returns, broken only by Gordie's occasional snuffling from the living room.

I pull on clean sweatpants while Lena hesitates by the pile of yesterday's clothes.

"You can borrow something of mine," I offer. "I like looking at you in my things."

She nods, and I dig through my dresser for a T-shirt and shorts. While she dresses, I head to the kitchen, determined to make her a breakfast worthy of the night we shared.

By the time she joins me, I've got coffee brewing and eggs sizzling on the stove. Her hair is damp around her shoulders, my Fury t-shirt hanging loose on her frame, the shorts revealing her lush thighs. She's never looked more beautiful.

"Cheesy eggs?" she asks, wrapping her arms around me from behind as I stand at the stove.

"With butter," I confirm, flipping one with a practiced motion. "And I have ketchup."

"Fancy," she teases, pressing a kiss to my shoulder before moving to pour coffee for us both.

We move around the kitchen in that same easy synchronicity, setting the table, feeding Gordie, and preparing breakfast together like we've done a hundred times before. I can't remember the last time I felt this comfortable with someone—certainly never with Adam, who always maintained a certain careful distance even at his most affectionate.

Over breakfast, we talk about nothing important—Gunnar and Emerson's wedding, whether anyone noticed our early departure, what we might do with the rest of our Sunday. We carefully avoid labeling whatever this is between us, though the "summer fling" designation feels increasingly inadequate for the warmth spreading through my chest whenever Lena laughs.

Gordie eventually joins us at the table, sitting hopefully at Lena's feet. She slips him a tiny piece of plain egg, earning a disapproving look from me.

"What? He gave me the eyes," she defends. "I'm only human."

"He's a master manipulator," I tell her seriously. "Don't fall for it."

"Too late," she says, smiling down at my dog with such affection that my heart constricts.

The doorbell rings, disrupting the moment. I glance at the clock—barely past ten on a Sunday morning. Who the hell is visiting now?

"I'll get it," I sigh, pushing back from the table.

When I open the door, Brian stands on my doorstep, impeccably dressed despite the hour, a tablet in one hand and coffee in the other. His expression is grim.

"Morning," I say warily. "What brings you here at the crack of dawn on a Sunday?"

"We have a situation." He walks past me without waiting for an invitation, his usual composure noticeably rattled. He stops abruptly when he sees Lena in my clothes at the table, her hair still damp from our shower.

"Dr. Sinclair," he says after a beat, his professional mask sliding into place. "Actually, this concerns you, too."

Lena and I exchange confused glances as Brian places his tablet on the kitchen counter and opens a website.

"Adam's been busy." He turns the screen toward us, revealing a sports blog with the headline: "Fury Defenseman's Bisexual 'Phase' Over? Sources Close to Ex Suggest Identity Was Career Move."

My stomach drops as I scan the article, which quotes an "anonymous source familiar with the relationship," claiming my bisexuality was "always more about image than identity" and suggesting I was "ready to return to a conventional life-style now that I've gotten the publicity I wanted."

"There's more." Brian swipes to another site, this one featuring screenshots from social media. LGBTQ hockey fans express disappointment, questioning whether I was ever really part of their community. One post from a popular queer hockey account reads: "Tough to see @AlderStag abandon the community that supported him, proving bisexuality stereotypes right. #JustAPhase"

"What the hell?" I grip the counter, anger rising. "This is—"

"Adam's work," Brian finishes for me. "His fingerprints are all over it. Not sure what you did to piss him off, but it's become a liability."

Lena has moved next to me, reading over my shoulder. Her face is flushed with indignation. "This is disgusting. How can he weaponize someone's identity like this?"

"Because he's a professional manipulator who knows exactly which buttons to push." Brian takes a sip of his coffee. "And because you two gave him the ammunition."

"It's just been petty prank shit," I protest, though the memory of holding Lena's hand, of the deliberately public display, undermines my argument.

"And now Adam's making sure everyone sees it as you rejecting your queer identity." Brian pulls up another article. "The bi-erasure narrative is getting traction. This morning, his firm released a statement about 'supporting authentic representation in sports' that's basically a thinly veiled shot at you."

I sink into a chair, the weight of this attack hitting me fully. It's one thing to be humiliated publicly by Adam's cheating, but to have my identity questioned, to be painted as someone who used the LGBTQ community for publicity—that cuts deeper than I would have expected.

"How do we respond?" Lena asks, her hand finding my shoulder, a gesture of support that would feel comforting if it weren't also part of what Adam is using against me.

"Carefully." Brian sets down his tablet. "Adam's strategy is obvious. He's redirecting the narrative, making himself the wounded party defending the community against your 'opportunism.' It's classic deflection."

"But it's complete bullshit," I say, my voice rising. "Being with Lena doesn't make me less bisexual. That's the whole point of bisexuality!"

Brian sighs. "I know that. You know that. Most reasonable people know that." A rare empathetic expression crosses his face. "But Adam is humiliated, and he doesn't deal in mailed dick pasta or singing telegrams. He's manipulating legitimate issues in the queer community to attack you personally."

I run a hand through my hair, frustration building. "So, what's the play?"

"First, we need to be strategic about your public appearances." Brian glances meaningfully between Lena and me. "The Black and Gold Charity Gala is in two weeks. Adam's firm is handling the PR, which means he'll be there, working the room, watching for any opportunity to reinforce his narrative."

"You want me to what—pretend I'm not with Lena?" The words come out before I fully process them, and I feel her stiffen beside me.

"We're not together, Alder," she says quietly. Her words slice at my soul.

Brian watches this exchange with shrewd eyes. "What you do privately is your business. However, professionally, you need to maintain appropriate boundaries at public events like the gala, where the entire organization will be present. Not just because of the fraternization policy, but because Adam is actively weaponizing your relationship—or whatever this is—against both of you."

Lena nods slowly. "He's right. I can't afford to lose my job, and you can't afford to be demonized like this.."

"So, we just let him win?" I ask, hating how defeated I sound.

"No," Brian says firmly. "We respond on our terms. I've already contacted Out Sports about an interview where you can address these accusations directly. We highlight your continued commitment to LGBTQ advocacy while emphasizing that bisexuality isn't a phase and doesn't disappear when you date someone of any gender."

He turns to Lena. "And Dr. Sinclair, I'm afraid this puts you in an awkward position. Any public association with Alder right now will be twisted to fuel this narrative."

I watch her face as she processes this, the professional mask I've come to recognize sliding into place. "I understand," she says. "I've been meaning to look more seriously for my own apartment anyway. This seems like the right time to prioritize that."

Her words hit me like a body check, even though I should have expected them. "You don't have to leave immediately," I say quickly. "The apartment hunt was going terribly, remember?"

"I know, but I need to make it a priority. Not just half-heartedly looking at listings." She sighs. "I need this job, Alder. I can't risk losing it because of this situation."

Brian watches our exchange with sympathy, which surprises me. "For what it's worth, I'd be happy for you two in another timeline. But right now, we need to be strategic."

"I'll send you the Out Sports questions later today," he continues, standing to leave. "And Alder—no more public appearances with Dr. Sinclair until we get this under control. Adam's looking for any angle to undermine you."

After Brian leaves, Lena and I sit in painful silence. Gordie whines from his bed, sensing the tension.

"I'm sorry," I finally say. "I didn't think Adam would go this far."

"It's not your fault," she replies, moving to check on Gordie. "He's playing dirty. That's on him, not you."

As I watch her gently care for my dog, her hands sure despite our difficult conversation, I'm struck by how quickly she's become essential to my life. The thought of her leaving —of going back to being just colleagues who nod politely in hallways—is like a physical ache.

"I'll help you look for apartments," I offer, moving to join her beside Gordie, who licks my hand. "Maybe there's something in this neighborhood that would work for your budget."

She smiles, but it doesn't reach her eyes. "Thank you. That would be helpful."

We sit silently for a moment, both petting Gordie, our hands occasionally brushing. Each touch feels precious now, knowing they're numbered.

"This doesn't change anything about how I feel," I say quietly. "About last night. About you."

She meets my eyes, vulnerability and regret mingling in her expression. "I know. But sometimes feelings aren't enough, are they?"

I don't have an answer for that because she's right. In the real world—our world of professional sports, public scrutiny, and manipulative exes—sometimes what we want takes a backseat to what's necessary.

Our hands touch again as we both stroke Gordie's fur, and neither of us pulls away. It's a small rebellion, but it's all we have right now.

CHAPTER 25
LENA

My FINGERS HOVER OVER THE KEYBOARD, AND THE SAME apartment listing I've been staring at for ten minutes is still open on my screen. The rent is too high, the location is too far from work, and judging by the carefully cropped photos, the bathroom probably hasn't been updated since the 1970s.

I close the tab with a sigh and lean back in my office chair. After yesterday's conversation with Alder and Brian's blunt assessment of our situation, my apartment search has taken on new urgency and produced even more stressful results.

No more half-hearted browsing. I need to find my own place—soon. Maybe I need to look at the suburbs…

The thought squeezes my heart as I consider how much further that would put me from Alder and, truly, his entire family.

A knock at my door interrupts my thoughts. I quickly switch to the dental records I should be reviewing and call, "Come in."

Coach Thompson enters, his imposing figure filling the doorway. "Dr. Sinclair. Got a minute?"

"Of course." I straighten in my chair, fighting the irrational fear that he somehow knows I was apartment hunting instead of working. "What can I do for you?"

He settles into the chair across from my desk, his expression unreadable. "Just checking in on mouthguard progress. I'm hearing that some of the guys are refusing to wear them."

I nod. "Yeah. And I swear I advised them otherwise. They insist some nonsense about rites of passage…"

Thompson groans. "I really had hoped that mindset would change from my day in the game. We really don't need to be fishing teeth from inside the Zamboni." He shakes his head, then fixes me with a direct look. "And how are you settling in with the team? Any… concerns I should be aware of?"

The careful emphasis makes my stomach clench. Is this another warning about the fraternization policy?

"Everything's going smoothly," I say, keeping my voice professional. "The equipment is excellent, and everyone's been very welcoming."

He studies me for a moment, then nods. "Glad to hear it. You've been a good addition to the staff, Dr. Sinclair. I'd hate to see anything interfere with that. There's a strong pool of trauma dentists in this city…"

The message couldn't be clearer: Don't mess this up.

"I appreciate that, Coach." I manage a smile. "I value this position very much."

"I know you do." He stands, straightening his Fury polo shirt. "By the way, the Black and Gold Gala is coming up. Important event for the organization. All team leadership are expected to attend. The donors genuinely like talking to our dentist at these shindigs. War stories and whatnot…"

"I'll be there," I assure him.

"Good. Keep up the good work." With a final pointed look, he leaves, closing the door behind him.

I bite back a groan. If I needed further confirmation that my relationship with Alder is under scrutiny, that was it. The team values discretion, and we've been anything but discreet.

My apartment search needs to be my top priority—not

just for my career but also for my sanity. Living with Alder while trying to maintain professional boundaries is becoming impossible, especially after this weekend.

My phone buzzes, my mother's name flashing on the screen—perfect timing, as usual.

"Hi, Mom," I answer, steeling myself.

"Lena, darling. I've been trying to reach you for days." Her voice has that tone where I can tell she's about to say something mean. "Too busy with famous athletes to call your mother?"

"Of course not. I've just been busy with the new job."

"The hockey position? How's that going? Have they realized they made a mistake yet?" She laughs lightly as if she's made a joke instead of questioning my competence.

"Actually, it's going really well," I say, ignoring the barb. "I'm getting settled in."

"And where are you living now? Did you work things out with Brad?"

I wince. "No, Mom. That's over."

"Hmm." She sounds disappointed as if my refusal to reconcile with a cheating boyfriend is somehow a failure on my part. "So you found your own place?"

"I'm in a temporary situation while I look for something permanent." Not technically a lie, though I doubt she'd approve of my current "situation."

"Well, don't wait too long. Good apartments are harder to come by than good men," she says as if I don't know this from weeks of searching. "And with your student loans, you can't be picky."

"I'm aware of my financial limitations, Mom."

"I'm just being realistic, darling." She sighs. "So, what else is new?"

I hesitate, then decide to mention the gala. If nothing else, maybe she'll have practical advice about formal wear: "The team is having a charity event soon. I need to find a dress."

"A formal event? Well, I'm sure you have something appropriate in your closet." Her voice takes on that careful tone she uses when discussing my appearance. "Something black and plain would be best. No need to draw attention to yourself."

Of course. Heaven forbid I wear something that might truly make me feel good about myself.

"I thought I might get something new," I say, surprising myself with the defiance in my voice.

"Oh, Lena." She sighs again. "You know how hard it is to find flattering formal wear in your size. Why waste the money? Just wear something dark and conservative that you already own."

I glance at the clock. "I should go, Mom. I have patients waiting."

"Alright, dear. Just remember what I said. Black, simple, no fuss. It's what works for you."

I hang up, feeling deflated yet irritated—the familiar emotional cocktail my mother specializes in serving. She's wrong, of course. I know she's wrong. But part of me still hears her voice when I shop for clothes and see myself through her critical eyes.

It's hard not to slip back to memories of my time in bed with Alder, the way he looked at my body with reverence, ran his hands along me like I was a precious work of art…

My phone buzzes again, this time with a text from an unknown number.

> Hi Lena! This is Emerson (Gunnar's wife). Got your number from Alder's phone. Hope that's okay! Fern's taking me shopping for the charity gala this weekend. Would love for you to join! Us curvy girls need to stick together.

I stare at the text, warmth blooming in my chest even as a knot forms in my stomach. Emerson and Fern—Wyatt's girlfriend, who is back from London for the wedding—are reaching out to include me, which feels unexpectedly nice. But the prolonged interaction with Alder's family is a painful reminder of my precarious position.

In another life, one where I wasn't the team dentist and Alder, and I didn't have a damning policy hanging over our heads, maybe I could have been friends with these women. Perhaps I could have truly been part of the Stag circle, joining them for dinners and holiday celebrations.

But that's not my reality.

Still, I could use help finding a dress, and the thought of facing formal wear shopping alone after my mother's comments is depressing.

> I'd love that

I reply.

> Could definitely use your expertise.

Emerson responds immediately:

> Perfect! Curvy Couture is on Walnut St in Shadyside tomorrow at around 5? They have amazing stuff.

> See you there

I confirm, trying to ignore the voice that whispers I'm only setting myself up for more pain by strengthening connections I'll eventually have to sever.

. . .

Curvy Couture is tucked between a high-end shoe store and a coffee shop on one of Shadyside's trendy shopping streets. It's right near the emergency vet where we took Gordie the other day, but I try not to think about those intimate moments where Alder was so vulnerable, and I loved being someone he could lean on.

The shop window display features mannequins with actual curves wearing beautiful, vibrant formal wear—not a shapeless black sack in sight.

Emerson and Fern are already waiting outside when I arrive, both looking effortlessly stylish. Emerson waves enthusiastically when she spots me.

"Lena! So glad you could make it." She pulls me into a hug like we're old friends instead of people who've met exactly twice. "You remember Fern."

Fern offers a warm smile and a handshake. "Nice to meet you properly. I saw you at the wedding, but things were a bit chaotic."

"You too," I say, taking in her classic style and bright colors. "How long have you been back from London?"

"Just a couple of days. Wyatt has a game this weekend so that we will fly back soon."

Emerson pats her arm. "The aunts are really going to be pressuring you two to get hitched now that we broke the seal."

Fern shakes her head. "No way. I'm finishing this PhD if it kills me. Wyatt can wait a few more years."

There's an easy camaraderie between them that makes me both envious and comfortable. They effortlessly include me in their banter as we enter the boutique, a cheerful bell announcing our arrival. Fern confesses that Wyatt used to be her student when she was a TA for his math class and I realize the Stag men seem to specialize in impossible relationships … and, evidently, figuring out how to make them work.

The store is a revelation—filled with beautiful, fashionable clothes designed for bodies like mine. There are no shapeless tents or matronly styles, just gorgeous, well-made garments that acknowledge curves as assets rather than flaws to be hidden.

"First-timers?" asks a stylish Asian woman who introduces herself as Vivian. "Welcome! Looking for anything in particular?"

"Formal wear for a charity gala," Emerson explains. "Something fabulous for the doc and myself."

Vivian grins. "I can definitely help with that. Let me pull some options."

As she bustles away, Fern turns to me. "So, you and Alder. How's that going?"

The directness of her question startles me. "Oh, we're not —I mean — it's complicated."

"It always is with the Stags," Emerson says knowingly. She turns to Fern. "Lena fixed Tucker's tooth and promised Gunny she'd prevent him from losing any."

"That seems like a big promise," Fern suggests.

I grin. "I believe what I said was that I would do my best to take care of his teeth." The conversation momentarily distracts me from my distress about my life choices.

Before Emerson can respond, Vivian returns with an armful of dresses. "Let's start with these. The fitting rooms are in the back."

The next hour passes in a whirl of fabric and zippers. Emerson and Fern are brutally honest yet encouraging critics, nixing a teal gown that makes me look "like a mermaid having an identity crisis" and enthusiastically approving a deep burgundy that "makes your boobs look phenomenal."

Despite my inner turmoil regarding Alder, I find myself enjoying their company. They're funny and kind, sharing stories about navigating Stag family dynamics and offering insider tips for the gala.

"Whatever you do, avoid the shrimp puffs," Emerson

advises. "No shellfish in Pittsburgh during months with no R. It's a rule."

"Totally a rule," Fern adds. "That's my best bartender tip."

"I'll keep that in mind," I say, emerging from the fitting room in a dark purple gown with a sweetheart neckline. "I'm absolutely hoping not to stand out at this event."

The words come out more wistful than intended, and both women exchange a glance.

"Trouble in paradise?" Emerson asks gently.

I hesitate, then decide on a partial truth. "Well, I mean, Alder is a wreck about the recent press stuff about him not being queer enough. And then, the team has a fraternization policy. It's... professionally complicated."

Understanding dawns on their faces. "It'll work out," Emerson says with confidence that seems unfounded given the circumstances. "The Stag family is nothing if not determined. When they want something, they find a way."

I don't share her optimism, but I appreciate the sentiment. "What do you think of this one?" I ask, changing the subject as I smooth the fabric over my hips.

"Stunning," Fern says immediately.

"Alder won't be able to keep his eyes off you," Emerson adds with a wink.

That's precisely the problem, but I don't say so. Instead, I study my reflection, hardly recognizing the woman looking back at me. The dress hugs my curves without constricting them, and the color makes my skin glow, and my eyes appear darker. I look powerful, confident, and beautiful.

Not at all like someone who should be hiding in plain black to avoid drawing attention.

"I'll take it," I decide impulsively.

The price tag makes me wince—more than I've ever spent on a single item of clothing—but after a lifetime of settling for whatever fit rather than what I actually wanted, it feels like a declaration—a statement that I deserve beautiful things, regardless of my size or relationship status.

As we leave the boutique, shopping bags in hand, Emerson links her arm through mine. "This was fun. We should do it more often."

"Definitely," Fern agrees. "Come to London and hang with me there."

I smile, not correcting their assumption that I'll be part of these future plans. Letting myself enjoy the fantasy for just a little longer.

"Oh, look at that," Fern says suddenly, pointing across the street. "For Rent."

I follow her gaze to a small sign in the window of a brick building. The location is nice—Shadyside is an upscale neighborhood within walking distance of shops and restaurants, though farther from the training facility than ideal.

"Are you looking?" Emerson asks, confused.

"Yes, actually. My current situation is … temporary." That much is true, regardless of how much I wish it weren't.

"You should check it out," Fern encourages. "Shadyside's fun. Very grownup."

Almost before I realize what I'm doing, I'm crossing the street, pulling out my phone to call the number on the sign. To my surprise, the landlord answers immediately.

"I'm essentially just around the corner," he says when I inquire about viewing the apartment. "Can you wait ten minutes?"

I agree, turning to wave at Emerson and Fern, who give me a thumbs-up from across the street before heading off with promises to text later.

The landlord, a middle-aged white guy named Jim, arrives shortly. He leads me through a side entrance and a narrow staircase to the second floor.

"It's not huge," he warns as he unlocks the door. "But it's

clean, utilities included, and I installed new appliances last year."

The apartment is indeed small—a studio with a kitchenette along one wall, a bathroom tucked behind a pocket door, and a main living space that would serve as both bedroom and living room. A bay window overlooking the street provides the only real architectural feature of note.

It's objectively less nice than the place I shared with Brad and certainly a far cry from Alder's spacious townhouse. The bathroom is dated, the kitchen cramped, and I can already tell the closet space will be woefully inadequate.

But it's available immediately. And it could be mine alone.

"What's the rent?" I ask, already mentally calculating if I can make it work.

Jim names a figure that's high for the square footage but still within my budget—barely.

"Could I have a minute to think?" I ask.

"Sure thing. I need to take a call anyway." He steps out into the hallway, leaving me alone in the empty apartment.

I move to the window, looking out at the tree-lined street below. Despite its limitations, the apartment has good natural light, and the neighborhood feels safe. I could walk to shops and restaurants. Parking may be a bit of a nightmare, a far cry from the assigned spots at Alder's.

Alder.

I close my eyes, allowing myself to remember this morning—waking in his bed, his arm thrown protectively across my waist, with Gordie snoring at our feet. Despite the lecture from Brian, we fell into bed together that evening, wordlessly. It all feels so right with him—the easy domesticity of making food together, his lips brushing my neck as he reaches past me for a mug or the salt. The way his eyes follow me across the room as if he can't quite believe I am there.

It would be so easy to stay. To keep pretending we can

make this work. To sink further into the comfort and connection.

But Brian's words echo in my mind: "You slip up there, it's not just your ass on the line."

I can't be responsible for damaging Alder's career. And I can't risk losing the job I worked so hard to secure. Three hundred thousand dollars in student loans doesn't leave room for romantic indulgence. And it's only a matter of time before Alder's breakup catches up with him emotionally.

What we have is temporary, by definition—a summer fling. Eventually, it would end anyway. Better to make a clean break now before I'm in too deep.

If I'm not already.

Jim returns, and the phone call is completed. "So, what do you think?"

"I'll take it," I say before I can change my mind.

He seems pleased, pulling rental documents from his messenger bag. "Great. I can get you keys today if you've got the deposit."

Twenty minutes later, I stand on the sidewalk outside my new apartment building, keys in one hand, dress bag in the other. A strange mix of emotions swirls through me—pride at taking this step toward independence, anxiety about telling Alder, and a hollow ache at the thought of no longer waking up beside him every morning.

My phone buzzes with a text from the man in question:

How's shopping? When will you be home?

Home. The word makes my heart clench. Alder's townhouse has felt more like home in two weeks than my apartment with Brad ever did in four years.

Shopping was successful

I reply, deliberately ignoring his second question.

Heading back soon.

I look down at the keys and then back at my phone. I should tell him. He deserves to know I've found a place.

But not yet. Not today. Today, I want one more night of pretending this summer fantasy could be real. Tomorrow will be soon enough for reality.

I slip the keys into my purse and head for the bus stop, the weight of my decision sitting heavy on my chest.

CHAPTER 26

ALDER

THE RIVER LOOKS DIFFERENT TODAY—CALMER, FLATTER, AND more inviting than it had been last week when Lena and I took Gordie for his morning walk—perfect kayaking conditions. Lena and I are supposed to keep things professional, but we're friends. I do shit with my friends.

And paddling seems like a healthy distraction from my current drama. Much better than driving to Adam's place and knocking him out.

I click through the rental options on my laptop, searching for a place away from the busy downtown spots where we might be recognized.

I find a small place up in North Park that offers private launches. More expensive, but worth it for the privacy. I imagine Lena's smile when I surprise her with another day on the water—just the two of us, sunshine and cool water. Maybe this time we can pack a picnic lunch, find a quiet spot near the lake, stretch out on a blanket...

Gordie whines softly, breaking my fantasy. He's recovering well from his surgery, the cone off, and his energy is returning to normal. I reach down to scratch his ears, earning a contented groan.

"She'll be home soon, buddy," I tell him as if he's been

wondering the same thing I have—when Lena will return from her shopping trip with Emerson and Fern.

Home. The word feels right when I think of Lena in my space with my dog. Despite the complications, despite Brian's warnings and the looming charity gala where we'll have to pretend we're nothing more than colleagues, having her here feels natural. Right. Our bodies just seem to go together.

I know it can't last. She needs her own place for both our careers' sake. But maybe we can stretch this summer a little longer and steal a few more weekends and a few more nights before reality intrudes. It all feels so precious, so fleeting. I'm probably delusional, but I'm planning these outings as if we can be a real couple.

I start to realize Lena and I are just as much of a dirty secret as me and Adam. But I like to hope that Lena's intentions are different. I remind myself that she's met my family. That she wants to be with me if she can figure out how.

The sound of a key in the lock sends Gordie scrambling toward the door, his nails clicking on the floor. I follow at a more measured pace, though my heartbeat picks up speed at the prospect of seeing her.

"Hey," I say as she enters, bag draped over an arm. "How was shopping?"

"Good." Her smile seems subdued, not quite reaching her eyes. "Found a dress for the gala."

"Can I see it?" I ask, reaching for the bag.

She pulls it back slightly. "Bad luck. You'll see it at the event."

Something feels off about her demeanor, but I press forward with my plans. "So, I was thinking… There's this kayak place up north that looks great. More secluded than where we went before. I thought maybe we could make a day of it, pack a lunch—"

"Alder." She cuts me off gently, setting her stuff down by the door. "I need to tell you something."

The tone of her voice—careful, measured—sends a chill through me. She reaches into her purse and pulls out a set of keys, holding them up to catch the afternoon light streaming through the windows.

"I found an apartment," she says quietly.

The words take a moment to penetrate, to make sense. "An apartment," I repeat, staring at the keys—concrete evidence of a decision already made.

"It's small, but it's available immediately." She closes her hand around the keys. "I'm going to move in tomorrow."

"Tomorrow?" My voice sounds strange to my ears, distant and hollow. "That's... fast."

She nods, not quite meeting my eyes. "It's for the best, Alder. We agreed I need my own place."

"Yeah, but I thought we'd have more time to, I don't know, look together. Find something that works for you." Something close to me is what I don't say.

"This works." She finally looks up, her expression a careful mask. "It's within my budget and in a safe neighborhood. It makes sense."

I swallow against the tightness in my throat. "When were you planning to tell me?"

"I'm telling you now." She sighs, setting her purse down and moving past me into the living room. "I thought moving while you were at training tomorrow would be easier. Clean break."

The phrase echoes in my head, sharp and painful. Is that what she wants? To be done with whatever this is between us?

I follow her into the living room, where she's kneeling to greet Gordie. The dog presses against her, sensing something's wrong.

"What about us?" I ask, the question bursting out before I can stop it.

She looks up at me, sadness etched in the lines around her

eyes. "There can't be an 'us,' Alder. Not the way things are. You know that."

"So that's it? You're just... leaving?" I hate how plaintive I sound, but I can't seem to control it. I sound like I sounded with Adam, always begging him to stay longer. Shit, I'm a pathetic wreck. Begging people to be with me.

"I have to." She stands, Gordie still pressed against her legs. "We both have careers we've worked hard for. This arrangement was always temporary."

"Right." My laugh sounds bitter even to my own ears. "I remember."

"It's not just that." She wraps her arms around herself as if suddenly cold. "This is getting complicated. Fast. And complicated is the one thing we can't afford to be."

I want to argue, to tell her we can figure this out, and to find a way to make it work. But the rational part of me knows she's right. We've been playing with fire, risking our careers for something we initially defined as temporary, petty revenge.

"I'll help you move," I say instead, surrendering to the inevitable.

She shakes her head. "I hired movers. My stuff that's here will fit in my car, and they're meeting me at the other place tomorrow at ten."

Of course, she has it all worked out. Lena is nothing if not efficient, even when breaking my heart.

The thought catches me off guard. Is that what's happening here? Is she breaking my heart?

"Will you at least stay tonight?" I ask, hating the desperation in my voice.

Her expression softens. "Yes. Tonight, I'll stay."

I know I'm making things harder for myself, but the second Lena walks toward my room instead of hers, I know I'm going to make love to her one last time. Wordlessly, she sheds her clothes and climbs into the bed. I follow, pulling her into my arms and covering her mouth with mine.

I'm achingly hard, and she reaches down, squeezing my cock until I moan into her mouth. When I trace a hand down Lena's body, I find her wet and wanting as well. She juts her hips against my fingers, and I fumble with the nightstand to grab a condom. I slide it on and roll on top of her, luxuriating in the feel of her body, of her softness surrounding me. I press my forehead against hers and thrust inside like it's the most natural, normal thing in the world.

It's never been like this, so easy. So natural. Lena digs her hands into my butt, urging me on, and I grunt as I drive into her. I want to do so many things, but I'm drawn by some unseen power just to thrust. Lena arches her back, finding the friction she needs against my pelvis, and I hear her tiny gasps and feel the flutters as she starts to come.

With my hand pressed to her chest and my mouth on her ear, I come, too, filling the condom with everything I'm unable to say at this moment.

After lying in my bed, our bodies still tangled together, skin cooling. I can't stop touching her, my fingers tracing patterns on her bare shoulder, memorizing every curve, every freckle as if I could somehow keep her with me through touch alone.

"This is so unfair," I whisper into the darkness, my voice rougher than intended. "I finally find someone who sees me— really sees me—and I can't have you."

Her body tenses against mine. "Alder—"

"No, let me say this." I prop myself up on one elbow, needing to see her face. Moonlight spills through the blinds, painting silver streaks across her skin. "I've spent my whole life being defined by hockey, by what I can do on the ice. Even with Adam, I was just the athlete, the trophy he kept hidden.

But with you..." My voice catches. "With you, I'm just me. All of me. And you accept that. You accept me."

Her eyes glisten in the darkness, her hand coming up to cup my cheek. "I do. That's why this hurts so much."

I turn to press a kiss into her palm. "I don't know what I'm going to do without you here. I know we said this was temporary, but it doesn't feel temporary. It feels like—" I stop myself, afraid to name what's growing between us.

Instead of words, I lower my mouth to hers, pouring everything I can't say into the kiss. She responds immediately, arms wrapping around my neck, pulling me closer. The kiss deepens and grows desperate as if we're both trying to imprint ourselves on each other before morning tears us apart.

I whisper against her lips when we break for air, "One more time. Please."

She nods, and I move down her body, worshipping every inch with my hands and mouth, committing her to memory. This time, we go slow, savoring each touch, each gasp, each shudder. I watch her face as she comes apart beneath me, and when I finally sink into her, the sensation is so overwhelming I have to close my eyes.

"Look at me," she whispers, and I do, our gazes locking as we move together. Something profound passes between us at that moment—something neither of us is ready to name, but both of us feel.

Later, she curls against my chest, her tears warm against my skin. I hold her tighter as if I could somehow keep morning from coming, keep her from leaving.

"I'll figure something out," I promise, though I have no idea what. "We'll figure something out."

She doesn't answer; she just presses a kiss over my heart as if we're both pretending to believe there's a solution waiting for us beyond this night.

CHAPTER 27
ALDER

THE TOWNHOUSE FEELS WRONG WITHOUT HER IN IT. AFTER training, I walk through the rooms, cataloging the empty spaces she's left behind. Her toothbrush is gone from the holder in the guest bathroom. The dresser drawers are empty, the closet is bare, and the bed is made with military precision as if she'd never slept there.

Gordie follows me, sniffing around corners, clearly searching for her scent. He looks up at me with confused eyes when he can't find her.

"I know, buddy," I tell him, scratching his ears. "I miss her too."

In the kitchen this morning, I found a note propped against the coffee maker. A plastic baggy of marijuana—our stolen booty from Brad's apartment—sits beside it. I pick up the note, recognizing Lena's neat handwriting:

Don't forget to floss. - L

That's it. Just four words and an initial. As if this summer meant nothing more to her than a dental cleaning. Staring at it now, I crumple the note in my fist, and unexpected anger rising in my chest.

Then, I smooth it out again and read the words once more. Is there something more here? Some hidden message I'm missing? Or is she really that detached, that clinical about what happened between us?

I shove the note in my pocket and grab my phone, my thumb hovering over her name in my contacts. What would I even say? "Come back"? "I miss you already"? "I think I might be falling for you"?

The last thought sends a jolt of panic through me. I'm not falling for Lena. I can't be. It's too soon after Adam. Too complicated with our professional relationship. What we had was physical, convenient, and mutual comfort during a diffi-cult time. Nothing more.

I set the phone down without calling. It's better this way—cleaner. We had our summer fling, brief as it was, and now we move on. We focus on our careers. We are adults about the whole thing.

Gordie whines at the back door, and I let him out into the yard, watching as he half-heartedly sniffs around the grass. Even my dog is moping.

"Get it together, Stag," I mutter to myself. I have a charity gala to attend tonight, and I need to be professional, polished, and completely unaffected by the sight of Lena across a crowded room.

I can do this. I have to.

CHAPTER 28
ALDER

The Black and Gold Charity Gala takes place at the Carnegie Museum of Art, where the grand hall is transformed with elegant lighting, ice sculptures, and enough flowers to fill a greenhouse. I adjust my bow tie for the third time as I enter, scanning the room automatically for familiar faces.

The event is a who's who of Pittsburgh sports—players from the Fury, the Black Sox, and the Forge, all in their formal best, mingling with donors, sponsors, and local celebrities. In years past, I've enjoyed these events, relishing the chance to dress up and socialize outside the locker room.

Tonight, I feel as if I'm wearing someone else's skin.

"A-Stag!" Banksy approaches, champagne in one hand, the other draped around his boyfriend. "Looking sharp, man."

"Thanks," I manage, accepting the glass he offers. "You too."

"Listen," he says, lowering his voice. "You good? Cam and I are here for you with all this anti-bi bullshit. You know we got you."

A wave of regret washes over me for not reaching out to Banksy after Brian came over. "Thanks, man." I put an arm on each of their shoulders. "I really appreciate that. And I'm good. Really."

Banksy looks at me and doesn't believe me for a second, but he's kind enough not to push. "Well, we're in if you want to get a tattoo or paint your house with the bi-flag colors. Whatever."

I nod, not actually listening, as he yacks about potential line changes for next season. My eyes are too busy scanning the crowd for the woman consuming my thoughts.

"There you are." Gunnar appears at my elbow, Emerson resplendent beside him in a deep green gown that shows off her curves. "You look like someone shot your dog."

"Thanks," I say dryly. "You're looking lovely, Em."

She gives me a sympathetic smile. "How are you doing, Alder?"

Something in her tone tells me she knows exactly what happened with the press and with Lena. Of course, she does —she was shopping with her when she decided to ditch me. "I'm fine," I say, the words sounding hollow even to my own ears. "Great event."

Gunnar snorts. "Yeah, you seem thrilled to be here. Try to look a little less miserable, will you? You're scaring the wait staff."

Emerson elbows him gently. "Be nice. He's having a rough day."

"Doesn't mean he gets to sulk like a big baby," Gunnar softens the criticism with a brotherly punch to my shoulder. "Come on, I need you to help me schmooze the Wilkins Foundation people. They're funding our youth hockey camp this summer."

I allow myself to be led through the crowd, grateful for the distraction. For the next hour, I force smiles, make small talk, and pretend to be the charming, carefree hockey star everyone expects. It's exhausting, but it's easier than thinking about Lena.

As the evening progresses, I find myself ordering something stronger than champagne at the bar. The bartender is just sliding my whiskey across the counter when I hear a commotion near the entrance.

I turn, and the world seems to slow down.

Lena stands in the doorway, a vision in a wine-colored dress that hugs her curves perfectly. The sweetheart neckline showcases the soft swell of her breasts. Her hair is swept up, exposing the elegant line of her neck—the same neck I was kissing just a few nights ago.

She's breathtaking, and from the hush that falls over those nearest the entrance, I'm not the only one who thinks so.

Our eyes meet across the room, a brief, electric connection before she looks away, moving further into the crowd. I watch as Coach Thompson greets her, introducing her to some donors with obvious pride. She's an asset to the organization, after all—a skilled professional who belongs here just as much as any of us.

Just not with me.

I down my whiskey in one swallow, welcoming the burn.

"Well, well. If it isn't Alder Stag."

I freeze at the familiar voice, then turn slowly to find Adam standing beside me at the bar. He's immaculate in a tailored tuxedo, perfectly styled dark hair, and a press badge hanging around his neck.

"Adam," I acknowledge coldly.

"All day long," he signals the bartender. Scotch, neat." He turns back to me with that smile I once found so charming. You're looking tense. Are you not enjoying the party?"

"It's fine." I focus on my empty glass, wishing I could order another without looking like I need it.

"I saw your dentist arrive. Quite the entrance." He accepts his drink from the bartender. "She seems to be settling in well with the team. Though I hear she's recently changed her living arrangements."

Of course, he knows. Adam makes it his business to know everything about everyone in Pittsburgh sports.

"Not your business," I say, my voice tight.

"Just making conversation." He takes a sip of his scotch. "Been seeing a lot of interesting comments from your fans online lately. The community never does like being used as PR."

I don't respond, but I can feel my jaw clenching.

"Tell me, how is life in the mainstream, straight guy?" Adam's voice is casual and conversational, but his eyes are calculating. "I wouldn't know..." His smile turns smug.

The accusation behind his words hits like a body check that I didn't see coming. "I've never been straight."

"No?" He laughs softly. "Could have fooled me." And then his demeanor changes. He's predatory, almost. "Actions have consequences, Alder," Adam says coolly. "You compromised my professional reputation. Only seemed fair to return the favor."

My eyes widen. "I made a mistake," I say through gritted teeth. "You orchestrated a campaign to humiliate me."

Adam shrugs. "Consider it a lesson in the power of strategic PR. Something you should have thought about before running your mouth."

My vision narrows, and blood rushes in my ears. Before I fully register what I'm doing, my fist connects with Adam's jaw, sending him stumbling backward.

There's a moment of stunned silence, then chaos. Adam recovers, lunging forward with a drink tray he snatches from a passing server. The edge catches me across the face, pain surging through my bones.

Hands grab at both of us, pulling us apart. I hear shouting and see flashes of light that must be camera phones. Someone shouts my name, trying to get my attention, but all I can focus on is the throbbing in my face and the cold satisfaction of having finally punched Adam Lawson.

"Alder." A firm voice cuts through the noise. "Alder, look at me."

I blink, focusing on the face in front of me. Lena, her expression professional but her eyes concerned.

"I need to check your jaw," she says, loud enough for others to hear. "Come with me."

She doesn't wait for a response. She just takes my arm and guides me away from the crowd through a side door into a quiet hallway lined with artifacts under glass.

"That was quite a statement," she says once we're alone, her tone caught between clinical and concerned. "Let me see."

Her fingers are cool against my skin as she gently probes my mouth. I wince when she hits a tender spot.

"Nothing broken," she declares after a moment. "But you're going to have a bruise." She steps back, creating distance between us. "What happened?"

"Adam happened," I say, the words coming out sharper than I intended. "He was running his mouth."

"About what?" she asks quietly.

"About us. Him and me. You and me." I sigh, the anger draining away, leaving only a bone-deep weariness. "Doesn't matter. I shouldn't have hit him."

"No, you shouldn't have." Her voice is soft but firm. "That's going to be all over social media in about five minutes."

"Add it to my list of poor decisions lately." I meet her eyes, finding them unreadable in the dim hallway lighting. "How's the new place?"

She seems startled by the question. "It's... fine. Small, but functional."

"Good." I don't know what else to say. There's so much and nothing at all.

We stand in awkward silence for a moment, both aware of how different this is from the easy intimacy we shared just days ago. She's so close I can smell her perfume, the same scent that lingered on my pillows this morning.

"You look beautiful," I say finally because it's true and

because I can't help but say it. That dress... it's perfect on you."

A blush spreads across her cheeks. "Thank you."

I step closer, unable to help myself. "Lena, I—"

"We should get back," she interrupts, taking a deliberate step backward. "People will talk."

"Let them," I say, the words escaping before I can stop them.

She shakes her head, a sad smile on her lips. "That's the problem, Alder. They already are."

She turns to go, but I gently catch her wrist. "I miss you," I admit, the words raw and honest. "I miss you in my house. In my bed. I miss waking up with you."

Her expression softens, vulnerability breaking through her professional mask. "I miss you too," she whispers. "But missing each other doesn't change anything."

"Doesn't it?" I ask, still holding her wrist, feeling her pulse race beneath my fingers. "If we both feel the same way—"

"We can't, Alder." She pulls her hand from my grasp. "I'm sorry about your jaw. Ice it when you get home. Twenty minutes on, twenty off."

And then she's gone, back through the door to the gala, leaving me alone in the hallway with the phantom sensation of her touch still lingering on my skin and the certainty that whatever I felt for her before she left, it's only grown stronger in her absence.

NIGHT IN THE NEW APARTMENT DRAGS ON FOR AGES. EVERY unfamiliar creak and hum keeps me from sleep, the strange shadows on unfamiliar walls playing tricks on my tired eyes. The bed—a hastily purchased foam mattress from the internet so I didn't have to sleep on something Brad touched—feels too firm, too empty.

At Alder's, I'd grown accustomed to sharing space with him and Gordie. The warmth of another body, the dog's gentle snoring at our feet. Even the guest bed there was the perfect firmness. The sense of safety and comfort I never realized I was missing until I had it.

Now, I'm alone again in a studio that feels both too small and too vast.

When my alarm finally buzzes at six, I've gotten maybe three hours of fitful sleep. I heave myself into the shower—a lackluster trickle compared to Alder's luxurious rainfall showerhead and missing the warm company of his beautiful body—and try to wash away the memory of last night's gala.

Of Alder's face when I examined his jaw, the hurt in his eyes that had nothing to do with physical pain.

Of the quiet "I miss you" still echoing in my head. It's even more painful knowing Alder is under attack for his sexuality.

My instincts scream at me to comfort him, defend him. Part of me fears I contributed to that unfair treatment by participating in the schemes that led Adam to take such nasty actions.

My dress hangs on the back of the bathroom door, the fabric catching the morning light. It seems out of place in this stark, undecorated apartment.

Kind of like me at the gala, if I'm being honest. Dressed up and trying to belong.

My phone buzzes as I make coffee on the single-cup machine I salvaged from my apartment. The screen lights up with notification after notification—texts, news alerts, social media mentions. I'd silenced it last night after getting home, unwilling to deal with the aftermath of the gala fight.

But there's no avoiding it now.

I scroll through the messages, most from numbers I don't recognize. Journalists are probably hoping for a comment about the altercation between Alder and Adam. The news alerts are even more direct:

"FURY STAR DECKS EX IN CHARITY GALA BRAWL"

"STAG VS. LAWSON: LOVERS' QUARREL TURNS VIOLENT"

I can't help but feel a wave of relief that I'm mentioned only in passing in most articles, if at all. A few notes that "team dentist Dr. Lena Sinclair was seen attending to Stag's injuries," but the focus is squarely on Alder and Adam.

Silver linings... I suppose. My career might survive this mess after all.

I hesitate for a moment, then open my messages and tap out a text to Alder:

> How's the jaw this morning?

Professional concern. That's all it is.

His response comes quicker than I expected: a photo of

Alder's face in profile, a spectacular bruise spreading along his jawline in mottled purple and blue. He's giving an exaggerated frown to the camera. Even injured and pouty, he's ridiculously handsome.

I shouldn't respond. I should maintain a professional distance. But my fingers are typing before I can stop them:

> Impressive bruise. Ice and ibuprofen. And maybe don't punch anyone else for a while.

Three dots appear, then:

> No promises. How's the new place?

The simple question carries more weight than it should. I stare at it for a long moment before replying:

> Quiet. Getting used to it.

Another pause, then:

> Gordie misses you.

What I want to write is *I miss him too. I miss you.* What I actually type is:

> Give him a scratch behind the ears from me.

> Will do

comes the reply, and then nothing more.

I set my phone down, determined to focus on work. The move to my place was the right decision, the necessary one. The fact that it feels wrong is irrelevant.

The drive to the Fury facility seems to take forever. When I arrive, the main space buzzes with youth hockey camps and frenzied talk between scouts and the coaching staff. I make my way to my office, nodding professionally to the staff I pass, relieved that Alder isn't here volunteering.

I throw myself into patient files and equipment inventory, grateful for the mundane tasks that require concentration without emotional investment. The morning passes in a blur of paperwork and consultations with the athletic trainers about face shield modifications.

Just before noon, there's a knock at my office door. I look up to find Sarah Collins, the assistant coach, leaning against the doorframe. Her dark hair is pulled back in her trademark sleek ponytail, and her Fury polo and slacks are impeccably wrinkle-free. I feel frumpy by comparison in my scrubs.

"Got a minute, Doc?" she asks.

"Of course." I gesture to the chair across from my desk. "What can I do for you?"

She closes the door before sitting down, which immediately puts me on alert. This isn't a casual visit.

"Quite a show last night," she says, her expression neutral. "How's A-Stag's jaw?"

"Bruised, but not broken." I keep my tone clinical. "He'll be fine."

"Good to hear." She studies me for a moment. "Just wanted to make sure. Can't have him taking more hits to the face while he's healing."

I nod. "He should be able to maintain his conditioning work."

Sarah taps her hands on my desk but makes no move to leave. "I'm Sorry I missed most of the excitement," she says after a moment. I was... held up."

Something in her tone makes me glance up. There's a knowing look in her eyes, almost a challenge.

"I noticed you arrived late," I say carefully. "Did you get caught in traffic?"

A small smile plays at her lips. "Something like that." She leans forward slightly. "Listen, not to pry, but—"

A sharp knock interrupts whatever she was about to say. The door opens without waiting for a response, and Coach Thompson sticks his head in.

"Collins. Need you in the video room. Going over defensive strategies with the new rookie class."

Sarah sighs but rises. "On my way." She turns back to me as she reaches the door. "Rain check on that conversation, Doc. Maybe coffee tomorrow?"

"Sure," I agree, curious despite myself.

She nods and follows Thompson out, but not before giving me a look that suggests she has more to say. I wonder what she was about to ask and why it required privacy.

My phone rings just as I'm gathering my things for lunch. My mother's name flashes on the screen, and I seriously consider letting it go to voicemail. But avoiding her will only lead to more persistent calls, so I answer with a resigned sigh.

"Hi, Mom."

"Lena Diane Sinclair." Her use of my full name immediately puts me on edge. "Would you care to explain why you're in the tabloids this morning?"

"The tabloids?" I repeat, confused. "I'm not—"

"Pittsburgh Press-Gazette. Page six." I can hear the rustling of newsprint. "There's a photo of you crouched in front of that hockey player with your skirt hiked up. It's humiliating."

I pull up the newspaper's website on my computer and quickly find the article. Sure enough, there's a photo of me examining Alder's jaw in the museum hallway. The angle makes it look intimate rather than professional, my hand on his face, his eyes locked with mine.

What strikes me most about the image, though, isn't the suggestive framing—it's the tenderness in my expression, the care evident in every line of my body. I look like a woman in love, not a doctor treating a patient. The headline is all about his fight with Adam, but anyone with eyes should see that it's me who is a goner for Alder Stag.

"It's not what it looks like," I say automatically. "I was checking his injury. It's my job."

"Well, you're certainly not dressed like you're doing your job," my mother sniffs. "We talked about plain black. That gown is far too revealing for someone of your size. Your chest is practically spilling out. What were you thinking, wearing something so inappropriate to a professional event?"

The familiar criticism stings, but instead of shrinking from it as I usually do, I feel a spark of anger ignite.

"What was I thinking?" I repeat, my voice rising. "I was thinking I wanted to wear something that made me feel beautiful. Something that celebrated my body."

"Lena, be realistic. Women like you need to—"

"No." The word comes out sharper than I intended, but I don't soften it. "I'm done with that kind of thinking, Mom. I'm done letting you make me feel bad about my body and my choices."

"I'm only trying to help you—"

"By criticizing everything about me? By teaching me to hate myself? That's not help, Mom. That's cruelty."

My outburst is followed by a shocked silence. I've never spoken to her this way before, never challenged her constant stream of "helpful" criticism.

"I'll call back when you're less emotional," she says finally, her voice tight.

"Don't bother unless you're ready to actually support me," I reply. "I'm done with the negativity. I deserve better." I end the call before she can respond, my hand shaking slightly, but my resolve is firm.

I stare at my phone for a long moment, stunned by my assertiveness. Standing up to my mother has been a dream scenario for years, one I've played out in my head but never had the courage to enact.

Until today.

Before I can process this shift, my phone rings again. I expect it to be my mother calling back to scold me for my "attitude," but instead, Brad's name flashes on the screen.

My instinct is, again, to ignore it, but something—perhaps the lingering adrenaline from standing up to my mother— makes me accept the call.

"What do you want, Brad?" I ask without preamble.

"Well, hello to you, too," he says, the familiar condescension in his voice instantly putting my teeth on edge. "I'm calling about the furniture."

"What furniture?"

"Our furniture. From the apartment. You took everything."

I blink, momentarily confused. Where has he been the past few days that he's just calling me about this now? "I took my stuff, Brad. Things I bought."

"The couch was ours. So was the dining table."

"No, Brad. They were mine. I paid for them."

"We were living together," he says as if explaining something to a child. "What was yours was ours."

"That's not how it works when only one person pays for everything." I can feel my patience thinning. "I bought that couch. And the dishes. And the dining table. Check your bank statements if you don't believe me."

"You're being unreasonable," he says. "Adam has a chipped orbital bone thanks to your hockey player's tantrum, and now I'm stuck taking care of him in an empty apartment."

The image of Adam and Brad playing house in what was once my home is so absurd I almost laugh. "First of all, he's not 'my' hockey player. Second, I give exactly zero shits about anything related to Adam. And third, if you need furniture, go buy some. You can use all the money you saved by living off me for four years."

"I can't believe you're being so petty about this," Brad says. "It's just stuff."

"Exactly. It's just stuff. Stuff that I bought with my money while you were freeloading."

"I was working on my dissertation!"

"And how's that going?" I ask sweetly. "Making progress now that you have to pay your own bills?"

His silence is answer enough.

"I have to get back to work," I say, a surge of satisfaction flowing through me. I've carried the crushing weight of my dental school loans alone for years while Brad contributed nothing—not even emotional support. Just endless critiques and expectations while I worked to exhaustion to keep us afloat. "Don't call me again unless it's to apologize for cheating on me and abusing me financially for years. And even then, I probably won't answer."

I hang up, a current of joy flowing through me. First, my mother, now Brad, and I'm on a roll today.

Maybe moving out of Alder's was exactly what I needed to find my backbone.

By the time I return to my apartment that evening, I'm exhausted but strangely energized. Standing up for myself has left me feeling stronger and more centered. I look around the sparse space with new eyes. It's not much, but it's mine. A blank canvas I can fill however I choose, without compromise.

I unpack a few more boxes, arrange my books on a shelf, and hang some framed prints I've had since dental school— small touches that begin to transform the studio from an anonymous space into my home.

My phone buzzes with a text from Sarah:

> Coffee tomorrow? Some things you should know.

I stare at the message, intrigued. What could the assistant coach possibly want to tell me? Something about Alder? About the team's reaction to last night's fight?

> I'll be there

I reply, curiosity getting the better of me, telling her a place named Jitters is convenient to my apartment.

I sit on my bed, scrolling through the evening's news coverage of the gala fight. Most outlets seem to be treating it as typical sports drama, emphasizing Alder's broken heart. I cringe at the sensationalism.

My thumb hovers over Alder's contact information. It would be so easy to call him, to hear his voice, to ask how Gordie's doing. To admit that I miss them both more than I expected.

But that would undo everything I'm trying to accomplish by moving out. The distance is necessary for both our careers and our sanity—a clean break, like ripping off a bandage.

Except it doesn't feel clean at all. It feels raw, painful, and unfinished.

As the single-cup coffee maker sputters out just enough for one travel mug, I catch myself glancing toward the door, expecting a cold nose to nudge my leg. The phantom sensation is so strong that I almost reach down to scratch behind ears that aren't there.

I check my phone one more time before leaving—no messages from Alder. The screen shows only the usual notifications—email, news alerts, and a text from my mother that I'll continue ignoring.

Relief and disappointment war in my chest. Relief that I don't have to navigate another carefully casual exchange. Disappointment that he's respecting my request for space.

The walk to Jitters takes me through Shadyside streets that feel nothing like the riverside path I walked with Alder and Gordie: different trees, different smells, different life. I pass a couple walking hand in hand, their shoulders brushing as they laugh at some private joke. The pang, I feel, is sharper than expected.

"This is temporary," I mutter to myself. "This feeling will pass. It's just withdrawal from physical intimacy. Nothing more."

If I repeat it enough times, I'll likely start believing it.

. . .

Sarah Collins is already at Jitters when I arrive, tucked into a corner table with her back to the wall. Unlike her usual poised and perfect self, today she fidgets with her coffee cup, her dark ponytail slightly askew. She has the unmistakable look of someone who hasn't been sleeping well.

"Thanks for coming," she says as I slide into the chair across from her. "I wasn't sure you would."

I order a latte from the server before turning my attention back to Sarah. "Your text was intriguing. What's up?"

Sarah glances around the coffee shop, ensuring no one is within earshot. "I need to talk to someone who might understand a... delicate situation. And after seeing you at the gala with A-Stag..." She trails off, observing my reaction.

"I was providing medical assessment," I say automatically. The lie feels stale on my tongue.

Sarah's mouth quirks into a humorless smile. She reaches into her bag and pulls out a manila envelope, sliding it across the table. "Medical assessment. Sure."

I open the envelope with trepidation. Inside are several glossy photos—images that weren't published in the papers. My breath catches. In one, my palm rests gently against Alder's jaw, but it's our eyes that tell the real story. We're looking at each other with undisguised longing, a tenderness that can't be mistaken for professional concern.

"Where did you get these?" I ask, my voice barely audible.

"A friend at the Press-Gazette owed me a favor. I convinced him these weren't newsworthy." Sarah leans forward. "He disagreed but respected my judgment."

I stare at the photos, unable to look away from the naked emotion on both our faces. We appear to be two people in love, not a doctor and patient.

"Thank you," I finally manage, sliding the photos back into the envelope. "That was... kind of you."

"Don't thank me yet." Sarah takes a deep breath.

I look up sharply. The moment is too pointed and too relevant to be coincidental.

"If you're implying there's something between Alder and me..." I begin cautiously.

"I'm saying I need to know I'm not the only one drowning here." The vulnerability in her voice surprises me. Sarah Collins has always seemed unflappable and in complete control.

Understanding dawns. "You have feelings for someone on the team?"

She nods once, sharply, not volunteering a name. "It's completely inappropriate. I'm a coach. It creates complicated power dynamics when you're in leadership." She runs a hand through her hair, further disheveling her usually perfect ponytail. "We're at the same level professionally, but the optics... it could destroy everything I've worked for. Everything she's worked for."

The pronoun surprises me, but I keep my expression intact, allowing her to continue.

"But then I saw you and A-Stag at the gala," she continues. "The way you looked at each other. And I thought maybe you'd figured something out that I haven't."

"I haven't figured out anything," I admit, surprising myself with my candor. "I moved out of his place because I was scared of losing my job. Scared of damaging his career."

"So there was something between you." It's not a question.

I look down at my coffee. "There was. Is. I don't know anymore."

Sarah leans back in her chair, studying me. "The fraternization policy is more complicated than most people realize," she says after a moment. She traces the rim of her mug with one finger. "But there are procedures for disclosure and recusal for some positions, for some staff. The problem is..."

"Perception and conflicts," I finish for her.

She nods. "As a coach, any relationship with another staff member raises questions about fairness and whether decisions are being made professionally. Who gets promoted, and who gets the choice assignments." She sighs. "And in my case, there are... additional complications."

I understand her implication without her needing to elaborate. A same-sex relationship in professional sports carries its challenges, even in today's more accepting climate.

"My situation with one of the athletic trainers... we've been so very careful. However, I see how you and Alder look at each other and how you're struggling, and I wonder if I'm making the right choice by hiding.

"I haven't acted on my feelings," Sarah continues, her voice dropping lower. "I'm trying to maintain professional distance. But it's killing me."

"Moving out hasn't helped," I confess. "It feels worse. Like I've cut off a limb."

Sarah's laugh is bitter. "Maybe sometimes the right professional choice isn't the right human choice."

"What are you going to do?" I ask. "About your situation?"

She checks her watch and begins gathering her things. "I don't know. But I wanted an ally...or anyway, another woman who maybe understands my current torture." She stands, slinging her bag over her shoulder. "Especially since yours isn't necessarily hopeless."

The implication is clear—my situation might have solutions that hers doesn't.

"Sarah," I call as she turns to leave. "Thank you. For the photos. For trusting me."

She pauses, looking back at me with a sad smile. "Don't

thank me. Just... don't give up without exploring all your options. Some things are worth fighting for." She hesitates, then adds, "And maybe someday I'll find the courage to take my own advice."

After Sarah leaves, I remain at the table, staring into my cooling coffee. The manila envelope sits beside my cup, its contents burning a hole in my awareness. I should destroy the photos. Instead, I open the envelope again, studying the image that captures precisely what I've been denying—the depth of feeling between Alder and me.

My chest aches with a longing so intense it feels physical. I miss his laugh, warmth, and how he smells after a shower. I miss Gordie's snoring at the foot of the bed. I miss feeling like I belong somewhere, with someone.

I've spent my entire life trying to be smaller, less demanding, and less trouble—with Brad, with my mother, with everyone. I shrank myself to fit the spaces others allowed me.

Until Alder. Until Gordie. Until the Stag family chaos, which somehow made me feel more at home than anywhere I've ever been.

But I can't lose sight of reality. My student loan payments don't care about my feelings. Over three hundred thousand dollars in debt means I need this job with the Fury. Professionally, physically, and financially—I can't afford to risk it all for romance, no matter how right it feels.

Maybe I gave up too easily. Perhaps we both did. I just don't know what to do about it.

CHAPTER 31
ALDER

Charles Sutton leans back in his leather chair, fingers steepled. His expression is the carefully neutral mask of a man who's spent decades negotiating with millionaire athletes and billionaire investors. The bruise on my jaw throbs under his scrutiny.

"Adam Lawson is threatening legal action," he continues. "Not just against you, but against the organization. His company is not happy, to put it mildly."

"He deserved it," I say, the words escaping before I can stop them.

Brian shifts nervously beside me. He's been hovering since we entered the office like he's afraid I might lunge across the desk and take a swing at the owner next.

Coach Thompson, who's been silently observing from the corner, steps forward. "Maybe he did. But that's not how professionals handle things off the ice." He pauses, then adds in a lower voice, "Even if I would've done the same in your position."

The unexpected show of solidarity doesn't soften the blow that follows.

"Public apology," Sutton declares. "Community service

with the youth hockey program. And you're covering any medical expenses for Lawson."

I nod, accepting the punishment without argument. Adam's probably going to milk me for a nose job. Jagoff. It could be worse. They could bench me next season, trade me to a team in the middle of nowhere, and completely end my career.

"We'll draft a statement," Brian jumps in. "Schedule a press conference."

"Fine," I say, just wanting this meeting to be over.

"One more thing." Sutton's eyes bore into mine. "This is your only warning, Stag. Next time, there won't be a conversation."

The implied threat hangs in the air as I'm dismissed.

"What were you thinking?" Brian explodes the moment we're alone in the hallway. "Do you have any idea the PR nightmare we're dealing with?"

I lean against the wall, suddenly exhausted. "It wasn't planned, Brian."

"No shit." He shoves a piece of paper into my hand. "Public statement. Memorize it. We're holding a press conference tomorrow morning."

I scan the typed paragraph—a generic apology full of corporate-speak about "regrettable actions" and "commitment to sportsmanship." There is nothing about Adam's smug face or his taunts about Lena. Nothing about how it felt to finally hit something that had been hurting me.

"This is bullshit," I say, crumpling the paper slightly in my fist.

Brian steps closer, lowering his voice. "This is your last chance, A-Stag. No more public outbursts, no more scenes. The team has been more than patient with the loss after the kiss cam and all the circus that followed."

I want to argue, but I know he's right. This isn't helping anyone, least of all me.

Brian's expression softens slightly. "Look, I get it. The guy's a dick. But this isn't helping you move on."

Move on… as if I haven't been trying to do exactly that.

"You really don't see what's going on here?" Brian asks, exasperated.

"Enlighten me," I spit back, pressing the ice pack to my jaw.

"After you blew his confidentiality at the barbecue, Adam lost a major account. The merger announcement was a mess. This whole thing—kissing that philosophy professor on camera, planting those stories questioning your bisexuality— it's strategic. It's revenge, A-Stag. He's trying to tank your public image like you accidentally tanked his career."

I rear back, the pieces finally clicking into place. "So, this isn't just about our breakup."

"You hurt him professionally. Now he's doing the same to you. The difference is, he's doing it deliberately."

I blink and adjust my weight. "I'll be at the press confer- ence," I promise, pocketing the statement. "I'll say what needs to be said."

Brian looks skeptical but nods. He walks away, muttering, "Pain in my ass."

I'm almost to the parking lot when a familiar voice calls out behind me.

"Heard management reamed you out." Tucker falls into step beside me, matching my stride as easily as he always has. "How bad was it?"

I fill him in on the consequences as we step through the doors into the bright afternoon sunshine. The mid-summer heat strikes like a physical wall after the air-conditioned facility.

"Public apology, community service, not bad." I shrug, trying to appear more casual about it than I feel.

Tucker nudges my shoulder. "Nice right hook, though. Dad would be horrified, Mom probably secretly proud."

Despite everything, I feel a smile tugging at my lips. "Dad would pretend to be horrified while Mom's around."

"Exactly."

We reach my car, and I expect Tucker to head toward his own. Instead, he hesitates, and his expression grows serious.

"Have you talked to her?" he asks.

I don't pretend not to know who he means. "No. She made her choice."

"You're both stubborn idiots." Tucker shakes his head. "I've seen the way she looks at you, A. And the way you've been moping."

"I need to clear my head," I say, changing the subject. "And you're one to talk." His brows fly up, and he shakes his head, starting to say something. I hold up a hand. "I can't talk about your shit right now, whatever it is. I'm going for a drive."

I spin on my heel away from my twin, feeling unmoored now more than ever.

I drive aimlessly at first, muscle memory carrying me through familiar streets. Only when I realize I'm approaching Shady-side—where Lena's new apartment is located—do I jerk the wheel, making a sharp turn away.

I don't even know exactly where she lives—just the neigh-borhood she mentioned. But the thought of accidentally driving past her building, maybe seeing her through a window or on the street, is both tempting and terrifying.

My heart races, and my thoughts swirl. If Tucker were here, he wouldn't have any experience with this kind of relationship fallout. I realize my older brothers do, though. I swallow the bile rising in my throat and veer toward Gunnar and Emerson's place. I haven't called ahead. Haven't even decided if I'm going there until I'm parking outside their building.

I hesitate in the car for a long moment, questioning what I'm even doing here. Gunnar and I have never been the "talk about our feelings" type of brothers.

But I need someone who'll understand. Someone who won't judge me for being a mess over a woman I've known for less than two months.

I knock on their door, perhaps harder than a normal person would. There's a muffled curse from inside, then followed by shuffling footsteps. The door swings open to reveal Gunnar, hair disheveled, wearing only sweatpants. Behind him, I glimpse a door slamming shut.

"Shit." I take a step back. "Bad timing. I didn't call—"

"Aldernator?" Gunnar blinks, then recovers. "No, it's—we were just—" He runs a hand through his hair, glancing down the hall. "Em, it's Alder."

Emerson's head pops out from behind the bedroom door, her face flushed. "Hi, Alder." She smooths down her shirt, which is definitely on backward. "I was just... napping."

"Right." I start to back away. "I'll go. Sorry to interrupt your... nap."

"Don't be stupid. She'd never fall asleep on my watch." Gunnar grabs my arm, pulling me inside.

Emerson throws a pillow at his head, which he catches with practiced ease.

He grins at her and turns back to me. "Give me two minutes to get decent, and then we can talk."

I stand awkwardly in their entryway while they straighten up, feeling like an intruder. After a moment, Emerson disappears into her music room. Her curls tamed into a messy bun.

Cello music begins to play behind the closed door, which I realize gives Gunnar and me an additional layer of privacy.

Gunnar retrieves two beers from the fridge, handing one to me. "So," he says, dropping onto the now-straightened couch. "What brings you to interrupt my afternoon delight?"

I wince. "Sorry about that."

"I'm kidding. Mostly." He takes a long drink, studying me over the bottle. "Management chewed you out good?"

"Fucker is a blabbermouth."

"He is, but…" Gun gestures toward my bruised jaw. "Figured there'd be consequences."

I collapse into the armchair across from him. "Community service, public apology, gotta pay for Adam's plastic surgery or whatever."

"Worth it, though?"

I consider the question longer than I should need to. "Yes. No. I don't know."

Gunnar watches me, his expression more serious than usual. "You wouldn't drive here unannounced about that, though."

"No," I admit after a long pause.

A beat of silence stretches between us. Then Gunnar says quietly, "So... the dentist."

I start to defend myself, but he cuts me off with a wave.

"I'm not judging. Em, and I like her. A lot." The sincerity in his voice surprises me. "The summer fling isn't such a carefree thing after all, is it?"

The phrase—my phrase, thrown back at me from that family dinner—lands like a punch. "Don't."

"Look, I saw you two at our wedding. The way you looked at each other." Gunnar leans forward. "She looks at you the way Em looks at me. That's rare, A."

My throat tightens. "Yeah, well, she also moved out the second things got complicated."

"I'd argue things have been complicated for you guys from the start."

A sharp knock interrupts whatever Gunnar was about to say. He rises to answer the door, and I'm not entirely surprised to see Tucker standing there, a six-pack dangling from his hand.

"Twin sense. Figured you'd end up here," he says to me before nodding at Gunnar. "G."

"Fucker." Gunnar takes the beer. "A's moping about the dentist."

"Yeah, well, he's been pathetic since she left," Tucker says, dropping onto the couch.

"I'm right here," I protest.

"Good." Tucker grabs a beer. "Then you can listen to people who actually care about you."

Gunnar retrieves his phone from the coffee table. "Want to see something interesting?" He scrolls for a moment, then turns the screen toward me. "Em got the first batch of wedding photos this morning."

I stare at the image—Lena and me on the dance floor, our bodies close, eyes locked. Even in the still photo, the intensity between us is palpable. Her hand on my shoulder, mine at her waist. The way we're leaning in, like magnets drawn together.

"Em said everyone at the wedding was talking about how you two couldn't keep your eyes off each other," Gunnar says.

"Or your hands," Tucker adds.

I look away from the photo. "It doesn't matter. She chose her career."

"So did you," Tucker says, unexpectedly serious. "She worked her ass off to get where she is. You, of all people, should understand that."

"It's different," I argue.

"Is it?" Gunnar challenges. "You've both dedicated your lives to your careers. You've both made sacrifices. The question is whether this sacrifice is worth it."

His words hit home in a way I wasn't expecting. I take a long pull of my beer, buying time to gather my thoughts.

"What if I'm not enough?" The question slips out before I can stop it, raw and honest in a way I rarely am with my brothers. "I wasn't for Adam."

"Adam's an asshole," Gunnar says firmly. "That doesn't reflect on you."

"You're comparing apples and garbage, bro," Tucker adds.

"You know what I was afraid of when Em and I first got serious?" Gunnar sets his beer down. "Not that I wasn't good enough for her. That what I was asking her to accept—the publicity, the travel, the scrutiny—wasn't worth it. That I was selfishly pulling her into a life she never asked for."

I look up, surprised by the admission. Gunnar and Emerson have always seemed so solid, so sure.

"What changed?" I ask.

"Nothing. I'm still afraid of that sometimes." He shrugs. "But I realized it wasn't my decision to make. It was hers. And she chose us, even knowing what it meant."

Tucker nods thoughtfully. "It's about trust, man. Trusting that she knows what she wants, what she's willing to risk." He hooks his gaze on mine, and I know he's got something on his mind, but I'm grateful that he's letting me focus on my exploding life.

"We don't know Lena like you do," Gunnar adds. "But that woman doesn't seem like the type to make decisions lightly."

"Or back down from a challenge," Tucker says.

Gunnar swipes to another wedding photo—this one of Lena talking with our mother, laughing about something.

"Mom loves her, by the way," he says. "Keeps saying she's never seen you so comfortable with someone."

"Even Odin approved, and he judges everyone," Tucker adds.

I stare at the photo, feeling a complex mix of emotions.

Seeing Lena laughing with my mother brings back memories of how easily she fit into my family and how naturally she became part of my life.

"The question is," Gunnar says, "what are you going to do about it?"

"I don't know yet." I pull Brian's crumpled statement from my pocket, smoothing it on my knee. "Can we talk about something else?"

Gunnar shrugs and crushes his beer can with a belch. "God, I love the off-season. Is that your press conference script? Let's see."

Tucker reads it over my shoulder. "This is corporate bullshit."

"You can't say this," Gunnar agrees. "If anything, the Fury should release a statement that bisexuality is real."

"Thanks, Gun," I say. I stare at the paper some more and sigh. "Maybe I need to find my own words." I'm surprised by the certainty I suddenly feel. "Something honest."

"Brian will hate that." Tucker claps me on the shoulder. "I love it."

We spend the next hour brainstorming what I could say instead, how I could be sincere while still being professional. By the time I'm ready to leave, I have the bones of something that feels right—something that acknowledges the mistake without denying the humanity behind it.

"Thanks," I say as my brothers walk me to the door. "For... you know."

"Anytime," Gunnar says. "And for what it's worth, I'm sure she misses you too."

I lean past Gunnar and conduct an eyebrow conversation with my twin, explaining that we will talk after things settle for me and that he can tell me whatever's been weighing on him.

Tucker nods. "At least talk to her. Clear the air. Maybe ask Uncle Tim for advice? I'm pretty sure he set up these rules after Aunt Lucy started banging Uncle Hawk when she coached the Forge…Tim probably knows the loopholes…"

I make a noncommittal gesture, but internally, something has shifted. Maybe Lena made the practical choice, the professional one. But I'm not convinced it was the right one—for either of us. The problem is, once I go to my uncle with this information, he's duty-bound to report that we're actually in a relationship. It feels inappropriate for me to go to him without consulting Lena first, and…I don't know if I'm ready to talk to her yet because she could freak out and end things before we settle this. I'm definitely not prepared for her to give up on us.

CHAPTER 32
LENA

THE STUDENT LOAN STATEMENT SITS ON MY NIGHTSTAND WHERE I left it, the number glaring at me even from inside the envelope: $325,742.16. A third of a million dollars in debt for a career I have worked my entire adult life to achieve. A job where I can support myself with my brains since I was told my looks would make love a challenge.

"This is what matters," I tell my reflection as I brush my teeth. "This job. This career. This life you built for yourself."

I've never been the type to make impulsive decisions. My relationship with Brad developed due to my mother's plans and meddling. Every step of my education and career has been carefully planned and meticulously executed—until Alder, when I let my heart override my head.

The manila envelope from Sarah sits beside the loan statement, and the photos inside serve as a tangible reminder of what I walked away from. However, that was the right choice. The professional choice. The only choice that ensures I can pay off my mountain of debt and build the career I sacrificed so much to create.

I brew a single cup of coffee in my cheap machine, and as I sip this mediocre brew, I reaffirm my decision: I need to secure my position as team dentist. No distractions. No complications. No Alder Stag.

No matter how much my chest aches at the thought.

When I arrive, the Fury training facility is buzzing with activity. The summer youth hockey camp is gearing up for its second session, and coaches are assessing which players show promise for hockey academies.

I pause to watch as a young boy, perhaps ten years old, struggles to insert his mouthguard. He grimaces at the generic shape, trying to make it fit comfortably. The coach calls him to attention, and he reluctantly puts it in, his expression clearly uncomfortable.

Something clicks in my mind.

In my office, I pull up research I've collected on innovations in protective equipment. Several universities have been experimenting with impact-sensing technology in football helmets and lacrosse gear, but application in hockey has been limited. Half the cases I saw at the emergency room were gruesome sports accidents gone awry, and at least half of those could have been prevented with proper mouth protection.

I sketch rapidly on my tablet, envisioning custom-fitted mouthguards created with advanced 3D printing technology and embedded sensors. The sensors could measure impact forces, tracking potentially dangerous hits and providing real-time data on player safety.

The concept isn't entirely new, but its implementation throughout an organization, beginning with youth programs, could revolutionize how we understand and prevent concussions and dental trauma.

"If I can't fix my personal life right now, at least I can excel professionally," I mutter, already drafting an implementation plan.

By mid-morning, I've outlined a comprehensive proposal: digital scans of each player's mouth, an advanced 3D printing of perfectly fitted mouthguards produced in-house rather than sent from a lab, and embedded sensors to collect impact data. Additionally, a partnership with Carnegie Mellon's biostatistics department to analyze the results.

The youth camp provides the perfect testing ground—a controlled environment, consistent supervision, and players at a crucial developmental stage when protecting their growing bodies is essential.

I sent a brief email to the facility manager asking about the leadership meeting schedule. The response came quickly: Fury's leadership team meets daily at three. Today, they'll discuss youth programs and community outreach.

Perfect timing.

I refine my proposal, add preliminary cost projections, and compile research supporting the technology's potential impact. By lunchtime, I've crafted a concise presentation that emphasizes both player safety and the organization's opportunity to pioneer cutting-edge protective technology.

As I review my notes, my phone buzzes with a text. For a heartbeat, I hope it's Alder. Instead, it's my mother, another thinly veiled criticism about my life choices. I silence the notification without responding.

Focus, Lena. This is what matters.

At precisely 2:55, I arrive outside the conference room. Through the glass, I can see Coach Thompson, Charles Sutton, and several other members of the Fury leadership team reviewing documents. My pulse quickens as I knock on the door.

Coach Sarah looks up, surprise flashing across her face before she gestures to me.

"Dr. Sinclair," she says. "We weren't expecting you."

"I apologize for the interruption," I say, keeping my voice steady despite my racing heart. "I have a player safety initiative I'd like to present if you can spare five minutes."

Sutton checks his watch, then nods. "You have the floor, Doctor."

I connect my tablet to the room's display and launch into my presentation. The nervousness in my stomach transforms into professional confidence as I outline the mouthguard innovation.

"Each player would receive a custom-fitted mouthguard created using advanced 3D printing technology," I explain, showing the mock-ups I've created. "But the embedded sensor technology is what makes this program truly innovative."

I advance to the next slide, displaying diagrams of the impact sensors.

"These sensors would measure force vectors, frequency, and intensity of impacts. The data would be collected and analyzed in partnership with Carnegie Mellon researchers, helping us identify patterns that could lead to injury."

The athletic trainer leans forward, visibly interested. "We've been looking at similar technology for helmets."

"Exactly," I nod. "The mouthguard application is particularly valuable because the jaw is so dynamic. And since mouthguards are already mandatory equipment for youth, we're not adding anything new to the player's gear."

Sutton, who I expected to focus on costs, asks, "Implementation timeline?"

"We could begin with the youth summer program as soon as we get a printer in," I say, relieved by his interest. "It's a perfect testing ground—controlled environment, consistent supervision, developing players who would benefit most from the protective technology and long-term data collection."

Coach Thompson shares a look with Sutton, then says,

"We're actually starting a community service initiative with the youth program. Alder Stag will be working with those kids as part of his... disciplinary action."

The sound of Alder's name sends a shock through my system, but I maintain my professional expression. "That timing works well. We could coordinate efforts."

Sutton taps his pen against the table thoughtfully. "We're holding a press conference tomorrow about Stag's community service. Would this be ready to announce by then? Show the organization's commitment to player safety alongside our disciplinary actions?"

My mouth goes dry at the thought of standing beside Alder at a press conference, but this is exactly the opportunity I need professionally.

"Absolutely," I hear myself say. "I can prepare all the necessary materials."

"Excellent." Sutton stands, signaling the end of the meeting. "Thompson, make sure Dr. Sinclair has whatever resources she needs for this. I want Pittsburgh leading the conversation on player safety."

As the room clears, Coach Thompson hangs back.

"Good initiative, Doctor," he says. The press conference is tomorrow at 11. The communications team will prep you beforehand."

"Thank you for the support," I say, gathering my tablet.

He studies me for a moment longer than feels comfortable. "Interesting timing."

"I'm not sure what you mean," I say, though I suspect I do.

"Nothing." He shrugs. "Just nice to see everyone focused on their professional contributions to this organization."

The emphasis on "professional" is subtle but unmistakable. Message received, Coach.

• • •

Back in my office, I close the door and lean against it, exhaling slowly. Professional success and personal turmoil are all tangled in a knot I can't seem to unravel.

Tomorrow, I'll stand alongside Alder before cameras and reporters. I'll need to maintain composure while ignoring the memory of his body against mine, his voice in the dark, and the way my body stretched to accommodate him.

I sink into my chair and start drafting emails to the equipment suppliers I'll need to contact. Focus on the work. Not on Alder's bruised jaw or how it felt to trace my fingers along it at the gala. Not on the way his eyes would crinkle when he laughed at something I said. Not on Gordie's excited greeting when we'd return home together.

Home. It felt like home in a way no place ever has.

I shake the thought away and continue working, losing myself in specifications and price quotes. By the time I finish, the facility has grown quieter, most of the staff having left for the day.

As I gather my things to leave, my phone buzzes with an email from the communications director: details for tomorrow's press conference, including a brief outline of what I should expect and what points to emphasize about the mouthguard program.

The reality sinks in. In less than twenty-four hours, I'll be face to face with Alder again, in front of cameras, reporters, and the entire Fury organization.

As I drive home through the evening traffic, my mind splits between rehearsing my talking points for tomorrow and wondering how I'll manage to look at Alder without revealing everything I feel.

The mouthguard program is a solid professional accomplishment—precisely what I need to secure my position. I should be celebrating this win. Instead, I'm dreading the moment I'll have to stand beside the man I walked away from and pretend he means nothing to me.

Tomorrow will be a test of everything I've worked for—my professionalism, my composure, my commitment to my career. I can't fail.

When I return, my apartment feels emptier than usual. I set my laptop on the kitchen counter and stare at the sparse furnishings and blank walls I haven't bothered to decorate. Despite my best efforts to make it home, the place still feels temporary.

I reheat leftover takeout and eat, standing at the counter and scrolling through my presentation notes one more time. The information blurs before my eyes, and my mind drifts to tomorrow's press conference—to Alder.

Will he look as tired as I feel? Has he been sleeping any better than I have? Will there be an opportunity to speak privately, or will we maintain this painful distance?

In bed, I stare at the ceiling, sleep eluding me despite my exhaustion. The apartment creaks and settles around me, the sounds still unfamiliar. I miss the soft snoring of Gordie at the foot of the bed, the steady breathing of Alder beside me.

Without fully thinking it through, I reach for my phone and type a message to Sarah:

> How do you handle seeing her every day?
> This is so much harder than I expected.

My thumb hovers over the send button, a moment of doubt. Sarah and I aren't friends, not really. We've had one meaningful conversation. This text is unprofessional, inappropriate even.

I send it anyway.

I immediately regretted it. Sarah reports directly to Coach Thompson. What if she shares this with management? What if this undermines everything I've worked for?

The three dots appear almost immediately. Sarah is typing. My heart pounds as I wait.

Her reply comes through:

> Being a woman in pro hockey is not for the weak. Neither is loving someone you shouldn't.

Loving.

The word jumps out at me, sending a shock through my system. Is that what this is? Love? The possibility has been hovering at the edges of my consciousness, but seeing it spelled out so plainly makes it impossible to ignore.

Before I can process this, another message appears:

> We'll talk after the press conference. Get some sleep. Your career and your heart both matter.

I reread the messages, then a third time. Sarah understands. Not just the professional constraints but also the emotional reality. And she hasn't dismissed either as unimportant.

Finding balance is the hard part.

I set my phone on the nightstand and curl onto my side, Sarah's words echoing in my mind—especially that one word: loving.

I've been operating under the assumption that I had to choose—career or Alder. Professional success or personal happiness. That achieving both was impossible under the circumstances.

But what if it's not? And if so, what am I willing to risk for it?

The answer follows me into dreams of blue eyes and strong arms.

CHAPTER 33

ALDER

Personal fight club, Coach said as if he doesn't encourage me to rough people up on the ice. But that's the ice. I know this.

Charles Sutton's voice echoes in my head as I clip Gordie's leash to his collar. The morning air is already thick with humidity, promising another scorching Pittsburgh summer day. Gordie tugs impatiently, eager for his morning routine despite the heat.

The crumpled statement from Brian sits on my counter, next to my handwritten notes—what I want to say at today's press conference. Words about mental health, vulnerability, and the pressure cooker of professional sports. Not the sanitized corporate apology Brian crafted.

"Come on, buddy," I murmur to Gordie. "Let's get you situated."

Outside, the neighborhood is coming alive. Kim waters her flower beds in a caftan, and LeMarcus is shooting hoops, already sweating in the morning heat.

"Morning, Alder!" Kim calls, giving Gordie a wide berth. She's never quite warmed to my peculiar-looking dog. "Beautiful day, isn't it?"

I force a smile and wave. "Sure is."

LeMarcus abandons his basketball to jog over. "Yo, A-Stag. How's it hanging?"

"Low and to the left," I reply automatically, earning an eye roll.

"Man, you have been moping since your roommate bounced," LeMarcus says, dropping into step beside me. "She coming back or what?"

The direct question catches me off guard. "It's complicated."

"Adult relationships usually are," Kim chimes in, proving she's been eavesdropping. "That woman had a glow about her when she was living with you."

I grunt noncommittally, not wanting to discuss Lena with my neighbors. Not today, when I'm hours away from seeing her again at the press conference. I follow Gordie as he circles a tree, looking for the perfect spot.

My phone buzzes in my pocket. Brian, predictably:

> Remember the script. No improvising.

I stare at the message for a long moment. I'm exhausted, but I know I can't read the statement Brian drafted. I also can't continue like this, seeing Lena at work, not kissing her, not pulling her into my arms. She is the one with the unique skills here, and she can't afford to lose this job.

So, I pull up stats on teams within driving distance of Pittsburgh. Cleveland. Columbus. Hell, Detroit is only five hours away. I start to wonder how quickly Brian could get me traded. I'd have to live away from my twin, from my family. From Lena. But the weekend visits would be worth it.

I am considering texting Brian about setting up a trade. I envision the steps afterward … leaving the team. Leaving the city that's always been my home. Can I bear it?

For Lena, yes. In a heartbeat.

But would she even want that sacrifice? Would she accept

it, knowing what the Fury means to me? I would make that trade if it meant keeping her in my life as a partner. Hockey is what I do, but Lena is becoming who I am.

I lie on the floor next to my dog and ask his opinion on moving. He stares at me like I'm nuts. "Well," I tell him. "Something's going to change tomorrow. Not sure what, but I'm at least going to tell the truth."

My new suit fits perfectly, as expected. The Stag brothers have kept the same tailor for years—an older Serbian man specializing in fitting enormous athletes. Even Tucker, who hates dressing up, admits that Gregor's suits make us look "less like hulking monsters, more like James Bond on growth hormones."

I adjust the jacket, checking my bruised jaw in the mirror. The discoloration has faded to a yellowish purple, still visible but no longer the angry red it was days ago. My knuckles have healed faster—the joys of access to professional medical support.

My phone rings—Brian again as if sensing my wavering commitment to his sanitized statement.

"Morning, sunshine," I answer.

"Tell me you're going to stick to the script." No greeting, just straight to the point. Classic Brian.

"Good morning to you too, Brian. Yes, I slept well, thanks for asking."

"Cut the crap, A-Stag. This is about damage control. Say the words, look contrite, move on. Don't you want a milk ad like your brother?"

I sink onto the edge of my bed, Gordie immediately jumping up to lay his head in my lap. "What if there's something more important than damage control?"

A long, exasperated sigh comes through the speaker. "There isn't. Not in professional sports."

"Maybe there should be."

"Save the philosophy for off-season charity galas—oh wait, you punched someone at the last one." Brian's tone sharpens. "Just stick to the script, Alder. Please."

I end the call without promising anything, which will drive him crazy. Good. Let him sweat a little.

My phone buzzes with a text from Tucker:

> Don't let Brian neuter you. Say what you need to say. We've got your back.

I smile and type back:

> Thanks, Fucker. See you there?

His response is immediate:

> Front row. Gun too. Even called Dad and Odin to watch online.

The support of my family steadies me as I finish getting ready. Whatever I decide to say today, I won't be standing alone.

The Fury facility has more media presence than I expected for what should be a routine disciplinary press conference. News vans from all the local stations crowd the parking lot, and a cluster of reporters hover near the entrance like vultures waiting for something to die.

"Quite the turnout," I mutter as I navigate them, ignoring shouted questions.

Once inside, I'm immediately intercepted by Melissa Chen, the team's PR director. Her expression is a familiar mix of professionalism and barely concealed stress.

"There's been a change to the program," she says, walking briskly beside me toward the conference room. "Dr. Sinclair will be presenting a new player safety initiative after your statement."

My step falters. "Lena will be there?"

Melissa gives me a sharp look at the familiarity but continues smoothly. "Dr. Sinclair will speak about a new mouthguard program for the youth hockey camp. You'll speak first about your community service. Then, she'll present her initiative. You'll both take questions afterward."

I nod, trying to process this unexpected development. I'd prepared myself to face the media, to decide whether to read Brian's statement or speak my truth. I hadn't prepared to do it with Lena in the room, watching me.

I catch a glimpse of her through the glass wall of a side conference room. She's seated at a table, surrounded by communication staff, reviewing notes. Her dark hair is pulled back, and she's wearing a black suit that somehow makes her look both professional and achingly beautiful.

As if sensing my gaze, she looks up. Our eyes meet briefly through the glass before we both look away, the moment electric despite its brevity.

"You're in here," Melissa says, opening a door to a smaller room. "We start in twenty minutes. Your agent said he's on his way."

Left alone, I pace the small space, alternating between reviewing Brian's script and my notes. The words swim before my eyes, my thoughts repeatedly drifting to Lena. Will she stay for my statement? Will she listen to what I have to say? Will it matter to her?

The door opens, and Gunnar and Tucker enter, both in suits that suggest they've come straight from a meeting with their financial advisor.

"You look like you're about to skate into Game 7 without a cup," Tucker says by way of greeting.

Gunnar studies my expression with more seriousness. "Whatever you're planning, just make sure you're ready for the consequences."

I stop pacing, looking between my brothers. "What if the consequences are worth it?"

They exchange a glance that speaks volumes about their familiarity with my stubborn streaks.

"Then you'll have no regrets," Gunnar says simply.

The door bursts open again, revealing Brian in a state of barely contained panic. "Five minutes. Stick to the script, A-Stag. I'm begging you."

I fold my notes and tuck them inside my jacket. "I'll say what needs to be said."

Brian looks to my brothers for support but finds none. "You're all going to be the death of me," he mutters.

"Drama queen," Tucker coughs into his fist.

Charles Sutton stands at the podium, his practiced owner's smile firmly in place as he addresses the assembled media.

"...commitment to the highest standards of conduct from every member of our organization," he's saying as I tune back in. "The Pittsburgh Fury believes in accountability, which is why Alder Stag has agreed to apologize for his actions and commit to community service with our youth hockey program."

I'm seated at a long table to the side of the podium, acutely aware of Lena, who is several seats away. She hasn't looked at me since we entered the room, her attention fixed on Sutton or her notes.

"Now, I'll turn the microphone over to Alder Stag." Sutton gestures toward me, his expression making it clear this is my one chance at redemption.

As I approach the podium, the weight of multiple expectations pressing down on me: Brian's desperate face in the corner, my brothers' supportive presence in the front row, Sutton's stern vigilance, and Lena, whose expression I can feel but don't dare look at directly.

I pull out Brian's statement and place it on the podium. The words stare back at me, hollow and impersonal. *I deeply regret my actions at the Black and Gold Charity Gala. My behavior fell short of the standards expected of a Pittsburgh Fury player...*

I look up at the assembled media, cameras trained on my face and recorders capturing every word. Then, I set the paper aside.

"I was supposed to read you an apology that someone else wrote," I begin. "About regrettable actions and commitment to sportsmanship. But that wouldn't be honest, and you deserve honesty."

A murmur ripples through the room. I see Brian cover his face with his hands in my peripheral vision.

"Yes, I hit Adam Lawson at the charity gala. No, it wasn't professional or appropriate. I take full responsibility for that action and accept the consequences."

I pause, feeling the familiar pre-game focus settling over me. This isn't a script anymore. This is real.

"But I'm not here to just apologize for losing my temper. I'm here to talk about something more important—the mental health of athletes."

Another ripple through the crowd, this one accompanied by the rapid clicking of cameras.

"When I first joined the Fury, I was twenty-one years old. I'd spent my entire life focused on hockey, defined by hockey. And suddenly, I was in the spotlight, not just as a player but as one of the first openly bisexual men in the league."

I can feel Lena's attention now, a subtle shift in her posture that draws my gaze briefly before I continue.

"I met someone who seemed to understand the pressures I was facing. Someone who, I later realized, was skilled at recognizing vulnerabilities and abusing them."

I'm careful not to accuse Adam of emotional manipulation directly but to make it clear that the relationship wasn't healthy. I take a big breath and turn the paper over. "In recent days, my identity as a bisexual man has been questioned and weaponized against me. Let me be absolutely clear: Who I date doesn't change who I am. Bisexuality doesn't disappear when you're with someone of any gender. It's not a phase, and it's not a publicity stunt.

"This isn't an excuse for my actions. It's context. Hockey players are conditioned to push through pain, to never show weakness. We're taught that emotions are a liability."

I look directly at my brothers now, drawing strength from their presence.

"But they're not. They're human. And pretending otherwise doesn't make us better athletes—it just makes us more dangerous to ourselves and others. Part of being truthful about my emotions means confronting the harmful stereotypes that bisexual people face. The idea that we're somehow less committed to the LGBTQ community based on who we're dating is deeply damaging - not just to me, but to every young athlete watching who might be questioning their own identity."

I shift gears, moving to safer territory. "That's why I'm actually excited about this community service. These kids deserve to learn not just how to play hockey, but how to be whole people who happen to play hockey."

Sutton is nodding slightly, which I take as a good sign. Coach Thompson, standing near the back, looks surprisingly approving.

"The Fury organization is already leading the way in physical player safety. I hope we can lead the way in player's emotional safety, too."

Now, I allow myself to look directly at Lena for the first time during my speech.

"We're fortunate to have professionals like Dr. Sinclair who are innovating in player protection. Her work protects our bodies. Now, we need to do the same for our minds."

Our eyes meet briefly, and something passes between us—understanding, perhaps—or at least acknowledgment.

"I'm sorry for letting my emotions manifest in a physical way. That's not who I want to be. Not the example I want to set. But I'm not sorry for having those emotions. None of us should be."

I take a breath, concluding my unscripted remarks. "I'm looking forward to working with these kids and being part of an organization that values the whole player—body and mind. And I'm proud of the Fury's commitment to protecting our athletes at every level."

Lena rises, approaching the podium with professional composure. She gives me a small smile and I wish I could kiss her so badly. Instead, I step back, taking the seat she vacated, and watch as she presents her mouthguard program with confidence and expertise. Pride wells in my chest, alongside a deep ache of longing. She's brilliant, passionate, and completely in her element. The media is responding enthusiastically, and I notice both Sutton and Thompson nodding along with her points.

Brian slides into the seat beside me, his expression a mix of relief and lingering annoyance. "That wasn't the script," he whispers, "but... it wasn't a disaster. Nice work tackling the bi-erasure."

"I wasn't playing an angle," I reply quietly. "I meant it."

He studies me for a moment, then sighs. "I know. That's why it worked."

Lena concludes her presentation, and the moderator opens the floor for questions. Most are about the mouthguard program, and some are about my community service. I answer the questions directed to me as honestly as possible without drifting into territory that might make the organization uncomfortable.

Then, a reporter from the Press-Gazette stands. "Mr. Stag, your comments seemed to reference issues between you and Adam Lawson. Care to elaborate?"

I lean toward the microphone. "The particulars of my love life aren't relevant to today's announcements. What's important is the work we're doing with youth hockey and player safety."

The reporter doesn't look satisfied but sits down. Another immediately rises, this one from a local TV station. She directs her question to Lena.

"It's interesting that Mr. A Stag brings up the Fury stance on player bodies *and* minds. Dr. Sinclair, there's been speculation about your personal relationship with Mr. A Stag. How do you respond?"

The room goes silent, all eyes turning to Lena. I hold my breath, knowing whatever she says next could change everything.

CHAPTER 34
LENA

THE REPORTER'S QUESTION HANGS IN THE AIR, A TICKING BOMB waiting to detonate my carefully constructed professional facade. The conference room falls silent, all eyes turning to me. I can feel Alder's gaze from where he sits at the table, the weight of his attention almost physical.

Time seems to stretch as I consider my options. Should I deny everything? Should I stick to the sterile script of "we're colleagues, nothing more"? Should I redirect to the mouth-guard program and ignore the personal question entirely?

Sarah's words from last night flashes in my mind: *Your career and your heart both matter.*

In this suspended moment, I realize that whatever I say next will define both my professional standing and my personal future. The path of least resistance would be to deny, deflect, and maintain the safe distance I've been struggling to create.

But I'm tired of shrinking myself, of making myself smaller to fit the spaces others allow me.

I take a measured breath, straighten my posture, and lean toward the microphone.

"My relationship with Mr. Stag is both professional and personal," I begin, my voice steadier than expected. "As professionals, we maintain appropriate boundaries in the workplace."

A murmur ripples through the media section. I continue more confidently.

"However, I won't deny that we've developed a friendship outside of work. It initially formed from shared emotional trauma, but developed because we understand one another in ways that make us well-rounded people." I glance briefly toward management, gauging their reaction. Sutton's expression remains neutral, but Coach Thompson's eyebrows rise slightly.

"What matters today is that both Mr. Stag and I are committed to player safety—physical and mental—within this organization. The mouthguard program represents a significant advance in how we protect our athletes, and I'd prefer to focus on those innovations."

I begin to pivot back to the technical aspects of the concussion sensors, ready to redirect the conversation away from personal territory, when Alder unexpectedly leans forward in his seat, grabbing the microphone. His expression is composed, but his eyes are intense.

"I'd like to add something, if I may," he says, his deep voice reverberating. "Dr. Sinclair has demonstrated nothing but the highest professional standards since joining this organization. She greets our athletes with empathy and skill. I'm not going to lie. Hockey is brutal on teeth, and our smiles are such an important part of our lives off the ice."

He pauses, and I can see him making a decision, crossing some internal threshold.

"On a personal note, her presence in my life has made me a better player and person." His gaze finds mine across the room, direct and unflinching. "Hockey is about the whole athlete—mind, body, and heart. I believe our organization understands this better than most."

My breath catches in my throat as he continues.

"I know I play better, more effectively, when I'm whole. When I'm not compartmentalizing or suppressing parts of myself, that's why I came out, with the full support of my team, and it's why I'm coming out now as having found a person I want to be with long term."

The room has gone utterly still, every reporter sensing the significance of what's happening. This isn't just about a fight at a charity gala anymore. It's about something much more fundamental.

"In fact," Alder continues, "I've asked the team's legal counsel to review personnel policies to ensure all players, including myself, are carefully considered when I pursue this relationship with Dr. Sinclair. Which," and here he winks. Winks! "As I said earlier, the specifics of my love life are not up for discussion today."

I feel a rush of emotion at his declaration, fighting to maintain my professional composure even as something shifts dramatically inside me. No one has ever spoken about me this way—as someone who makes them better, stronger, more whole.

The moderator quickly steps in, sensing the moment has become too charged for a standard press conference.

"Thank you, Mr. Stag, Dr. Sinclair. This concludes our formal statements. Press packets with additional information on the community service initiative and the mouthguard program are available at the back of the room."

There's scattered applause as the press conference officially ends, immediately followed by a surge of reporters trying to get follow-up questions. The PR team creates a buffer, Melissa Chen efficiently directing staff to escort Alder and me to separate side rooms.

As I'm led away, I catch Alder's eyes across the chaos of bodies and cameras. Something unspoken passes between us —an acknowledgment that whatever happens next, something significant has changed.

. . .

"Well, that was certainly interesting."

I turn to find Sarah standing in the doorway of the small conference room where the PR team had deposited me "to decompress." She dismisses the remaining staff member with a coach's authority and closes the door behind her.

"Did I just end my career?" I ask the adrenaline of the press conference finally giving way to anxiety.

Sarah smiles, leaning against the table. "No. You just started being honest about your life."

"Is there a difference in professional sports?"

"More than you'd think." She crosses her arms, studying me. "For what it's worth, I thought you handled that perfectly. Professional but authentic."

I sink into a chair, the weight of the morning catching up with me. "What happens now?"

"Professionally? Not sure." Sarah takes the seat across from me. "It's true that Alder asked Tim Stag to take a look at our policies. Well…first, he apparently called demanding we trade him to Columbus." She rolls her eyes, and I gasp, horrified at the idea of him moving away from his team and family.

Noting my reaction, Sarah laughs. "I promise, Alder Stag isn't going anywhere. Well, at least not without his twin and a very high transfer fee."

"What…" I shake my head as if the thoughts rolling around were physical shapes that need to settle. "What, um, happens in other teams? With romantic relationships?"

Something flickers across her face—a quick, carefully concealed reaction. "It's tricky. Pro sports is a unique environment, and it's not easy to prevent abuses of power. Ensure athletes aren't pressured or coerced by those with authority over them."

The subtext is clear. As a coach, Sarah's situation with

whoever she's involved with is far more complicated than mine with Alder.

"So I'm not getting canned for admitting I have a personal relationship with a player?"

"No. But there will be guidelines. Boundaries." She straightens as a knock sounds on the door. "And I think you're about to hear about those now."

The door opens to reveal Melissa Chen. "Dr. Sinclair? Mr. Sutton and Coach Thompson would like to speak with you in the main conference room."

Sarah encourages me as I stand: "Remember what I said last night. Balance is hard, but not impossible."

The walk to the conference room feels like the longest of my life, each step carrying me toward what I assume will be a professional reckoning. To my surprise, when I enter, both Sutton and Thompson stand to greet me, their expressions not nearly as severe as I expected.

"Dr. Sinclair," Sutton says, gesturing to a chair. "Thank you for speaking with us."

I sit, hands folded in my lap to hide their slight tremor. "Of course."

"I want to start by saying your mouthguard presentation was excellent," Sutton begins. "The board is extremely enthusiastic about implementing the program."

"Thank you," I say cautiously, waiting for the other shoe to drop.

Thompson leans forward. "We also appreciate your honesty out there. Handling personal questions in a professional setting is never easy."

Sutton nods in agreement. "As mentioned, we've evaluated our organizational policies with legal counsel. Your... situation with Alder Stag has highlighted areas that need updating."

He slides a folder across the table to me. Inside are several documents, topped by what appears to be a formal disclosure form.

"Tim Stag has been particularly vocal about modernizing our approach," Thompson explains. "He's been quite insistent on these revisions, meeting with player advocates and industry experts."

"Mental health and well-being weren't always part of the conversation." Sutton sucks on his teeth as I open the folder.

I scan the documents, my heart rate gradually slowing as I realize this isn't a termination meeting.

"If you choose to pursue a personal relationship with a player," Thompson says carefully, "these are the professional boundaries we'd expect: disclosure, recusal from certain medical decisions, and regular check-ins with HR."

"We're not in the business of controlling our employees' personal lives," Sutton adds. "But we do need to ensure that professional integrity is maintained."

I look up from the papers, hardly daring to believe what I'm hearing. "So I'm not being fired?"

Thompson laughs at that. "Fired? We just announced your mouthguard program to the media. The timing would be terrible."

"Not to mention," Sutton adds, more seriously, "we value your contributions, Dr. Sinclair. Trust me, it's not easy to find a dentist who can handle the mouth trauma we see out here. And Alder Stag is one of our most valuable players, and he was right about one thing—he plays better when he's whole."

The meeting concludes with specifics about the mouthguard program implementation and a timeline for the policy revisions. As I turn to leave, the door opens, revealing Tim Stag himself in an impeccably tailored suit, tablet in hand, and an uncharacteristic grin spreading across his usually serious face.

"Charles, you might want to see this," he says, striding

into the room and placing the tablet on the conference table. "Public response is... significant."

Sutton frowns, pulling the tablet closer. "What are we looking at here?"

"Social media reaction to the press conference. The clip of Alder and Dr. Sinclair has gone viral. Over two million views in the last forty minutes alone." Tim swipes to another screen. I can see the strong family resemblance to Alder and smile despite the gravity of the situation. "And this is the Fury's website traffic. It's crashed twice already."

Thompson leans in to look. "Is this bad press? Do we need to issue a statement?"

Tim's smile widens. "Quite the opposite. The fans are over-whelmingly supportive. Hashtag 'FuryLove' is trending nationally, with all the Pride flag emojis. Some industrious fan has begun 3D printing fake teeth with little A's and L's on them."

Sutton scrolls through the tablet, eyebrows climbing higher. "This is... unexpected."

"There's more." Tim pulls his phone from his pocket. "The switchboard is being flooded with calls. The email server crashed about ten minutes ago. Most are variations on the same theme—don't stand in the way of the dentist and the defender."

I feel my face heating as I realize they're discussing public reaction to my relationship with Alder.

"Seems your policy review came just in time, Tim," Sutton says dryly. "I guess the fans have spoken."

Tim slips his phone back into his pocket. "Funny how quickly public sentiment can clarify organizational values, right?" He turns to me, extending his hand. "Dr. Sinclair, welcome to the family, so to speak. I believe my nephew is waiting for you."

Confused but cautiously optimistic, I thank them and exit the conference room. As I walk through the facility halls, staff members smile at me knowingly, and a few give me a thumbs up or say quiet congratulations.

What is happening?

The parking lot is nearly empty when I reach it, most of the staff and media have left. I'm halfway to my car when I spot a familiar figure leaning against it, hands in pockets, expression uncertain.

Alder straightens as I approach, his suit jacket discarded, tie loosened—the corporate veneer slipping away to reveal the man I've missed so desperately.

We stand facing each other, the space between us charged with everything said and unsaid at the press conference.

"I'm sorry," he begins, "for speaking about you without permission. I should have—"

"You said you play better when you're whole," I interrupt. "What did you mean?"

He blinks, then his expression shifts to something more open, more vulnerable. "I meant that I'm better at everything when you're in my life. Happier. More focused. More... me."

The simplicity of his answer, the raw honesty of it, makes my chest ache.

I press a palm to his face, his skin smooth and soft. "You told them to trade you." My voice is a cracked whisper.

He purses his lips. "That was impulsive. And they shot that idea down real quick. Turns out it's better to address the actual problem head-on."

"I have something to show you," I say, pulling the folder from my bag. I hand him the disclosure forms, watching as he scans them, understanding dawning in his eyes.

"Management gave me these. It's not either/or, Alder. It's complicated, but possible." I take a breath. "There's a path forward if we want it."

He looks up from the papers, hope and caution warring in his expression. "So where does that leave us?"

The question hangs between us, encompassing so much more than this moment, this parking garage, this day of revelations.

"It leaves us with a choice," I say, my voice steady despite my racing heart. "And I think I'm ready to make mine."

I step forward, closing the distance I've been so careful to maintain. His hands come up instinctively to steady me, warm and solid against my waist.

"I've spent my whole life making myself smaller," I whisper. "For Brad. For my mother. For my career. I don't want to do that anymore."

Alder's eyes never leave mine, intense and blue and full of a longing that matches mine. "You should never be anything but exactly who you are, Lena. That's who I—" He stops and swallows. "That's who I've fallen for."

The word hangs unspoken between us: fallen. Not a summer fling. Not a convenient arrangement. Something real and lasting and worth fighting for.

A small commotion draws my attention past Alder's shoulder. To my astonishment, a group of fans has gathered at the edge of the parking lot, some holding hastily made signs. "Hockey Heart Healer" reads one. "Let The Fury Love!" proclaims another.

"What in the world?" I murmur.

Alder glances behind him, shaking his head with a bemused smile. "Fury fans move fast." He turns back to me, his expression serious despite the growing crowd. "Does it bother you? The attention?"

I consider this, watching as more fans arrive, most keeping a respectful distance but making their support clear. A few months ago, this kind of public scrutiny would have terrified me and sent me retreating into invisibility.

But today, I find I don't mind being seen. Not if I'm being seen with him.

A cheer erupts from the crowd as he pulls me into his arms, lips finding mine in a kiss that feels like coming home. The sound barely registers—all I can focus on is Alder, solid and real against me, his hands steady on my waist, his heartbeat strong beneath my palm.

When we finally break apart, breathless and laughing, he rests his forehead against mine. "That was very unprofessional, Dr. Sinclair."

"I have paperwork," I remind him with a smile. "We're allowed now."

More fans have gathered, and their cheers are a soundtrack to this moment that feels entirely private and strangely public. But for once, I don't feel the need to make myself smaller, to hide from view. With Alder's arm around me, I think it is exactly the right size.

The word hangs unspoken between us: love. Not a summer fling. Not a convenient arrangement. Something real and lasting and worth fighting for.

I reach up and grip his shoulders. "Take me home, Alder."

CHAPTER 35
ALDER

I can't stop looking at her. All the way to my townhouse, I steal glances at Lena in the passenger seat—the curve of her jaw, her fingers tap nervously against her thigh, the slight smile that appears and disappears as she processes everything that just happened. Neither of us speaks, the air between us electric with anticipation. We've said what matters in front of cameras and management; now we need to say the rest with our bodies.

Gordie greets us at the door with the appropriate enthusiasm, his entire body wiggling with joy. He circles Lena's legs, whining and snuffling, ecstatic that she's back where he believes she belongs.

"I think someone missed you," I say, the first words either of us has spoken since leaving the parking garage.

"I missed him too," Lena says, crouching to scratch behind Gordie's ears. When she looks up at me, her eyes are bright with emotion. "I missed both of you."

The press conference feels like it happened in another lifetime. The carefully worded statements, the professional posturing, the tension of waiting for consequences—all of it fades in the face of this moment. Lena, back in my home. Our home, if she wants it to be.

"Are you hungry?" I ask because I need to say something... anything to keep from grabbing her right here in the entryway.

She straightens, stepping closer to me. "Not for food."

My breath catches in my throat. Gordie, oblivious to the tension building between us, chooses this moment to bring over his favorite chew toy, dropping it at our feet with an expectant woof.

"Not now, buddy," I tell him, not taking my eyes off Lena.

"We should probably..." she begins.

"Yeah," I agree, understanding immediately.

I scoop up Gordie, who protests with a confused whine, and carry him to my bedroom. I grab his favorite treats from the dresser, scatter them on the floor, and then add his second-favorite toy for good measure.

"Stay," I tell him firmly, backing out of the room and closing the door.

The soft click of the latch is like a starting gun. When I turn, Lena is there, just steps away in the hallway, her eyes dark with want. We stare at each other for one suspended moment, the last thread of restraint stretched between us.

Then she moves. Her hands come up to my chest, pushing me back against the wall with surprising force. I go willingly, my back hitting the framed family photos with a thud.

"I've missed you so much," she whispers against my mouth, and then she's kissing me, fierce and claiming.

I respond instantly, my hands framing her face, then sliding into her hair, destroying whatever professional style she'd carefully created this morning. She tastes like she is coming home after too long away.

The kiss deepens, months of longing and forced separation disappearing as our bodies remember each other. Her tongue slides against mine, and I groan, pulling her closer until there's not a whisper of space between us. She can feel exactly what she does to me, how quickly she brings me to aching hardness.

"Bedroom," I manage between kisses, though I'm already working at the buttons of her blouse.

"Too far," she gasps as my lips find her neck, her head tipping back to give me better access.

She's right. Ten steps to what was once her room—it might as well be miles. We're not going to make it.

My hands slide under her thighs, lifting her against me. Her legs wrap around my waist as I spin us, pressing her against the opposite wall. Frames rattle. Something falls. Neither of us cares.

We sink to the floor in a tangle of limbs and half-removed clothing. My tie is strangling me, and my jacket is twisted behind me like a straitjacket. Lena isn't faring much better; her blouse is hanging open but caught at her wrists, and her skirt hikes up around her hips.

I curse as I yank at my tie, somehow making the knot tighter. Lena laughs, the sound turning to a gasp as I give up on the tie and palm her breast through her bra instead.

"Let me," she says, reaching for the tie. Her fingers deftly loosen the knot that had defeated me, sliding the silk free from my collar.

The moment of pause allows me to look at her—hair mussed, lips swollen from my kisses, blouse falling open to reveal the curves I imagined. She's more beautiful than my memory, more real. And she's choosing to be here with me.

"You're gorgeous," I tell her, my voice rough.

"So are you," she says, working at the buttons of my shirt. "But you're wearing too many clothes."

We're not gentle with each other. Can't be, after everything. This isn't the tender exploration of our first time together or the comfortable familiarity of the mornings that followed. This is claiming. Reclaiming. A physical declaration of what we've both finally admitted we want.

My shirt joins my tie and jacket on the hallway floor. Her blouse and bra follow. My hands slide up her thighs, pushing her skirt higher, finding the edge of her underwear—simple black cotton that somehow drives me crazier than any lace could.

"These need to go," I mutter, hooking my fingers in the waistband and dragging them down her legs.

She kicks them away, then reaches for my belt, her fingers clumsy with urgency. "Fair is fair."

I help her, lifting my hips to shove my pants and boxers down, not bothering to take them all the way off. I need her too badly for finesse.

But when I move to climb over her, she plants a hand on my chest, holding me back. "Not yet."

Confused, I pause. "Lena?"

Her eyes are dark and determined. "I want to taste you first."

The words send a jolt of heat through me. But as she starts to move down my body, I catch her shoulders, gently stopping her.

"Me first," I say, and before she can protest, I shift our positions, laying her back on the hallway floor.

I take my time with her body, even as my own throbs with need. I press kisses to her neck, her collarbones, the soft swell of her breasts. She arches beneath me, hands in my hair, trying to direct me where she wants me.

"Patience," I murmur against her skin, though I have none myself.

When I finally reach her thighs, I can't help myself. I've fantasized about this since the day she moved out—about marking her pale skin, leaving evidence of my possession that only we would know about. I bite down, not hard enough to hurt but firm enough to leave a mark.

She cries out, but not in protest. Her hands tighten in my hair, pulling me closer rather than pushing me away. I do it again, a little higher, a little harder. The sound she makes is primal and needy.

"More," she demands, and it unlocks something savage inside me.

I've always been careful with lovers, mindful of my size and strength. But Lena isn't fragile and doesn't want me to be gentle right now. She wants the defender, the man who protects what's his on the ice and off it.

I nip and suck at the tender skin of her inner thighs, painting a constellation of marks that bloom pink and then darker beneath my mouth. Each one draws a gasp or moan from her, her thick legs falling wider to give me better access.

When I finally move higher, tasting her where she's wet and wanting, she nearly flies off the floor. Her back arches beautifully, a string of curses falling from her lips that would make my teammates blush.

I grip her hips, holding her in place as I devour her. There's no teasing, no drawing it out—just relentless pressure and rhythm that has her climbing toward release with stunning speed.

"Alder," she gasps, her thighs trembling against my shoulders. "I'm going to—"

"Let go," I urge against her most sensitive spot. "Let me feel you."

Her orgasm crashes through her with an intensity that surprises us both. She cries out my name, her body shaking, hands fisted in my hair almost painfully. I work her through it, easing only when she tugs me away, suddenly oversensitive.

I rise to my knees, lifting her with me. We're still in the hallway, half-clothed and fully desperate. I want more space and more comfort for what comes next.

"Living room," I decide, scooping her into my arms.

She comes willingly, wrapping around me as I carry her the short distance to the larger space. I lay her on the soft rug in front of the couch, taking a moment to admire the mess I've made of her.

This time, I take a more measured approach. I kiss each part of her methodically, relearning the geography of her body. The curve of her waist, the soft plane of her stomach, the undersides of her breasts. She watches me through heavy-lidded eyes, letting me explore without rushing me.

"I missed touching you," I confess between kisses. "Missed the way you feel under my hands."

"Show me," she whispers.

I slide my fingers between her legs, finding her still sensitive but already building toward another peak. Her breath hitches as I circle her most sensitive spot, then dip lower to tease her entrance.

"Yes," she hisses, her hips lifting to meet my touch.

I work her with my fingers, watching her face as pleasure builds again. She's more vocal now, less inhibited, directing me with words and movements. More of me. Faster. Harder. There.

Her second orgasm is slower to build but stronger when it hits. Her inner muscles clench around my fingers as she pulses and shudders. I press my lips to her neck, feeling her pulse race beneath my mouth.

"You're incredible," I murmur against her skin.

She comes down slowly, her breathing gradually steadying. When she opens her eyes, they are filled with new determination.

"My turn," she says, pushing at my shoulders.

I allow her to maneuver me onto my back, curious to see what she has in mind. She straddles my thighs, her hands splayed across my chest. I'm almost painfully hard, have been since we started, but I don't rush her.

She explores me with the same thoroughness I showed her, tracing the contours of my muscles, the ridges of old scars, and the fresh bruises from stick work with my brothers.

Her touch is both reverent and possessive, claiming me as hers as surely as I marked her.

I'm suddenly overcome with a need to connect with Lena. I reach for her, pulling her up for a kiss that says everything I can't find words for.

When we break apart, she's breathing hard, her pupils dilated with desire. "I want you," she says. "Now."

"How do you want me?" I ask, needing to hear her say it.

"Inside me." She shifts, straddling my hips. "Like this."

I groan as she positions herself above me, the head of my cock brushing against her heat. "Wait," I manage. "Protection—"

"I'm on birth control," she says. "And there hasn't been anyone but you, Alder."

I look up at her, hardly daring to believe what she's suggesting. "Are you sure?"

Her answer is to lower herself slightly, letting me feel how wet she is, how ready. "I want to feel all of you, Alder. No barriers."

The thought nearly undoes me. We never did this before—always used condoms, always played it safe. The idea of being inside her with nothing between us makes my cock twitch eagerly.

"Come here first," I say, tugging her higher up my body.

She looks confused but follows my guidance until she's straddling my chest. I continue urging her forward until my meaning becomes clear.

"Oh," she breathes, eyes widening. "You don't have to—"

"I want to drown in this body," I assure her, my hands on her hips guiding her the rest of the way. "Ride my face, Lena."

She blushes but doesn't resist, carefully positioning herself above my mouth. I pull her down that final inch, my tongue finding her immediately. The angle is different, deeper, letting me taste her more fully.

She braces herself against the couch, her plush thighs

trembling on either side of my head as I work her toward a third orgasm. This one builds slower, more deliberately. I take my time, exploring every fold and hollow, enjoying what makes her moan and what makes her curse my name.

I've got my hands on her ass, palming that amazing soft skin. When she comes, it's with a deep, guttural sound that I feel in my bones. Her body shakes above me, one hand fisted in my hair, her thighs clamping around my ears. I stay with her through it, easing only when she tugs at my hair in a wordless signal.

She slides down my body, kissing me deeply, tasting herself on my lips. Then she reaches between us, taking me in hand, positioning me at her entrance.

"I'm yours," I tell her, needing her to know. "Always have been."

She sinks onto me with agonizing slowness, both of us gasping as I fill her. Nothing has ever felt like this—the wet heat of her surrounding me, no latex barrier dulling the sensation. I can feel every flutter of her inner muscles, every heartbeat.

For a moment, neither of us moves, overwhelmed by the connection. Then she rolls her hips experimentally, and I groan, my hands flying to her waist.

"Fuck, Lena. You feel incredible."

She smiles a slow, wicked curve of her lips and does it again. "So do you."

We find our rhythm quickly, her rising and falling as I thrust up to meet her. The familiar choreography of our bodies coming together, but deeper, more intense. I'm not going to last, not with how long I've waited for this, how good she feels.

"I'm close," I warn her, my hands tightening on her hips.

Instead of speeding up, she lifts off me entirely. Before I can protest, her hand wraps around the base of my cock, stroking firmly.

"Come for me," she says, her eyes locked with mine. "I want to see you. I want you all over me."

The words trigger something primal. I buck into her hand, my release building at the base of my spine.

"I'm going to—"my own roar cuts me off as I come harder than I can ever remember, painting her stomach and breasts with long stripes of white.

She continues stroking me, drawing out every last pulse until I'm completely spent. When I can focus again, I look up to see her watching me with awe and satisfaction.

"Christ, Lena," I breathe. "You're incredible."

She smiles, a slight flush highlighting her cheekbones. "So are you."

I reach for her, pulling her down to lie beside me on the rug. We're both sticky and sweaty, but I can't bear to be separated from her yet. I trace lazy patterns on her skin, unable to stop touching her.

In the distance, I can hear Gordie scratching at the bedroom door, probably wondering why he's been banished while we're clearly having fun without him. I pause my hand where it's stroking Lena's back. "Okay, if we relocate to the bed?"

She nods against my chest. "I think I can make it. In a minute."

With a groan and tremendous effort, I stand, then I bend and scoop her up, carrying her down the hall, mess and all, to deposit her in our bed. Gordie joins us and immediately passes out near my feet, snoring. "Very romantic," I whisper to Lena.

"I don't want to be anywhere but here," she says quietly, her head resting on my chest.

I tighten my arm around her, pressing a kiss to her hair. "Then stay. Forever."

She looks up at me, her eyes soft with emotion. She smiles and kisses me with a nod.

CHAPTER 36
LENA

FIVE WEEKS LATER

"Here we are," Alder says, the car tires crunching on gravel as we pull up to the Stag family ski house.

My breath catches at the sight of it. "Cabin" was the word Alder used, but this is no cabin. The structure rises from the mountainside with multi-story windows reflecting the late summer sunset, a sprawling edifice of wood and stone that commands the hillside.

"This is stunning," I whisper, watching Gordie's nose press against the car window, his tail wagging furiously.

Alder parks and claps his hands. "Wait until you see inside," he says, squeezing my hand before getting out to retrieve our bags.

I follow him up the stone path, Gordie racing ahead to sniff every bush and tree. When Alder pushes open the massive wooden door, I enter a great room with vaulted ceilings that soar two stories high. A wall of windows provides a breathtaking view of the mountain. A stone fireplace dominates one wall, with a comfortable-looking leather sectional arranged around it. The space flows into an impressive kitchen with a granite island and an enormous wooden table that could easily seat twenty people.

"This is where you vacation?" I ask, trying not to gape.

Alder grins, setting down our bags. "Dad and his brothers all bought it when my Uncle Tim turned 40." He moves toward a wall panel, pressing buttons illuminating the space and starting a fire in the fireplace with a gentle whoosh.

"Nice touch," I say, admiring the flames.

Gordie has already claimed a spot on the rug before the fire, circling three times before flopping down with a contented sigh.

"Smart dog," I murmur, joining Alder in the kitchen as he starts unpacking groceries. "Can I help?"

"You can open this," he says, handing me a bottle of wine. "I checked the calendar three times to make sure we'd have the place to ourselves. My brothers and cousins have a bad habit of showing up unannounced."

I laugh, reaching for the wine opener he points out in a drawer. "Is that a common problem?"

"You have no idea. Wyatt once brought Fern here for a romantic weekend and ended up with half the family walking in while they were... occupied." Alder's eyes crinkle with mischief as he unpacks steaks for tomorrow.

"What did he do?"

"Tried to get them to leave, but they all sat around and ate breakfast while Fern tried not to explode." Alder takes the open wine and pours a glass on each of us. "To have the place all to ourselves," he says, clinking his glass against mine.

"To proper scheduling," I counter, taking a sip.

After we put away the groceries and had our wine, Alder gives me the full tour. The downstairs level boasts a theater room with plush recliners, a foosball table, and gaming consoles. Outside, there's a heated pool and a hot tub large enough for at least eight people. The upper floors contain bedrooms—some with bunks for cousins, others with king beds for the original Stag brothers and their partners.

"This one's ours...for now," Alder says, pushing open the door to reveal a spacious room with a king-sized bed and a private balcony overlooking the woods. Each door has a small chalkboard, and I watch Alder write "A Stag + Lena" in his surprisingly tidy handwriting.

I step inside, running my hand along the deer-patterned quilt that covers the bed. "It's perfect."

Alder wraps his arms around me from behind, resting his chin on my shoulder. "I've never brought anyone here before," he says quietly.

The admission sends warmth spreading through my chest. "Thank you for sharing it with me."

We unpack in comfortable silence, moving around each other with the ease of people who have learned each other's rhythms. I hang my clothes in the closet beside his and arrange my toiletries alongside his in the bathroom. Such simple acts of domesticity, yet each one feels significant—another thread binding us together.

Later, we eat a quick meal of pasta and salad at the counter, sharing stories and laughing as Gordie tries to convince us he's never been fed.

"I can see why you love it here," I say, glancing around at the secluded luxury of the space. "It feels... peaceful."

"It's my favorite place to recharge before the season starts," Alder admits. "No press, no pressure. Just mountains and quiet."

This easy companionship with Alder feels like breathing after years of suffocation.

"Want to try the pool?" he asks suddenly, eyes bright with boyish excitement.

I hesitate, thinking of how I'd look in a swimsuit, then catch myself. This is Alder, who has seen every inch of me, touches me with reverence, and never once made me feel anything but desired.

"Race you there," I say instead, and his delighted laugh follows me as I head to change.

. . .

The heated pool gleams under the moonlight, steam rising gently from its surface into the cool mountain air. Alder dives in with athletic grace, surfacing with water streaming from his golden hair. I cautiously enter via the steps, but the perfect temperature soon lures me deeper.

"Come here," he says, floating in the center. "Look up."

I paddle over and try to mimic his position but keep sinking.

"Like this," he says, sliding his hands beneath me, supporting my weight. "Relax your neck... that's it... now look."

I gaze upward and gasp. Away from the city and the stadium lights, the night sky spreads in infinite darkness, punctuated by stars that seem close enough to touch.

"It's incredible," I breathe, focusing on staying afloat as he slowly removes his supporting hands.

"You sure are," Alder murmurs, his lips finding my neck.

The water makes everything weightless and dreamlike. His hands roam my body as we float, kiss, and touch. When the heat between us builds too high, we move to the hot tub, where the jets pulse against our skin and steam rises around us like a private cloud.

Once properly pruned, we emerge from the water, wrapped in plush robes, and drink more wine by the fire, Gordie snoring at our feet. I tuck myself against Alder's side, marveling at how naturally we fit together—my curves against his angles, my softness against his hardness.

"Happy?" he asks, pressing a kiss to my temple.

"Perfectly," I answer, and I mean it.

I wake to sunlight streaming through the windows and the scent of coffee and bacon. Alder's side of the bed is empty but still warm. Wrapping myself in one of his T-shirts, I pad downstairs to find him in the kitchen, wearing only loose shorts, flipping pancakes on the griddle.

"Morning, beautiful," he says, sliding a mug of coffee across the counter to me.

"Morning," I reply, accepting the mug gratefully. Gordie trots over to greet me, his whole body wiggling with excitement.

"He's already been out," Alder says, nodding toward the dog. "Chased three squirrels and lost every time."

"Poor baby," I coo, scratching behind Gordie's ears. "Those mean squirrels don't play fair."

The domesticity of the moment strikes me—Alder cooking breakfast, Gordie at my feet, mountain sunshine spilling across the wooden floors. Six months ago, I wouldn't have believed this could be my life.

"So," Alder says, sliding a plate of pancakes in front of me, "I was thinking we could hike up to the ridge today. The view is incredible, and there's a little mountain pond for swimming if we get hot."

I sip my coffee, watching him move confidently around the kitchen. "Sounds perfect. Though I can't promise to keep up with your athlete pace."

"I like going at your pace," he says with a suggestive wink that makes me blush despite everything we've done together.

We eat breakfast discussing practical matters—the upcoming season schedule, my mother's impending first visit to meet the Stags, and my role in helping to interview sports psychologists for the Fury staff. The conversation flows easily, punctuated by Gordie's attempts to score fallen bits of bacon.

After we finish eating, I stand to help clear the dishes. We work side by side at the sink, Alder washing while I dry, our hips occasionally bumping in the comfortable choreography we've developed.

"This is nice," he says quietly, handing me a clean plate.

"The ski house?" I ask.

"All of it. Being here with you. Waking up together. The normal, everyday stuff." He rinses a glass, his expression thoughtful. "I never had this with Adam. He always kept me at a distance, emotionally and physically."

I set down the dish towel, turning to face him fully. "I know what you mean. With Brad, everything felt like a transaction. What could I do to earn his approval and his attention? It was exhausting."

Alder turns off the water, drying his hands before taking mine. "Thank you for taking a chance on us. On me. I know it wasn't easy with the team policies and everything."

"Best risk I've ever taken," I say honestly.

He cups my face with one hand, his thumb tracing my cheekbone. "I need you to know that this isn't temporary for me. I'm in love with you, Lena."

Though we've been living together for weeks and shared our bodies and lives, neither of us has said those words directly until now. Hearing them sends a cascade of emotions through me—joy, relief, and a lingering hint of fear that I push aside.

"I love you too," I say, the words coming easier than I expected. "So much that it terrifies me sometimes."

He leans his forehead against mine. "What terrifies you about it?"

"Loving someone means they have the power to hurt you," I admit. "And I've been hurt before."

"Me too," he says softly. "But I'm not going anywhere, Lena. I'm all in."

"I'm all in, too," I whisper, meaning it with every fiber of my being.

Alder lifts me onto the counter, stepping between my thighs as he kisses me deeply. My arms wrap around his neck, pulling him closer, heat building between us rapidly.

"I love how you feel," he murmurs against my neck. "Every curve, every inch of you."

His hands slide under my shirt, spanning my waist, and I lean into his touch, lost in the sensation.

We're so absorbed in each other that we don't hear the front door open. It's only when Gordie suddenly barks in excitement that we break apart, turning toward the sound.

And there, standing in the doorway with wide eyes and dropped jaws, are Odin, Thora, Gunnar, and Emerson, arms laden with grocery bags and coolers.

For a frozen moment, no one speaks. Then Gunnar grins wickedly. "Well, well. Looks like we're interrupting dessert."

I bury my face in Alder's shoulder, mortification washing over me. But then I feel him shaking with silent laughter, and somehow, the absurdity of the situation hits me, too.

"I used the damn calendar," Alder says, not bothering to move away from me.

"Clearly," Odin drawls, setting down his bags. His girlfriend Thora is fighting a smile beside him.

Emerson steps forward, radiating warmth despite the awkward circumstances. "We can come back later if you two need some time to... finish your conversation."

Gunnar snorts. "No, we can't. I just drove an hour with your cello rattling in the trunk."

"I told you to check the calendar," Thora mutters to Odin.

"I did check it!" he protests. "And I noticed that Alder and Lena were hogging it all to themselves."

Alder groans. Gunnar raises his hands in innocence. "Don't look at me. Dad wanted a family weekend."

"Minus Tucker," Odin adds, shaking his head.

From the doorway, Juniper Stag appears, followed by her husband Ty, who sends Gordie into a frenzy of excitement.

"Well, don't stop on our account," Juniper says cheerfully, taking in the scene. "You were saying something about love and forever?" She beams at me.

· · ·

And just like that, our romantic getaway transforms into a family weekend. Bags are carried upstairs, and groceries are unpacked. The quiet sanctuary fills with laughter, teasing, and stories.

I help Juniper prepare lunch, chopping vegetables while she tells me stories of young Alder. Gunnar and Odin set up a horseshoe game outside, their competitive banter carrying through the open windows. Emerson and Thora discuss music on the couch, their conversation punctuated by Thora's distinctive laugh.

Alder catches my eye through the window, where he's helping his father set up the grill on the deck. He mouths "Sorry" with a rueful smile.

But I'm not sorry, not really. There's something magical about being enveloped in this family's warmth, about being treated as if I've always belonged here.

Later, when the family has spread out across the property —Gunnar and Emerson swimming, Odin and Thora hiking, Ty and Juniper napping—Alder and I find a quiet moment on the deck. The mountains spread before us, bathed in late afternoon sunlight.

"I'm sorry about the change of plans," he says, wrapping an arm around my shoulders. "I promise the next trip will be just us."

I lean into him, watching a male deer feel its way through the trees. "It's okay. I don't mind sharing you sometimes."

He studies my face. "Really? You're not just saying that?"

"Really." I turn to face him fully. "I meant what I said this morning. I love you. And I love your family, chaos and all."

"Even when they barge in unannounced?" he asks, eyebrows raised.

"Especially then," I admit. "It means I'm finally part of something real."

His expression softens, and I see the depth of his feelings written plainly across his face.

"You know," I say, intertwining my fingers with his, "for so long, I tried to make myself smaller. Literally and figuratively. With Brad, with my mother, with everyone. I shrank myself to fit the spaces others allowed me."

Alder squeezes my hand encouragingly.

"But for the first time in my life, I don't feel too big, too loud, or too much," I continue. "With you, with this family, I'm exactly the right size."

He pulls me into his arms, his embrace solid and sure. "You could never be too much for me, Lena. You're everything I never knew I needed."

Behind us, the door slides open, and Juniper calls, "Dinner is served, lovebirds!"

We both laugh at the moment of intensity breaking.

"Coming, Mom," Alder calls back.

As we head inside, I realize that the word "love" no longer terrifies me. Not when it's wrapped in this—family and belonging and the certainty that I am accepted exactly as I am.

For the first time, I feel truly, completely whole.

EPILOGUE: ALDER

FOUR MONTHS LATER

There's blood on the ice. Again.

This time, it's Cappy sprawled on his back, red pooling beneath his head as he groans. Trainers surround him, but I watch Lena kneel on the ice in her scrubs, her movements calm and precise as she examines our captain's mouth.

It happened fast—high stick from a Buffalo defenseman, no penalty called, and Cappy dropped like a stone. Now, the whistle has blown, and all of us are standing on the bench, watching Lena work.

"She's a fucking miracle worker," Banksy mutters beside me. "Remember when Doc Bowman would have guys spitting teeth into a towel and sending them back out?"

I nod, trying to maintain professional distance even as pride surges through me. I fidget with my stick, covered in rainbow pride tape. On the ice, Lena extracts something from Cappy's mouth—a splintered piece of the offending stick, I realize—and drops it into a metal pan held by a trainer. She says something that makes Cappy laugh despite his pain, then administers an injection with practiced efficiency.

"Dental block," Coach says, appearing at my shoulder, tugging at his tie covered in rainbow hockey sticks–a new regular part of his game-day ensemble. "He'll be numb in about thirty seconds."

Sure enough, within a minute, Cappy is being helped to his feet. The crowd cheers as he skates toward the bench, where Lena gives him final instructions. When she turns to head back through the tunnel, our eyes meet briefly. Professional on the surface, but I catch the glint of something warmer beneath.

"Stop looking at her ass," Tucker hisses, elbowing me as we prepare for the faceoff.

"I'm admiring her professional demeanor," I counter, readjusting my helmet.

"Sure you are."

Coach shouts our line change, and we hop the boards together, all business once more. But as I settle into position for the faceoff, I can't help the small smile beneath my mouthguard. Months with Lena, and I still get a kick out of watching her work.

We won the season opener 3-1, with Cappy returning to score the insurance goal in the third period. The locker room was electric afterward, with everyone riding the high of starting the season right. I rushed through my shower, fielded a few questions from the media about our defensive strategy, and politely declined offers from the guys to grab celebratory drinks.

"Hot date with the tooth fairy?" Banksy teases as I throw on a T-shirt and jeans while the rest of the team gets dressed for the clubs.

"Just tired," I lie, avoiding Tucker's knowing smirk from across the room.

The arena has mostly emptied by the time I slip through the door at the back of the locker room. According to the disclosure agreement we filed with the team, Lena and I maintain strict professionalism during working hours. She handles other players' dental emergencies and recuses herself for mine–not that I've had any–while I keep my hands to myself until we're off the clock.

Technically, we're still on the clock, but over the past few months, we've gotten pretty creative with our definition of "working hours."

Light spills from her arena office into the darkened corridor. Inside, I find her cleaning instruments, her back to the door, still in her professional attire—black scrubs with "Dr. Sinclair" embroidered above the pocket in gold thread.

I close the door behind me, turning the lock with an audible click. She doesn't turn around, but I see her shoulders straighten and a slight pause in her movements.

"Dr. Sinclair," I say, keeping my voice formal. "Got a minute?"

"That depends, Mr. Stag." She sets down an instrument and turns to face me, her expression serious except for the spark in her eyes. "Is this a professional consultation?"

I close the distance between us, backing her against the leather chair. "Strictly personal."

Her hands come up to my chest, not quite pushing me away. "The disclosure agreement specifically states—"

"That working hours end when the final buzzer sounds," I finish for her. "That was twenty-seven minutes ago."

"Was it?" A smile plays at her lips. "I must have lost track of time."

"Let me help you find it." I cup her face in my hands and kiss her, soft at first, then deeper as she melts against me.

"Congratulations on the win," she says when we part, her cheeks flushed in that way I've come to adore.

"Thanks for saving our captain." My hands find her waist, lifting her onto the counter with ease. "It's so wild to me how you just reach into all that gore and clean it up."

She wraps her legs around me, pulling me closer. "Just doing my job."

"Speaking of jobs..." My lips find the sensitive spot below

her ear that always makes her shiver. "I saw you watching me on that second-period penalty kill."

"You were extremely competent," she says with mock indifference, even as her head tips back to give me better access to her neck.

"Competent?" I nip at her throat in retaliation. "I blocked two shots in thirty seconds."

Her laugh turns to a gasp as my hands slide beneath her top. "Perhaps slightly above average performance."

"I'll show you above average," I growl, and then we're both laughing and kissing, hands fumbling with buttons and zippers, heedless of our surroundings.

We've become experts at this—finding moments and spaces to be together despite our demanding schedules. Sometimes, it's rushed and desperate, like now, with Lena's scrub pants flopping around one ankle and my jeans barely pulled down, her dental chair reclined to the perfect height. Other times, we take our time, spending whole weekends barely leaving my bed, exploring each other at the leisurely pace of people who know they have all the time in the world.

"God, I love you," I breathe against her neck as we move together, her knees spread as wide as the chair arms allow while she straddles me.

"I love you too," she gasps, fingers digging into my shoulders through my shirt. "Faster."

I comply, plowing up into her, my bare ass on the leather, and soon she's shuddering against me, biting my shoulder to muffle her cries. I follow shortly after, burying my face in her hair to stay quiet.

For a moment, we simply breathe together, foreheads touching, heartbeats gradually slowing. Then Lena laughs softly, kissing the corner of my mouth.

"So much for professional boundaries," she whispers.

"We're off the clock," I remind her, helping her straighten

her clothes before fixing my own. "Besides, no one's around this late after a game."

As if the universe wants to prove me wrong, we hear a noise from the adjoining locker room—between a curse and a sob.

Lena and I exchange concerned glances. I hop up to pull up my pants while she smooths her hair.

"Probably a custodian," I whisper, but neither of us believes it.

We move cautiously toward the connecting door, following the sound to the shower area. What we find stops us in our tracks.

Tucker sits huddled in the farthest stall, still half-dressed in pads, hunched forward, shoulders shaking.

"Tuck?" I approach slowly, worry replacing the post-coital haze. "What's wrong? Are you hurt?"

He looks up, startled, seemingly unsurprised to find us together. His eyes are red, and his face blotchy in a way I haven't seen since our grandfather died.

"She's pregnant," he says, voice raw.

I exchange a look with Lena, who seems as concerned as me.

I climb into the shower with my twin, wrapping my arms around him.

Lena mimes, packing a bag, and I nod as she steps out, giving us privacy.

"Tuck, what's going on, man?"

My brother takes a shaking breath. "I fucked up, Aldy." He drags a hand down his face. "And he knows it's me..."

"What can I do?"

"Nothing," he wails, leaning his head against my shoulder.

Eventually, I convince him that he reeks. I step out to let him shower, and then Lena and I drive him home, promising to get his car with him in the morning.

. . .

Back at the townhouse, I can't help but compare Tucker's anguish to my happiness. Six months ago, I couldn't imagine anyone filling the emptiness I felt before Lena. Now, I can't imagine my life without her in it.

As she slides into bed beside me, I'm reminded of the small velvet box hidden in my sock drawer, waiting for the perfect moment. Not yet, but soon.

"What are you thinking about?" she asks, curling against my side.

"How grateful I am that we found each other," I say, kissing her forehead. As she drifts off to sleep in my arms, I think about how whatever comes next—Tucker's drama, the long season ahead, the ring in my drawer—I know we'll face it together. Lena and I are no longer playing for payback but forever.

Want to know what Tucker's upset about? One-click his book,
Playing with Fire!

Hungry for more Lena and Alder? My newsletter subscribers get a
steamy bonus scene. Visit LaineyDavis.com to sign up or scan the
QR code below.

AUTHOR'S NOTE

The idea for this book came to me when my kids were watching YouTube shorts about dentists in the NHL. Before that, I never considered the people who tend the teeth of our hockey heroes and heroines. I had so much fun learning about dental trauma in the sport. Dr. Ray White from UNC's School of Dentistry graciously lent me his expertise on the tooth stuff.

I'm grateful for Elizabeth Perry, Karen Grey, and Liz Lincoln's critiques of early drafts and structure advice from Liz Alden. Val Sweeney and Dana Rosvanis provided insight into hockey authenticity every step of the way.

Many of you might have been nervous as Gordie suffered his ordeal, so I apologize for that stress. And I'm sorry so many of the names in this book begin with A. By the time a reader pointed this out, the characters were already fully formed people in my head.

ALSO BY LAINEY DAVIS

Stag Brothers Series

Sweet Distraction (Tim and Alice)

Filled Potential (Ty and Juniper)

Fragile Illusion (Thatcher and Emma)

A Stag Family Christmas

Beautiful Game (Hawk and Lucy)

Stag Generations Books

Forging Passion (Wes and Cara prequel)

Forging Glory (Wes and Cara)

Forging Legacy (Wyatt and Fern)

Forging Chaos (Odin and Thora)

Playing for Keeps (Gunnar and Emerson)

Playing for Payback (Alder and Lena)

Playing for Power (Tucker and …)

Bridges and Bitters series

Fireball: An Enemies to Lovers Romance (Sam and AJ)

Liquid Courage: A Marriage in Crisis Romance (Chloe and Teddy)

Speed Rail: A Single Dad Romance (Piper and Cash)

Last Call: A Marriage of Convenience Romance (Esther and Koa)

Planted and Plowed series

Against the Grain (Eila and Ben)

The Burgh and the Bees (Eden and Nate)

Yule Be Sorry (Eliza and ???)

Sappy Go Lucky (Eva and Asher)

Since You've Bean Gone (Ethan and Lia) *part of the Farm 2 Forking series

Binge the following series in eBook, paperback, or audio!

Brady Family Series

Foundation: A Grouchy Geek Romance (Zack and Nicole)

Suspension: An Opposites Attract Romance (Liam and Maddie)

Inspection: A Silver Fox Romance (Kellen and Elizabeth)

Vibration: An Accidental Roommates Romance (Cal and Logan)

Current: A Secret Baby Romance (Orla and Walt)

Restoration: A Silver Fox Redemption Romance (Mick and Celeste)

Oak Creek Series

The Nerd and the Neighbor (Hunter and Abigail)

The Botanist and the Billionaire (Diana and Asa)

The Midwife and the Money (Archer and Opal)

The Planner and the Player (Fletcher and Thistle)

Stone Creek University

Deep in the Pocket: A Football Romance

Hard Edge: A Hockey Romance

Possession: A Football Romance